The Hamish Macbeth series

DEATH of a POISON PEN

A Hamish Macbeth Murder Mystery

M. C. BEATON

ROBINSON
London

Constable & Robinson Ltd
3 The Lanchesters
162 Fulham Palace Road
London W6 9ER
www.constablerobinson.com

First published in the USA by Grand Central Publishing,
a division of Hachette Book Group USA, Inc.

This edition published by Robinson,
an imprint of Constable & Robinson, 2009

A copy of the British Library Cataloguing in
Publication data is available from the British Library

UK ISBN: 978-1-84901-277-5

Printed and bound in the EU

1 3 5 7 9 10 8 6 4 2

This book is for my husband,
Harry Scott Gibbons, and my son,
Charles David Bravos Gibbons, with love.

Hamish Macbeth fans share their reviews . . .

'Treat yourself to an adventure in the Highlands; remember your coffee and scones – for you'll want to stay a while!'

'I do believe I am in love with Hamish.'

'M. C. Beaton's stories are absolutely excellent . . . Hamish is a pure delight!'

'A highly entertaining read that will have me hunting out the others in the series.'

'A new Hamish Macbeth novel is always a treat.'

'Once I read the first mystery I was hooked . . . I love her characters.'

Share your own reviews and comments at www.constablerobinson.com

Chapter One

*I'm not a jealous woman, but I can't see
what he sees in her, I can't see what he sees
in her, I can't see what he sees in her!*
                        – Sir Alan Patrick Herbert

Jenny Ogilvie was curled up on a sofa in her friend Priscilla Halburton-Smythe's London flat. They had been talking for most of the evening. Jenny was secretly jealous of Priscilla's cool blonde looks. Although an attractive girl herself with her mop of black curls and rosy cheeks, she longed to look as stylish and composed as her friend.

A desire to rattle her friend's calm prompted her to say, 'You've talked an awful lot about this village policeman, Hamish Macbeth. I mean, you've barely mentioned your fiancé. Come on. What gives? I think you're still in love with this copper.'

A faint tide of pink rose up Priscilla's face. 'I was engaged to him once and we shared a lot of adventures. But that's all. What about *your* love life? You've been letting me do all the talking.'

'Oh, you know me. I like to shop around,' said Jenny. 'I'm not prepared to settle down yet.'

'What happened to Giles? You did seem frightfully keen on him.'

'He bored me after a bit,' lied Jenny, who had no intention of letting Priscilla know that Giles had broken off with her the minute she had hinted at marriage.

'You'll find someone. Don't worry,' said Priscilla with all the calm assurance of someone about to be married.

Jenny returned to her own flat, feeling jealous and cross. It was a pity, she thought, that Priscilla's policeman should live in some remote Highland village or she would be tempted to have a go at him herself. He must be one hell of a man to occupy so much of Priscilla's thoughts. She went to her bookshelves and pulled down an atlas of the British Isles. Now, where had Priscilla said that village was? Lochdoo or something. She scanned the index. There was a Lochdubh. That must be it. Maybe like 'skeandhu', the dagger Highlanders wore with full dress. She looked it up in the dictionary. That was pronounced *skeandoo*. Also spelt 'skeandubh'. So it followed that Lochdubh must be the place. She knew Priscilla's parents owned the Tommel Castle Hotel there. Just to be sure, she phoned directory inquiries and got the number of the Tommel Castle Hotel and asked for the exact location of Lochdubh. Got it! She replaced the receiver.

She put down the atlas and sat cross-legged on the floor. She had holiday owing. What if – just what if – she went to this village and romanced the copper? How would Priscilla like that?

Not a bit, she thought with a grin. She would ask for leave in the morning.

The subject of Jenny's plotting took a stroll along Lochdubh's waterfront the next morning with his dog, Lugs. PC Hamish Macbeth was preoccupied with a nasty case. The nearby town of Braikie had been subjected to a rash of poison-pen letters. At first people had ignored them because the accusations in some of them were so weird and wild and inaccurate that they hadn't been taken seriously. But as the letters continued to arrive, tempers were rising.

Mrs Dunne, who owned a bed and breakfast on the waterfront called Sea View, hailed him. She was a fussy little woman who looked perpetually anxious and tired.

'Morning,' said Mrs Dunne. 'Terrible business about those nasty letters.'

'You havenae had one, have you?' asked Hamish.

'No, but I just heard that herself, Mrs Wellington, got one this morning.'

'I'd better go and see her. Business good?'

'Not a bad summer, but nobody really books in now it's autumn. I've got a couple of the forestry workers as regulars. Though mind you, a lassie from London is coming for a couple of weeks, a Miss Ogilvie. She phoned this morning.'

Hamish touched his cap and walked off in the direction of the manse, for Mrs Wellington, large, tweedy and respectable, was the minister's wife.

Mrs Wellington was pulling up weeds in her garden. She straightened up when she saw Hamish.

'I've just heard you've had one o' thae letters.' Hamish fixed her with a gimlet stare to distract her from the sight of his dog urinating against the roots of one of her prize roses. 'Why didn't you phone the police station?'

She looked flustered. 'It was nothing but a spiteful piece of nonsense. I threw it on the fire.'

'I can do with all the evidence I can get,' said Hamish severely. 'Now, you've got to tell me what was in that letter. Furthermore, I've

4

never known you to light a fire before the end of October.'

Mrs Wellington capitulated. 'Oh, very well. I'll get it. Wait there. And keep that dog of yours away from my flowers.'

Hamish waited, wondering what could possibly be so bad as to make the upright minister's wife initially lie to him.

Mrs Wellington came back and handed him a letter. On the envelope was her name and address in handwriting now familiar to Hamish from the other letters he had in a file back at the police station. He opened it and took out a piece of cheap stationery and began to read. Then he roared with laughter. For the poison-pen letter writer had accused Mrs Wellington of having an adulterous affair with the Lochdubh policeman – Hamish Macbeth.

When he had recovered, he wiped his eyes and said, 'This is so daft. Why didnae you want to show it to me?'

'I know your reputation as a womanizer, Hamish Macbeth, and I thought this letter might give you ideas.'

Hamish's good humour left and his hazel eyes held a malicious gleam. 'I am in my thirties and you are – what – in your fifties? Don't you think you are suffering from a wee bit o' vanity?'

Her face flamed. 'There are winter–summer relationships, you know. I read about them in

5

Cosmopolitan – at the dentist's. And when I was in the cinema with my husband the other week, a young man on the other side of me put a hand on my knee!'

'Michty me,' said Hamish. 'What happened when the lights went up?'

'He had left by that time,' said Mrs Wellington stiffly, not wanting to tell this jeering policeman that during a bright scene on the screen, the young man had leant forward and looked at her and fled.

'And I am not a womanizer,' pursued Hamish.

'Ho, no? You broke off your engagement to poor Priscilla, and since then you've been playing fast and loose.'

'I'll take this letter with me,' said Hamish, suddenly weary. 'But rest assured, I have not the designs on you, not now, not ever!'

Back at the police station, he added the letter to the others in the file. There was a knock at the kitchen door. He went to answer it and found Elspeth Grant, the local reporter and astrologer for the *Highland Times*, standing there. She was dressed in her usual mixture of charity shop clothes: old baggy sweater, long Indian cotton skirt and clumpy boots.

'What brings you?' asked Hamish. 'I have-nae seen you for a while.'

'I've been showing the new reporter the ropes.'

'Pat Mallone,' said Hamish. 'The attractive Irishman.'

'Yes, him. And he is attractive. Are you going to ask me in?'

'Sure.' He stood aside. Elspeth sat down at the kitchen table. The day was misty and drops of moisture hung like little pearls in her frizzy hair. Her large grey eyes, gypsy eyes, surveyed him curiously. He felt a little pang of loss. At one time, Elspeth had shown him that she was attracted to him but he had rejected her and by the time he had changed his mind about her, she was no longer interested.

'So,' began Elspeth, 'I hear Mrs Wellington got one of those letters.'

'How did you learn that?'

'She told Nessie Currie, who told everyone in Patel's grocery. What on earth was in it?'

'Mind your own business.'

'All right, copper. What are you doing about these letters? They're weird and wild in their accusations, but one day one's going to hit the mark and there'll be a death. Haven't you asked for a handwriting expert?'

'Oh, I've asked headquarters, right enough, but it is always the same thing. Handwriting experts cost money. The budget is tight. It's chust a village storm in a teacup and will soon blow over, that's what they say.' Hamish's

Highland accent always became more sibilant when he was excited or upset. 'So I sit on my bum collecting nasty letters.'

'There is something you could do and I'll tell you if you make me a cup of tea.'

Hamish put the kettle on top of the stove and lifted down two mugs from the kitchen cabinet. 'So what's your idea?'

'It's like this. Someone always knows something. You could call an emergency meeting at the community centre in Braikie and appeal to the people of Braikie to help you. I could run off flyers at the newspaper and we could post them up in shops and on lamp posts. Someone knows something, I'm sure of that. Go on, Hamish. I feel in my bones that death is going to come and come quickly.'

Hamish looked at her uneasily. He had experienced Elspeth's psychic powers and had learned that, at times, they were uncanny.

'All right,' he said. 'I'll do it. Let's see. This is Monday. We'll make it for next Saturday evening.'

'No, make it around lunchtime, say one o'clock. There's a big bingo game on Saturday evening.'

'Okay. I'll leave it to you.'

Hamish made tea. 'What sort of person would you say was behind these letters?'

'Someone living alone, no family. Maybe

someone retired who once had some power over people. Probably a woman.'

'There are an awful lot of widows and spinsters in Braikie.'

'Never mind. Let's hope this meeting flushes something out.'

After Elspeth had left, he noticed she had left him a copy of the *Highland Times*. Curiously, he turned to her astrology column and looked under 'Libra'. He read: 'Romance is heading your way but it is a romance you will not want. You will suffer from headaches on Wednesday morning. You are not working hard enough. You are congenitally lazy, but remember always that mistakes caused by laziness can cause death.'

Hamish scratched his fiery hair. What on earth was the lassie on about?

On Saturday morning, Jenny Ogilvie looked out of the window of the bus that was bearing her northwards and felt she was leaving civilization behind. She had flown to Inverness and caught the Lochinver bus. She had been told, however, that the bus to take her on to Lochdubh from Lochinver would have left by the time she arrived, but a local taxi could take her the rest of the way. Moorland and mountain stretched on either side. Foaming waterfalls plunged down craggy slopes. Red deer stood as if posing for Landseer on the top of hills as the bus wound its way round twisting roads, breaking sharply to avoid the occasional suicidal sheep.

She had decided to book into a bed and breakfast in Lochdubh rather than stay at the Tommel Castle Hotel, in case Priscilla might learn from her parents of her arrival. The bus finally ground its way down into Lochinver and stopped on the waterfront. It was a fine day and sunlight was sparkling on the water.

Jenny climbed stiffly down from the bus and retrieved her luggage. She took out her mobile phone and dialled the number of a taxi service in Lochdubh she had tracked down by dint of phoning the Sutherland tourist board. Better to have someone from Lochdubh to collect her than get a cab from Lochinver.

A pleasant Highland voice on the other end of the line informed her that he would be with her in three-quarters of an hour and if she sat in the café on the waterfront, he would find her.

Jenny went into the café and ordered a coffee, forcing her eyes away from a tempting display of home-baked cakes. It was all right for Priscilla, she thought bitterly. Priscilla could eat anything and never even put on an ounce, whereas she, Jenny, could feel her waistband tightening by just looking at the things.

She was the only customer in the café. She noticed there was a large glass ashtray on the table in front of her. Jenny was trying to cut down on smoking, but she hadn't been able to have one all day. She lit one up and felt dizzy, but after two more, felt better. The sun was already disappearing and the water outside darkening to black when a man popped his head round the door. 'Miss Ogilvie?'

Jenny rose and indicated her luggage. 'The cab is outside,' he said. 'I would help you with your luggage, but my back's bad.'

Hoisting her two large suitcases outside, Jenny stared in dismay at the 'cab'. It was a minibus painted bright red on the front, but because the owner, Iain Chisholm, had run out of paint, the rest was painted a sulphurous yellow. Inside, the seats were covered in brightly coloured chintz with flounces at the bottom of each seat.

Jenny heaved her luggage in the side door and then decided to sit up in the front with Iain and see if she could pump him for some information.

The engine coughed and spluttered to life and the bus started its journey out of Lochinver and headed up the Sutherland coast to Lochdubh. 'I'm up from London,' said Jenny.

'Is that a fact?' said Iain, negotiating a hair-pin bend. Jenny glanced nervously down a cliff edge to where the Atlantic boiled against jagged rocks.

'What's Lochdubh like?' asked Jenny.

'Oh, it's the grand place. Nice and quiet.'

'No crime?'

'Nothing much. Bit of a scare now, mind you. Some damp poison-pen letter writer's on the loose.'

'How scary. Do you have a policeman?'

'Yes. Hamish Macbeth.'

'What's he like?'

'A fine man. Solved a lot of crimes.'

'What's such a clever copper doing being stuck up here?'

'He likes it and so do I,' said Iain crossly.

Jenny was dying to ask what Hamish looked like, but she didn't dare show any more curiosity. Surely, someone who could attract such as Priscilla must be really handsome. He was probably tall and dark with a craggy Highland face and piercing green eyes. When not in uniform, he probably wore a kilt and played the bagpipes. Jenny clutched the side of the old minibus as it hurtled onwards towards Lochdubh, wrapped in rosy dreams.

Earlier that day, Hamish addressed the inhabitants of Braikie in the community hall. 'Some of you must know something – have an idea who is sending out these poisonous letters,' he said. He noticed uneasily that people were beginning to glare around the hall. 'Now, don't go leaping to conclusions because you just don't like someone,' he said quickly. 'Maybe if you all go home and think hard, you might remember –' he held up an envelope – 'someone posting one of these in a pillar box. Just on the chance that our letter writer is here in this hall, I would caution you that when you are caught – and you will be caught, mark my words – then you will be facing a prison sentence. I am going to engage the services of a handwriting expert –'

'What took ye so long?' demanded an angry voice from the front. 'You should ha' done it afore this.'

'I was told that because of cutbacks in the police budget, they were not prepared to let me hire one,' said Hamish. 'On your way out, you will see a petition on the table at the door requesting the services of a handwriting expert from police headquarters. I want you all to sign it.'

Hamish was mildly annoyed to see Elspeth in the front row accompanied by Pat Mallone, the new reporter. It only took one reporter to cover this. Did she have to go everywhere with him? He was whispering in her ear and she was giggling like a schoolgirl.

'This is a serious matter,' he went on, raising his voice. 'And should be taken seriously by our local press as well.' Elspeth looked up and composed her features and made several squiggles in her notebook. 'The accusations in these letters so far are silly and untrue, but if by any chance this poison-pen letter writer should hit on the truth about someone, maybe by accident, then at the least it could cause misery and at the worst, death. Now sign that petition. It is your civic duty.'

The audience rose to their feet. Aware of Hamish, still standing on the stage watching them, one by one they all signed the petition as they filed out.

When the hall was empty, Hamish leapt down from the stage and collected the petition. He would take it down to Strathbane in the morning and see if it prompted them to give him a handwriting expert.

Jenny Ogilvie was dropped outside Sea View. She hefted her suitcases up to the door, rang the bell, and waited. The village was very quiet and great stars blazed in the sky above. A chill wind was blowing off the loch. She shivered and rang the bell again. At last she heard footsteps approaching the door from the other side. 'Who is it?' called a voice.

'It's me. Jenny Ogilvie from London.'

The grumbles coming from the other side of the door reminded Jenny of the cartoon dog Muttley. Then the door opened. 'What time of night d'ye call this?' demanded Mrs Dunne.

'I have come all the way from London,' said Jenny coldly. 'And if this is the sort of welcome you give visitors, perhaps I would be better off at the hotel.'

In the light streaming out from the door, Jenny had seemed to Mrs Dunne like a small girl. But the cold authority in Jenny's voice made her say hurriedly, 'Come in, lassie. You must forgive me. We aye keep early hours. I'll show you to your room. I only serve the bed and breakfast, mind, but if you're hungry, I've got some food I can give you.'

'Just a sandwich and some coffee would be fine,' said Jenny.

'Right. Pick up your suitcases and follow me.'

This was obviously a world where no one carried anyone's luggage, thought Jenny as she struggled up the wooden staircase after Mrs Dunne.

Mrs Dunne opened the door. 'This is your room. I've given you the best one, it being quiet this time of year.'

Jenny looked dismally round, wondering, if this was the best room, what on earth the others were like. A forty watt bulb burned in a pink and white glass shade. There was a narrow bed under a slippery quilt against one wall. A closet covered by a curtain, which Mrs Dunne pulled back with a magician's proud flourish, was where she would hang her clothes. A wash-hand basin of Victorian vintage with a pink glass mirror above it was over in one far corner, and in the other stood a desk and a hard upright chair. In front of the fireplace, filled with orange crêpe paper in the shape of a fan, stood a one-bar electric heater. The floor was covered in shiny green linoleum, on which were two islands of round rugs.

'You put fifty pence in the meter to start the fire,' said Mrs Dunne. 'Breakfast is from seven o'clock until nine o'clock, no later. I'll expect you to be out of your room by ten because I have to clean it and I don't want guests underfoot. You can sit in the lounge downstairs if it's a wet day. We have the telly – colour, it is. Now I'll show you the bathroom.'

Jenny followed her along the corridor outside to a room at the end of it. The bathroom held an enormous Victorian bath. Above it was a cylindrical gas heater. 'When you want a bath, put fifty pence in the meter above the door, turn this lever to the right, and light the geyser.'

'Do you mean I don't have my own bathroom?' asked Jenny.

'No, but there's only the two forestry workers and they're out early and don't use the bath much.'

16

Jenny repressed a shudder. 'What about laundry?'

'What about it? Can't you be doing your smalls in the hand basin?'

'No, I would prefer to do them in a washing machine with a tumble dryer.'

Mrs Dunne sighed. 'Well, you can use the one in the kitchen downstairs, but only if I don't need it. There's no tumble dryer but you'll find a clothes line in the back garden. Go and unpack and come downstairs and have something to eat.'

Jenny returned to her room. She felt thoroughly tired and depressed. She hoped this policeman would prove to be worth all this suffering. She opened one suitcase and unpacked a diaphanous nightgown and a silk dressing gown and laid them on the bed. Then she began to hang away some clothes and put underwear in the drawers.

When she heard Mrs Dunne calling her, she went reluctantly downstairs. 'I've put your food on a tray in the lounge,' said Mrs Dunne. 'When you're finished, put the tray in the kitchen – it's at the back of the hall – and don't forget to switch out all the lights. Good night.'

'Good night,' echoed Jenny. She went into the lounge. It was an uncomfortable-looking room with an acid three-piece suite which seemed to swear at the orange and sulphurous-yellow carpet. Above the cold fireplace some amateur had tried to copy the *Stag at Bay* and failed miserably. The television was operated by a coin box. A tray on the coffee table held a plate of ham sandwiches, two fairy cakes and a pot of tea. The ham sandwiches turned out to be delicious and the tea was hot and fragrant. Slightly cheered, Jenny finished her supper and carried the tray through to the kitchen. Then, carefully switching out all the lights behind her, she made her way up to her room.

It was very cold. London had been enjoying an Indian summer. She had not expected it to be so cold. She scrabbled in her purse looking for a fifty-pence piece but could not find one. She washed her face and hands, deciding to put off a bath until the following day. Shivering in her flimsy nightgown, she crawled into bed. There were two hot-water bottles in the bed and the sheets smelled faintly of pine soap. The bed was amazingly soft and comfortable. Jenny, normally a restless sleeper, plunged down into a deep and dreamless sleep.

Hamish drove towards Strathbane the following morning with Lugs beside him on the passenger seat of the police Land Rover and with the petition in a briefcase in the back. It was a beautiful clear day. Not even a single cloud wreathed the soaring mountain tops. A heron flew across the road in front of him, slow and graceful. The air was heavy with the smells of pine, wood smoke and wild thyme.

But his heart sank as the Land Rover crested a rise on the road and he saw Strathbane lying below him – the City of Dreadful Night. It had originally been a thriving fishing port, but European Union regulations and a decline in fishing stocks had put the fishermen out of business. Stalinist tower blocks reared up to the sky, monuments to failure and bad architecture.

He was lucky it was a Sunday. The bane of his life, Detective Chief Inspector Blair, hardly ever worked on Sunday. Hamish knew Blair would block any proposal of his out of sheer spite. He was even luckier to meet Chief Superintendent Peter Daviot in the reception area.

'What brings you, Hamish?' asked Daviot.

It was a good sign that he had used Hamish's first name. Hamish held out the petition and explained his need for the services of a handwriting expert.

'We have an overstretched budget,' said Daviot. 'Don't you think it'll just blow over?'

'No, I don't,' said Hamish.

'Don't what?'

'I mean, I don't think it'll blow over, *sir*. It's been going on for some time. My concern is this: If we don't track down this poison-pen letter writer soon, he or she, instead of wild

accusations, might hit on a truth that someone doesn't want known. Braikie's a very
churchy place. Everyone prides themselves on
their respectability. It could be that one of
these letters could drive a man or woman to
suicide.'

Daviot looked at the tall policeman with the
flaming-red hair. He knew that when it came
to cases, Hamish Macbeth often showed
remarkable powers of intuition.

'Type up a report and give it with the petition to Helen.'

'Thank you, sir.'

Hamish made his way up to the detectives'
room where Detective Jimmy Anderson sat
with his feet up on his desk.

'I was just thinking of going out for a dram,'
he said when he saw Hamish.

'Give me a minute, Jimmy,' said Hamish.
'I've got to type something out for Daviot.'

'So what's so important the big cheese has to
see it himself?'

Hamish told him as he switched on a
computer.

'Hardly earth-shaking stuff, laddie. Tell you
what. I'll be along at the Wee Man's. Join me
when you're finished.'

No one could remember why the nearest
pub, the Fraser Arms, had been nicknamed the
Wee Man's.

Jimmy left. Hamish rapidly typed up his

report and nipped up the stairs to where Helen, Daviot's secretary, gave him a sour look.

'Working on the Sabbath, Helen?' asked Hamish.

'If you have something for Mr Daviot, leave it with me and do not waste my valuable time.'

Hamish gazed on her fondly. 'You know something, Helen? You're right ugly when you're angry.' And then he scampered off before she could think of a reply.

Despite Jimmy's urging, Hamish would only drink mineral water at the pub. He often wondered why Jimmy had never been done for drunk driving. He set off again, stopping outside the town to give Lugs a walk on the heather. As usual, when he approached Lochdubh, his spirits lifted even though the day was darkening. Mist was rolling down the flanks of the mountainsides, and thin black fingers of rain clouds were streaming in from the west on a rising wind. The crisp feel of the day had gone and he could feel a damp warmth in the air blowing in from the Gulf Stream.

He parked outside the police station and went into the kitchen – and glared at the figure of Elspeth Grant, sitting at his kitchen table.

'How did you get in?' he demanded.

'You left the door open,' said Elspeth. 'An open invitation.'

'Well, next time, wait until I'm at home.' I'll need to keep remembering to lock the door, thought Hamish. He was so used to leaving it open while he went to feed his hens and check on his sheep that he often forgot to lock it when he was out at work.

'How did you get on with the petition?'

'I gave it to Daviot. He says he'll see what he can do.'

'It'll be too late,' said Elspeth, looking at him with her silver eyes.

'I think he'll get moving on it.'

'Oh, Hamish, you know what the red tape is like. They'll pass memos back and forth and it'll take weeks.'

'Well, let's see how it goes.'

There was a knock at the door. Hamish opened it and found an attractive face staring up at him. Jenny Ogilvie held out one small hand. 'I would like to speak to Hamish Macbeth.'

'I am Hamish Macbeth.'

He was surprised to see disappointment flash across her large brown eyes. The pair surveyed each other.

Jenny *was* disappointed. Gone was the craggy Highlander of her dreams. She saw a tall, gangling, red-haired man with hazel eyes and a gentle face. Hamish, for his part, saw an attractive girl with black curly hair, large eyes and a curvaceous figure. She was dressed in a smart skirt and jacket and flimsy high heels.

'What can I do for you?' he asked.

'I'm a tourist here,' said Jenny, 'and I arrived yesterday. I don't know this neck of the woods and I wondered if you could tell me good places to visit.'

'Come in,' said Hamish.

He introduced Jenny to Elspeth. 'Sit down,' said Hamish. Both regarded each other with the wary suspicion of cats. 'Drink?'

'Yes, thank you.'

'Jenny here is a tourist and wants to know where she should visit,' said Hamish, lifting down a bottle of whisky and glasses. 'Elspeth here is our local reporter. She'll help you out.' Elspeth glared at Hamish's back.

Lugs, roused from slumber by the sound of voices, came up to the table, put a large paw on Jenny's leg, and drew it downwards, leaving white ladders on her ten-denier tights.

Jenny squeaked with alarm and drew her legs under the table. 'Come here, Lugs,' ordered Elspeth. 'Good dog. Settle down.' She turned her clear gaze on Jenny. 'If you really want to sightsee, you'll need a car. Do you have one?'

'No, I did the last of the journey by taxi, a chap called Iain Chisholm.'

'I think you'll find he has a spare car to rent, and his prices are low.'

'Thank you. I'll try him in the morning.'

'Mostly, people who come up here are walkers, hill climbers or fishermen. They have some sort of hobby. But if you drive around, there's some wonderful scenery. Where are you staying?'

'Sea View.'

'You're right next to the *Highland Times* offices. Drop in tomorrow morning and I'll give you some maps and tourist brochures.'

Hamish joined them at the table and poured whisky into three glasses. 'Do you drink it neat?' asked Jenny.

'Aye, but I can put water in it if you like.'

'It's all right,' said Jenny quickly, not to be outdone by Elspeth. Was Elspeth his girl-friend? If she was, then her plot was doomed from the start.

'So what made you decide to come this far north?' asked Hamish. His Highland voice was soft and lilting. Jenny began to understand a little of why her friend Priscilla appeared to be so fascinated with this man.

'I came up from London. Just felt like getting as far away as possible.'

'Broken heart?' asked Elspeth.

'No,' said Jenny crossly.

Elspeth finished her whisky and stood up. 'I'd best be getting along.' She walked to the door and then turned and said to Jenny, 'Good hunting, but you'll find the prey is difficult to catch.'

Jenny's face flamed. 'What do you mean?'

'Just a Highland expression,' said Elspeth, and she went out and closed the kitchen door behind her.

'I'm sorry I butted in on you and your girl-friend,' said Jenny.

'Just a friend. So what do you do in London?'

'I work for a computer company.'

'And what's the name of it?'

Jenny looked at him, startled. She worked for the same company as Priscilla. 'I work for Johnson and Betterson in the City,' she said, inventing a name.

'Ah. If you've finished your drink, I'll walk you back. Lugs needs some exercise.'

Lugs needs to be put down, thought Jenny, standing up and ruefully looking down at the wreck of her tights.

Hamish opened the door. The rain still hadn't arrived, but he could sense it coming.

They walked together along the quiet water-front. 'I hope you won't be too bored here,' said Hamish as they approached Sea View.

Jenny stopped suddenly and stared.

'What's the matter?' asked Hamish.

He looked and saw Jessie and Nessie Currie, the local twin spinsters, the minister's wife, and Mrs Dunne, standing together at the gate of the boarding house. Mrs Dunne was holding up a piece of Jenny's underwear, a black silk thong. 'Now, what in the name o' the wee man would you say that was?' she was asking.

Hamish reached out a long arm and snatched it from Mrs Dunne. 'That is the makings of a catapult for Miss Ogilvie's nephew. You should not be going through her things.'

'I didn't,' protested Mrs Dunne. She turned to Jenny, who was standing there wishing an earthquake would strike Lochdubh and bury them all. 'It was lying in the corner of your room. I found it when I was cleaning. I didn't know what it was and I thought it might have been left by the previous tenant.'

Hamish handed the thong to Jenny. She stuffed it in her handbag, marched past them, and went up to her room. She sank down on the edge of her bed and buried her head in her hands. This holiday had all been a terrible mistake.

Hamish went back to the police station, mildly amused. From the washing lines of Lochdubh, he knew that the usual female underwear consisted of large cotton knickers with elastic at the knee.

When he walked into the police station, the phone in the office was ringing. He rushed to answer it.

It was Elspeth. 'You'd best get over to Braikie,' she said. 'Miss Beattie, who worked in the post office, has been found hanged. And there's one of those poison-pen letters lying on the floor under her body.'

Chapter Two

*There are certain persons for whom pure
truth is a poison.*

— André Maurois

Hamish drove to Braikie through a rising
storm. Rain slashed against the windscreen
and great buffets of wind rocked the Land
Rover.

He cursed police headquarters for their
penny-pinching ways. He pulled up outside
the post office. It was a sub post office and sold
groceries as well. He knew Miss Beattie lived
in a flat above the shop. A thin little woman
was huddled in a doorway. 'Are you Mrs
Harris who found the body?' asked Hamish.

'Aye, and a terrible sight it is.'

'What on earth were you thinking of to
report it to the *Highland Times* and not to the
police?'

'I could only get your answering machine,'
she whined.

Hamish heard the distant sound of a siren. He had reported the death to the ambulance service and to police headquarters before he had driven off from Lochdubh. 'You'd better show me where you found her.'

Mrs Harris emerged from her doorway and led him to a lane at the side of the post office and pushed open a door, revealing a flight of stairs leading up to Miss Beattie's flat.

He went first, saying over his shoulder, 'I hope you didn't touch anything.'

'I was that feart, I couldnae,' she said.

'How did you find her? Do you have a key?'

'No, but herself promised me some of her homemade cakes. I couldnae get a reply, so I went up the stairs and there she was. The door was open.'

When they got to the landing, Hamish ordered, 'You stay there.'

He opened the door and went in. The light was on and Miss Beattie's body hung from a hook in the ceiling. One of the poison-pen letters was lying on the floor. Hamish took out a pair of forensic gloves and slipped them on.

He read: 'I have proof that you're a bastard. Your father never married your mother and I'll tell everyone.'

He looked up at the contorted face swinging above him. A window behind the body was open, sending it turning in the wind.

He heard the thud of feet on the stairs. He

went out to meet the ambulance men. 'I'm afraid there's nothing you can do,' he said. 'They'll be arriving from Strathbane soon. I hope they're not long. I want to get that poor woman's body down.'

As they waited, he hoped Blair would consider a mere suicide beneath him. To his relief, when the police arrived, they were headed by Detective Jimmy Anderson.

The police photographer took pictures and then the ambulance men took the body down. Hamish cast his eyes around the room. There was no note that he could see, only that poison-pen letter on the floor.

The pathologist arrived and began his examination. Hamish scowled. Something was nagging at the back of his brain. Jimmy Anderson was reading the letter.

'For heaven's sake,' he said. 'The Highlands have aye been crawling with bastards and nobody gives a toss.'

Hamish wandered through to the kitchen. 'Still, I suppose,' came Jimmy's voice from the other room, 'respectability to that poor biddy was her whole life.'

Hamish looked at the draining board beside the sink. Two cups and saucers were on the draining board. Two beads of water were on the draining board under them. He conjured up a picture of Miss Amy Beattie as he remembered her. A bustling, cheerful woman.

He went back in and said to the pathologist, 'I can't believe it was suicide.'

The pathologist, Mr Sinclair, looked up at Hamish. 'Poor woman. Clear case of suicide.'

'I don't think so,' said Hamish slowly.

Jimmy Anderson swung round and glared at him. 'Come on, Hamish,' he said. 'What else could it be?'

'Murder.'

'Whit?'

Hamish said to Mr Sinclair, 'You might find she was drugged afore she was strung up.'

'And what makes you think that?'

'Okay, she stood on a chair or something, put the rope over that hook, and kicked the chair or whatever away. So where is what she was standing on?'

He went to the landing where Mrs Harris was standing with a policewoman. 'Mrs Harris, are you sure you didn't touch anything, move any of the furniture?'

'Me? Och, no. I telt ye, I was too feart.'

Hamish went back into the flat.

'What makes you think she was drugged?' asked the pathologist.

'Chust a hunch,' said Hamish, his Highland accent becoming stronger, a sign of his distress. 'There are two cups on the draining board that have recently been washed. I knew Miss Beattie. She wasnae the sort o' body to take her own life over a letter like that.'

'The forensic team'll be here in the morning,' said Jimmy. 'I wish you wouldn't complicate things, Hamish.'

'I may be wrong,' said Hamish, 'but it's as well to make sure.'

The police waited until the body was removed and the letter taken off to Strathbane by Jimmy. Then they sealed off the flat and left.

'I'm going to Strathbane in the morning,' said Hamish. 'I've got to get to a handwriting expert.'

He drove back through the buffeting storm to Lochdubh. He realized he had not had any dinner but felt too tired to make anything other than a sandwich. He fried some liver for Lugs, not seeing the irony that he would cook for his dog, no matter how tired he was, but not for himself.

Jenny tossed and turned and the wind screamed and shook the boarding house. She felt she had come to some remote, pitiless, savage land. Waves on the sea loch outside were pounding the pebbly shore, adding to the tumult. Before she finally went off to sleep, she had decided to leave Lochdubh the following morning and get back to civilization.

But when she awoke, sunlight was streaming in through a crack in the curtains and the wind had dropped. She struggled out of bed and drew back the curtains. Waves still chased each other down the long sea loch all the way from the Atlantic, but apart from that, there was no sign of the storm of the night before. She pulled up the window and leant out. The air was sweet and warm, as if the winds had blown away the earlier autumnal chill.

She decided to put off the idea of leaving. She went down to the dining room. Mrs Dunne supplied enough breakfast to keep anyone from needing more food for the rest of the day. Jenny found that this morning her appetite was sharp, and she demolished a plate of eggs, bacon, sausage and fried haggis with enjoyment. The tea, as usual, was delicious, not at all like tea in London. Must be the water, thought Jenny.

'I'm right sorry about that catapult of yours,' said Mrs Dunne, coming in to take her empty plate away. 'But it shows what a good-hearted girl you are to be thinking of your nephew.'

Jenny blushed and Mrs Dunne smiled on her with approval. It showed modesty when a pretty girl like Miss Ogilvie could blush at a compliment.

'Sad, sad business over at Braikie,' she said.
'What's that?'

'Poor Miss Beattie, her what ran the post office, hanged herself last night. They say it was because she got one o' thae poison-pen letters.'

'I suppose Hamish Macbeth is dealing with it.'

'Aye, himself's gone off to Strathbane to plead for one o' thae handwriting experts.'

Mrs Dunne bustled out and Jenny sat back in her chair and lit a cigarette. What a relief to see ashtrays everywhere. As the smoke curled upwards in the shafts of sunlight, she remembered how proud Priscilla had been about sharing investigations with Hamish. Wouldn't it be marvellous to put Priscilla's elegant nose out of joint by joining in one of these investigations herself?

She remembered that she was supposed to go to the *Highland Times* to pick up maps and tourist brochures. May as well. She would study a map and find the road to Strathbane and maybe bump into Hamish 'by accident'.

Also, she needed some sensible clothes: flat walking shoes, trousers and a warm weatherproof coat, all the essential items of clothing she had not brought. There was no point in wearing a siren's wardrobe in the Highlands.

Ten minutes later she walked into the offices of the *Highland Times*. Elspeth and a very attractive young man were studying pull sheets of the paper.

'Oh, there you are,' said Elspeth. 'Jenny, this is Pat Mallone. Pat, Jenny Ogilvie.' Pat had dark curly hair like Jenny's, but his eyes were bright blue. 'I've got the stuff on my desk,' said Elspeth. Jenny smiled bewitchingly at Pat Mallone, but he was watching Elspeth with a dopey smile on his face.

Amazing, thought Jenny sourly. Elspeth's clothes were a disgrace.

Elspeth handed her some maps and tourist brochures. 'I thought I might go to Strathbane first and buy some warm clothes and some walking shoes,' said Jenny.

'Good idea. You won't get very far in those,' said Elspeth, looking down at Jenny's flimsy high heels. 'I thought all you London ladies had taken to wearing sensible shoes.'

Not if we're trying to seduce someone, thought Jenny. 'I forgot to pack any,' she said. 'I left in such a rush. How do I get to Strathbane?'

'That's easy. Go out of the village over the bridge and up past the Tommel Castle Hotel. A mile along the road you'll come to a cross-roads. One way leads along the coast to Lochinver, but take the one on the right that leads inland to Strathbane.'

'Isn't it signposted?'

'Can't remember.'

Jenny thanked her and walked along to Iain Chisholm's garage. Iain was bent over the engine of an old Rover. She tapped him on the shoulder and he jumped and straightened up and banged his head on the underside of the bonnet.

'You fair gave me a start,' he said. 'What can I do for you?'

'I wondered whether you had a car I could rent.'

'You've come to the right place. I've got the very thing.'

'How much will it cost?'

'Twenty-five pounds a week.'

Jenny brightened. Amazingly cheap. 'I'll take it,' she said.

'Just you wait outside and I'll be bringing her round the front.'

Jenny felt that she could actually get to like this place after all. The sun was glittering on the surface of the calming loch, and only the faintest of breezes now lifted her dark curls.

She heard the sound of an engine. Down from a lane at the side of the garage came Iain, driving a Robin Reliant, one of those three-wheeler cars, beloved by some and treated as a joke by many.

It was painted bright pink, not car paint, but with what looked like a flat emulsion.

'Haven't you anything else?' asked Jenny as Iain stopped the car and got out.

'You can't do better than this. Of course, you could be taking the bus to Strathbane to one o' the big companies. They might charge you twenty-five pounds a day.'

Jenny looked at the car doubtfully. 'Does it go all right?'

'Like a bomb.'

May as well take it, thought Jenny. It does look ridiculous, but no one up here knows me.

'All right,' she said. She took out her cheque book.

'Haven't you got cash?' asked Iain.

Jenny fished out her wallet and extracted two twenties and a ten. Iain gave her a crumpled five-pound note as change.

She smoothed it out. 'What sort of money is this?'

'It's a Scottish five-pound note,' said Iain.

'I didn't know you people had your own money,' said Jenny, as if talking to the member of some strange aboriginal tribe.

Iain shook his head as if in disbelief at her ignorance and handed her the car keys. 'This one's for the ignition and that little one's for the petrol. You need leaded petrol.'

Jenny thanked him and got in the car. The seats, like the seats in the minibus, had been covered in loose chintz. 'I feel like a travelling circus,' she muttered as she put the key in the ignition. The engine roared to life, but the needle on the dashboard showed that the car was nearly out of petrol. She switched off the engine and got out again. Iain came out of the garage. 'What's up?'

'Practically no petrol,' said Jenny.

'Och, well, wait there. I'll get you a gallon. That'll get you to the nearest garage. These Robins don't use much.'

He went into the garage and came back with a gallon can, took the keys from her, and poured the petrol into the tank. He handed her the keys and said, 'That'll be five pounds.'

'What! That's a disgraceful price!'

'Did nobody tell you that petrol was expensive up here?'

'Oh, very well.' Jenny took out the Scottish five-pound note he had given her and handed it to him.

He gave her a cheery wave as she drove off. The dogged pink car chugged along nicely, up and over the braes. She passed the Tommel Castle Hotel entrance and drove on to the crossroads and turned off for Strathbane. She had to admit that the scenery was worth the visit. What mountains! What majestic scenery!

But when she crested the top of the hill to give her a view of Strathbane, like Hamish Macbeth, she experienced a sinking of the spirits. How awful that such a rundown industrial slagheap of a place should be dumped among the finest scenery in Britain. She saw a small garage by the side of the road and checked the petrol prices. Iain had overcharged her, but not by much. Why did the Scots put up with it? The prices were higher than in England. She filled up the tank and went into the garage shop to pay.

A giant of a man loomed behind the counter. She handed him her credit card and felt relief when it was accepted. She had begun to think that maybe in these primitive parts they didn't use credit cards. 'English?' he asked.

'Yes,' said Jenny brightly. 'I'm visiting.'

'You should stay in your own damn country.'

Before Jenny could think of an angry retort, a little woman shot out of the back shop. 'You behave yourself, Angus. I haff neffer heard the like. Go along with you, lassie, and welcome to the Highlands.'

She rounded on her giant of a husband. 'And as for you, you great scunner, you get off tae yir bed and stop insulting the customers.'

Jenny fled. No, it had been a mistake. One more night and back to civilization tomorrow morning.

Hamish Macbeth kicked his heels in Strathbane police headquarters all day. He had left Lugs with Angela Brodie, the doctor's wife, and hoped she wasn't overfeeding the animal. Angela was apt to be absent-minded, so that every time Lugs rattled his food bowl, she thought she hadn't fed him and would feed him again.

At last he was summoned up to Daviot's office. 'We have a handwriting expert who will see you this evening at seven. You will find him over in the forensic laboratory on the Scotsdale Road. You did bring the file of letters with you?'

'Yes, sir,' said Hamish. 'What's the man's name?'

'Mr Glass. Ask for Mr Roger Glass.'

'Any news of the autopsy?'

'Sinclair is still working on it. We should have a result by tomorrow. You're going to look very silly if it turns out to be plain suicide.'

'I'll take that chance, sir.'

Hamish went back to the police canteen to pass the time. He collected a tray containing egg and chips and tea and made for a table by the window.

He looked down into the street outside before he sat down. Across the road stood a shocking-pink Robin Reliant. I wonder what Iain is doing in Strathbane, thought Hamish, and then put it out of his mind.

Outside, Jenny decided to give up waiting for Hamish Macbeth. Robin Reliant enthusiasts were constantly knocking on her window to get her attention so that they could reminisce about the glories of their youth when they had owned such a car.

She glanced at her watch. If she was going to buy clothes, she'd better get a move on. She parked the car in a multi-storey in the centre which was built over a shopping arcade. In the arcade were several shops selling sporting goods, but they all seemed dreadfully expensive and she had no desire to buy clothes she would not be likely to wear again. Somehow the non-appearance of Hamish Macbeth had made her decide to stay on a bit.

At the end of the arcade, she found a store called Murphy's, full of cheap clothes and surprisingly cheap woollens. She bought two sweaters and a warm pair of wool trousers and an anorak. Then she moved to the shoe department and tried on shoes until she found a serviceable walking pair. On to the underwear department to purchase several pairs of white cotton briefs. I may look like a frump, she thought, but I'll be a comfortable frump.

She went into the toilet in the car park and changed her clothes and then surveyed herself in the mirror. The anorak, a garment she had once sworn never to be seen dead in, was cherry red. One of the new sweaters she had bought and now put on was lambswool and a dull gold colour. The trousers were dark brown and the flat shoes, brown.

Jenny walked to her car with a new feeling of freedom. Everything felt amazingly comfortable.

Her only regret was that her new anorak clashed violently with the colour of her car, but with an odd feeling of belonging, she headed out of Strathbane and took the road to Lochdubh.

At seven o'clock precisely, Hamish was ushered into Mr Glass's office. He had expected to meet a scholarly man wearing an old tweed jacket and thick glasses. Instead, he found himself looking at a man about his own age, mid-thirties, with sandy hair and a round cherubic face, wearing an open-necked checked shirt and jeans.

His voice, in contrast to his appearance, was dry and precise. 'You have the letters? It is Hamish Macbeth, is it not?'

'Yes, it is. I have the letters here.'

'It will take me some time '

Hamish sighed. 'It's an urgent case. Can't you at least try to give me some analysis of the type of person who wrote the letters?'

'I'll do my best. You'll find coffee in the pot over there. Help yourself.'

Mr Glass sat down and opened the file. Hamish poured a cup of coffee, sat down in a chair in the corner of the cluttered office, and tried to be patient.

At last he said, 'How can you really tell a person's character from their handwriting?'

'Attitudes and feelings influence the formations of handwriting. Handwriting is a sort of mental photograph of what's going on inside you.'

'What if someone deliberately disguised their handwriting?'

'Makes it a bit harder. But the real traits of character have a way of showing through.'

Silence again while Hamish fidgeted. There was a large plain clock on the wall, like the clocks you sometimes still see in Highland school classrooms. It had a loud tick-tock which seemed to get louder as the minutes dragged by.

'Ahum,' said Mr Glass.

'You've got something?' asked Hamish eagerly.

'Too early.'

Hamish's patience gave out. 'Look, man, one woman's dead and that woman was a postmistress and it's my guess it was murder and there'll be others if you don't get a move on. Give me an idea!'

'All right.' Glass capitulated. 'See this letter to a Mrs Wellington accusing her of having an affair with you?' He looked up at Hamish and a little gleam of malice darted through his eyes.

'Aye. You would pick that one. Go on. I'm looking.' Hamish bent over him.

'As far as I can see, she has made no effort to disguise her handwriting.'

'She? You're sure?'

'Pretty sure. She suffers from a low opinion of herself and never really feels safe.'

'I'm not surprised the biddy doesnae feel safe, writing letters like that.'

'No, that's not what I mean. She is always frightened of people finding out what her character really is like so that then they won't like her. She is often depressed. See how the lines of her writing descend and how the letters turn back? Look at the low *t*-bars. She wears a mask the whole time.'

'Like the Phantom of the Opera?'

'No, no. She assumes a role, possibly that of a strong, confident woman, and has probably been playing that part all her life.'

'She's old?'

'I think so. She has an overstretched personality. Because she thinks so little of herself, she tries to achieve more than she is capable of.'

'So even though she may be retired, she may have worked at something. I mean, not married and had children and been a housewife?'

'I can't go as far as that. You'll need to give me more time.'

'Phone me at Lochdubh when you've got something more.'

The following morning Hamish telephoned headquarters but was told that the results from the pathologist would not be ready until later that day.

There was a knock at the door. He opened it and recognized Jenny. The day was crisp and clear and she was dressed in her new 'sensible' clothes.

'What is it?' asked Hamish. He was anxious to get off to Braikie.

Jenny blinked. She had forgotten to come armed with an excuse. She thought of one rapidly.

'It's very remote up here,' she began, batting a pair of eyelashes, heavy with waterproof mascara, at him.

'So?' asked Hamish.

'I wonder if it's safe for a woman on her own to travel around?'

'Safest place in the world. Now, if you don't mind . . .'

Jenny's face reddened. 'Are you usually so rude to visitors?'

Hamish took another look at her. She was very pretty. 'I'm sorry,' he said. 'I've got a case that's worrying me. Look, I'll take you for dinner tonight.'

Jenny brightened. This was more than she had hoped for. 'Where?'

'That Italian restaurant on the waterfront. At eight this evening? I should be free then.'

'Lovely. I'll look forward to it.'

As she walked off, Hamish shook his head. A pretty girl lands on your doorstep, he chided himself, and you practically tell her to get lost.

Jenny had left the door open. He went to close it and found Elspeth standing there, staring up at him. He had not heard her arrive. But Elspeth always seemed to *materialize*.

'What now?' he asked.

'The handwriting expert. Did you see him?'

'Yes. Oh, come in. I'm trying to get off on the road to Braikie, but maybe it would be a good idea for you to hear what the man said.'

Elspeth followed him into the kitchen. 'What was she doing here?'

'Who?'

'The newcomer, Jenny Ogilvie.'

'Wanted some advice, that's all. Now, here's what the handwriting expert said.' He told her of Glass's findings. 'So,' he said, 'what is there in Braikie for an over-achiever? Maybe it is some woman who left and went to London, say, and made a success of whatever she did, then retired and returned to Braikie.'

'I don't think so. She's obviously had a lifetime of studying the locals.'

47

'Okay, Sherlock, come up with a better idea.'

'I think it would be someone with some sort of local power. The minister isn't a woman. The bank manager's a man and a newcomer at that. I have it!'

'Have what?'

'What about a schoolteacher? Braikie School is small and the headmistress has a lot of power.'

'They don't call them headmistresses any more,' said Hamish. 'It's "head teacher" in this politically correct world.'

'Bugger political correctness,' said Elspeth. 'Who do we know?'

Hamish thought about it. 'Miss McAndrew retired last year. I never really knew her.'

'Try her,' urged Elspeth.

'All right. But from the little I know of her, she seems a highly respectable lady.'

'I'd better get off.' Elspeth walked to the door and then hesitated. She turned round. 'We haven't had dinner together for a while. What about this evening?'

'I have a date.'

'Oh, Hamish. There's something odd there. She's stalking you.' And with that she was gone, leaving Hamish staring at the empty space where she had been standing only a second before.

* * *

Hamish fed Lugs but decided not to take his dog with him. It was going to be a tricky call. He could hardly walk into Miss McAndrew's home and accuse her of being a poison-pen writer. Maybe he should pretend he wanted her advice.

He drove off to Braikie, enjoying the splendid day, wondering how long it would last before the weather broke again. He drove along the shore road, noticing that for once the sea was calm, smooth glassy waves tumbling on to the rocky beach.

He called at the school and asked a teacher if he might have Miss McAndrew's address. He was told she lived in a bungalow called Braikie Manor on the shore road.

Interested to meet this woman who wanted to give the impression that she lived in a manor house, Hamish drove back out again on the shore road. He had been told that the bungalow was situated on a rise, just beyond the edge of Braikie.

It was a small square box of a house with one large bay window. The views out over the sea must be magnificent, he thought, as he parked the Land Rover at the side of the road and got out.

There was a short tarmac drive up to the front door. The garden was scrubby grass and a few trees permanently bent into a crouch by the Atlantic gales. The front door was slightly ajar.

He rang the doorbell in the wall on the side and listened as Westminster chimes sounded inside the house. No one came to the door. There was a garage at the side of the house. He walked up to it. There was a window at the side of the garage. It was grimy. He rubbed it with his sleeve and peered in. A small Ford Escort was inside. So she hadn't driven off anywhere.

He returned to the door and rang the bell again. Behind him, waves crashed on the beach and a seagull screamed overhead. He pushed the door wider and called, 'Miss McAndrew!'

Silence.

He took off his cap and tucked it under his arm. Perhaps she was asleep. He walked inside. There was a narrow hall. He looked down. The morning post was lying on the floor. He could feel his heartbeat quicken.

'Miss McAndrew!' he shouted again.

He opened a door on his left. The living room. No one there. A door on his right opened into the lounge, musty and slightly damp, obviously the 'best' room, used only on special occasions. There was an open door at the back of the hall leading into the kitchen. Before it, on the left and right, were two more doors. He opened the first.

It was a bedroom, the curtains tightly drawn. He fumbled for the light switch beside the door and switched it on. Light glared down on an awful figure on the bed soaked in blood. He walked forward. Dead eyes stared up at him. To make sure, he felt for her pulse and found none.

Miss McAndrew had been viciously and violently stabbed to death – a frenzy of stabbing. He took out his phone and called Strathbane. He pulled on a pair of thin gloves and went through to the living room. There was a desk by the window. On the top were a few bills and circulars. He slid open the desk drawers, one after the other. In the bottom drawer he found a packet of cheap stationery and a packet of envelopes. In one at the left top of the desk he found the beginning of a letter. 'Dear Effie,' it began, 'I have not heard from you for a while.' The handwriting looked like the writing on the anonymous letters.

He walked outside the bungalow and breathed in great gulps of fresh air. A car drove up and Jimmy Anderson got out, followed by his sidekick, MacNab, and two police officers. Hamish went to meet them. 'How did you get here so quickly?'

'Blair'll be along in a minute,' said Jimmy. 'We were in Braikie when we got your message. We were investigating that other murder.'

'You mean Miss Beattie?'

'Aye, that's the one. You were right. She'd been heavily drugged.'

'But I phoned this morning and was told the results weren't through.'

'I don't know who told you that, but it turns out you were right. So what've we got here?'

'A fatal stabbing.'

'Victim?'

'A Miss McAndrew, retired schoolteacher.'

'We've got the forensic team with us. They were going over the postmistress's flat again. We'll wait until they arrive. Any idea who murdered her or why?'

'I don't know who,' said Hamish heavily. 'But I know why.'

A car screeched to a halt at the foot of the garden and Detective Chief Inspector Blair heaved his bulk out of it.

'Why?' Jimmy asked Hamish.

'Miss McAndrew was the poison-pen writer and somebody found out.'

Chapter Three

Methought I heard a voice cy, 'Sleep no more!
Macbeth does murder sleep!' the innocent sleep,
Sleep that knits up the ravel'd sleeve of care.
                    – William Shakespeare

Blair was in a bad mood. He felt resentful that somehow Hamish Macbeth had turned what had appeared to be a simple suicide into a murder. And now that long drip of water, that glaikit Highland teuchter, had found another dead body.

He brushed past Hamish and said to Jimmy, 'Let's be having a look at the body.'

'Well, sir, the forensic team's just coming. Might be as well to wait for them.'

Blair's eyes bulged with fury, but he saw the wisdom of what Jimmy was saying and he rounded on Hamish. 'What prompted ye to call on her?'

Hamish patiently went through what the handwriting expert had told him and how he

53

thought a retired schoolteacher might fit the profile. Blair listened to him, his great bull head on one side.

The police photographer arrived, then the forensic team, and then the pathologist, Mr Sinclair. 'As soon as you're finished, I want a look inside the place,' growled Blair. 'And as for you, laddie, you may as well get back to your sheep or whatever.'

He stood to attention as a sleek black BMW halted behind the row of cars. Daviot got out. 'I was on my way to Braikie when I got a phone call telling me the news. You found the body, Macbeth?'

'Yes, sir.'

'Tell me about it.'

So Hamish told him how he had come to believe that Miss McAndrew might be the poison-pen writer and how he had found stationery which matched the paper used by the poison-pen writer in her desk.

'As you know by now, you were right about Miss Beattie's death. It's estimated the murder took place on the Saturday evening, maybe somewhere between nine and ten,' said Daviot.

'Aye, and I'm wondering why I wasnae told that the findings were in when I phoned this morning,' said Hamish.

Blair scowled at the sky. He had been passing by when he heard the girl taking Hamish's call and had told her to say that nothing had been discovered yet. Blair was jealous of Hamish and was always afraid that this peculiar policeman might one day decide not to sidestep promotion, move to Strathbane, and replace him.

'I don't know how that happened,' said Daviot. 'I think the best idea is for you to question people in Braikie and try to find out whether anyone was seen going up the stairs to Miss Beattie's flat. When we're finished here, I'll have some men released to help you.'

'I take it that countermands Mr Blair's order?'

'What order?'

'I was told to go back to my sheep, sir.'

Blair forced a jolly laugh. 'The trouble wi' you Highlanders,' he said, 'is that you cannae take a joke.'

'There you are, Macbeth. Now off you go.'

Another car screeched to a halt, and Elspeth and Pat Mallone got out. 'And get rid of those press,' ordered Daviot.

Hamish went up to Elspeth. 'She's dead, isn't she?' she asked.

'I'm supposed to get rid of you,' said Hamish. 'Follow me to Braikie and I'll tell you about it, but mind, you didn't hear it from me.'

They went into a dingy pub in Braikie called the Red Rory. In a puritan place like Braikie, thought Hamish, it followed that any drinking establishment should be as grim as possible.

55

They ordered soft drinks and sat down at a table by the window.

Hamish explained what he had found out.

'A double murder!' Pat's Irish eyes gleamed with excitement. 'I never thought I'd find such excitement up here.'

'Where are you from?' asked Hamish.

'Dublin.'

'And what brought you here?'

'I saw Sam's advertisement in the National Union of Journalists magazine and applied.' He grinned. 'I think I was the cheapest he could get, and I didn't have any experience in newspapers. I had been an advertising copy-writer since I left university. Mind you, when I saw Lochdubh and the *Highland Times*, I thought, what a dump. I can't live here. But then Elspeth walked in.' He smiled blindingly at her. Elspeth looked vaguely out of the grimy bar window.

'So you have the facts,' said Hamish. 'But don't quote me, not even as a source. Go out there and get quotes from the townspeople and quotes from Strathbane. Now I'm off to see what I can find out.'

'Are you sweet on him?' asked Pat after Hamish had left the pub.

'The only thing I'm sweet on,' said Elspeth coldly, 'is this story. Why don't we finish our drinks and see what we can find out so that we can print the stuff without betraying that Hamish told us.'

'Okay. It's going to be a long day. Why don't we have dinner at the Italian's tonight? Come on, Elspeth. You've been good taking me around and showing me the ropes. But we've got to relax sometime.'

Elspeth suddenly smiled. Why not? she thought. It wasn't as if Hamish Macbeth had shown any desire for her company recently.

'Fine. Let's get on.'

Pat grinned happily. He tried to remember whether the restaurant had candlelight. Candlelight was so romantic.

Hamish went first to see Mrs Harris, who had found Miss Beattie's body. 'It's yourself again,' she said, opening the door to him. 'Why are all the polis swarming all ower the place?'

'Can we go inside? I'll tell you about it.'

She lived in a flat above the shops near the post office. She led the way into a neat parlour where a budgie sang in a cage by the window and a large fat cat purred in front of the peat fire. 'Sit down,' said Mrs Harris. 'I'll get some tea.'

Hamish sank down in a comfortable, battered armchair by the fire. The cat purred, the clock on the mantel ticked, and he felt suddenly weary of the whole business.

He half-closed his eyes and thought hard. Miss Beattie, the postmistress, had been murdered. Who better to have guessed the identity of the poison-pen writer than the postmistress? But Miss McAndrew had been killed, and not in a planned and calculated manner, as in the murder of Miss Beattie, but by a frenzied stabbing. He felt he could now be looking for two murderers.

Mrs Harris came back in, carrying a laden tray. Hamish jumped to his feet and relieved her of it. 'Just set it on the table by the window,' she said.

'You shouldnae ha' gone to all this trouble,' said Hamish, looking down at plates of cakes and scones and a large pot of tea.

'It's not often I get the company, and now herself has gone, there's really nobody.' A tear rolled down Mrs Harris's withered cheek and she wiped it away with a corner of her flowered apron.

She poured tea. Hamish drew up a chair at the table. She sat down to the left of him, twisting her apron in her hands.

'Don't you have any family?' asked Hamish gently.

'My husband died twenty years ago. I never had the weans. My sister's gone as well.'

Hamish made a mental note to find out if there was some sort of old folks' club in Braikie and then asked, between bites of scone, 'Did Miss Beattie ever hint to you that she might have guessed the identity of the poison-pen writer?'

She frowned in thought. 'Wait a bittie. When you made that speech at the community hall, she says to me as we left, "It's all very well being asked to do your civic duty, but what if you've only got a suspicion and some poor respectable body is going to end up grilled by the police and maybe lose her reputation for nothing?"

'Well, I didn't think that much of it at the time because folks were guessing all over the place. I thought her question was . . . was . . .'

'Academic?'

'Aye, just a theory.'

'When did you last see her before you found her dead?'

'Outside the post office. She was locking up. Afore she left, she says, "Come round tomorrow and I'll give you some of my cakes." She had a rare light hand.'

'What of yourself? Did you ever have any suspicions about anyone?'

She shook her head. 'To tell the truth, I got fair sickened wi' all the accusations flying around. Why all these questions and why all the polis?'

'We like to be thorough,' said Hamish. He couldn't really tell her that her friend had been murdered until after the official announcement. She would find out soon enough, he thought.

'Did Miss Beattie have any relatives?'

'She had a sister, down in Perth. I think she's on her way up to the procurator fiscal's in Strathbane.' Scotland has a system based on Roman law, and the procurator fiscal is the coroner and public prosecutor of a Scottish district.

Hamish finished his tea and stood up. 'I'll be back to see you as soon as I have any news.'

Another tear rolled down her cheek. 'What's to tell? She took her ain life. I didnae know she was that unhappy. She should ha' told me.'

Hamish longed to tell her the truth, that her friend had not committed suicide, but still dared not tell her anything before it was all made official.

He left and went straight to the schoolhouse. It was an old-fashioned Victorian building of grey stone. He entered and wandered along a dingy corridor looking for a door marked head teacher, or headmistress or headmaster. He came to a door with a pane of frosted glass in it bearing the legend 'Head Teacher' in black painted letters. He knocked and a masculine voice said, 'Come!'

Hamish detested people who said 'Come.'

He opened the door and walked in. A small fussy man with gold-rimmed spectacles and thinning grey hair pasted across a freckled scalp was sitting behind a desk. He went on correcting papers.

Hamish felt his irritation growing. 'Now that you've impressed me with your importance, perhaps you might be able to answer a few questions, Mr . . .?'

The man looked up. 'Arkle,' he said. 'I am a very busy man. I've just taken over here. If you think I was trying to impress you, then you are much mistaken.'

'Good. Now, Mr Arkle, did you know Miss McAndrew?'

'We met at her leaving party. There was no need for me to see her before that. The school secretary explained everything to me.'

'I'd like a word with the secretary after I've finished with you. Now, Miss McAndrew has been found brutally stabbed to death this morning.'

'Dear me. Dear, dear me. What a shock! How can I help you?'

That's got your attention, you pompous git, thought Hamish. 'I am trying to get someone to describe her to me,' he said. 'What impression did you form of her?'

He frowned and placed the tips of his fingers together and peered wisely over them at Hamish. He always sees himself in a film, thought Hamish. 'Hmm. Let me see,' Mr Arkle said. 'Woman of the old school of teaching. Stern disciplinarian. She produced good results. Not a sympathetic type. I can't tell you much more than that.'

'May I be having a word with your secretary?'

'Yes, yes, of course.' He picked up the phone and dialled an extension. 'Miss Mather? Could you step into my office? The police would like to interview you.' He put the phone down. 'She will be along presently.'

'Where is her office?'

'Next door.'

And you couldn't just have shouted for her, could you, you twerp, thought Hamish. He saw a shadow outside the frosted glass of the door and jerked it open. A pale wispy girl stood there. 'Miss Mather?'

She looked up at him with wide frightened eyes. 'We'll just step outside,' said Hamish quickly. He had no desire to ask her questions with the head teacher listening and probably interrupting.

'Shall we go to my office?' she asked, casting a nervous glance at the head teacher's door.

'It's a grand day. Let's take a wee walk outside.'

She followed him meekly out of the school and stood beside him on the grey asphalt of the playground.

'Now, Miss Mather, my name is Hamish. And you are?'

'Freda.'

'Why are you looking so frightened?'

'When a policeman calls, it's almost always bad news. My mother . . .?'

'No, nothing about your family. The fact is that Miss McAndrew was found murdered this morning.'

She turned white and swayed. He caught her round the waist and led her to a bench at the edge of the playground. 'Put your head between your knees. That's a good girl. Now straighten up and take deep breaths.'

He waited until a little colour had come back to her face and then asked, 'Did you work for her?'

'Ye-es. For . . . for the past five years.'

'Think carefully and tell me honestly, what was she like?'

'Oh, she was a fine woman and got good results for the school.'

'Forget she's dead and tell me honestly what you really thought of her.'

A seagull landed on the ground at their feet, cocked its prehistoric head on one side, and, seeing no evidence of food, flew off with a contemptuous screech.

Freda bent her head. She was a drab-looking girl: hair of an indeterminate colour, neither fair nor brown, eyes of a washed-out blue, thin hunched figure.

'She was a bully,' said Freda. She gave a choked little sob. 'She would give little parties at her home and make me act as waitress, pouring out tea, handing round cakes, and she never paid me for it.'

'If she was such a bully, I'm surprised people wanted to visit her.'

'Oh, she was nice as pie to everyone, except maybe me and one of the other teachers.'

'There are four teachers, aren't there?'

'Yes, there's Miss Maisie Hart, Mrs Henrietta McNicol, Mr Jamie Burns, and a newcomer, Mr Matthew Eskdale.'

'And which one did she bully?'

'Mr Burns. He's quite old, you see, and he wants to hang on to get his pension.'

'You and Mr Burns could find other jobs?'

'Mr Burns is stubborn and swore she wasn't going to drive him out. As for me, my mother is not in good health, and finding another job would mean moving to Strathbane. I like to stay close.'

'Did anyone ever threaten Miss McAndrew?'

'I don't think anyone would dare.'

'What about the parents?'

'There was an incident last year at parents' day. Mr Joseph Cromarty, who runs the ironmonger's shop in the main street: His son, Geordie, had not been chosen for the school play and he shouted at her and accused her of having a down on the boy.'

'And did she?'

'You'd need to ask the boy's teacher, Mr Burns. I don't know about that.'

The dinner bell shrilled out from the school. Dinner was still in the middle of the day. Some children streamed out into the playground towards parents waiting at the gates. Other children carrying lunch boxes sat down on benches on the other side of the school yard. A harassed-looking elderly man came out and stood on the school steps.

'That's Mr Burns,' whispered Freda.

'Thanks for your time. I'll just have a word with him. Would you give me your home address and telephone number?'

She gave them to him. He thanked her again and she scuttled off into the school, her head bent.

Poor wee soul, thought Hamish. One bullying boss replaced by another.

He rose and approached Mr Burns. 'I've just heard the news about Miss McAndrew,' said Mr Burns. He had obviously once been a powerfully built man, but age had rounded his shoulders and turned muscle into fat. He had a thick shock of white hair and sagging jowls, his face marred by red broken veins.

'Who told you?' asked Hamish.

'Arkle.'

'Are you surprised? You don't seem surprised.'

'I hated the auld biddy. Mind you, I would have thought everyone was too scared of her to murder her.'

'Someone obviously wasn't. Do you know of anyone in particular who might have hated her enough?'

'Apart from me? No, not a clue. What a goings-on for a wee place like Braikie. First poor Miss Beattie murdered and now this.'

'Who told you Miss Beattie was murdered?' demanded Hamish sharply.

'Maisie Hart. She was late for school because she had a dental appointment and the nurse at the dentist's told her.'

'And who,' demanded Hamish impatiently, 'told the nurse?'

'She passed the post office on her way to the dentist's and got chatting to the policeman on duty and he told her.'

'I suppose it's all over the town,' said Hamish.

'Of course.'

If the cat's out of the bag, I may as well go the whole hog, thought Hamish with a wild mix of metaphors.

'So did you know that Miss McAndrew was our poison-pen letter writer?'

He looked stunned. 'Never! I mean, she was a bully, but she was all up front, if you know what I mean. Writing those letters was a poisonous, sneaky thing to do. Come to think about it, they started just around the time she retired.'

'Did you get one?'

'Yes. I sent it to you.'

'Refresh my memory. What was it about?'

'She accused me of having an affair with Maisie Hart. Maisie's a pretty wee thing. I was flattered.'

Hamish felt a tap on the shoulder and turned round. Blair stood there with Jimmy Anderson, MacNab, and a policeman and policewoman. 'We'll take over here, Macbeth.'

'Don't you want to know what I've got?' asked Hamish.

'I'll approach this with a fresh mind, laddie. Get off with you and talk to folks in the shops around the post office and people in the flats above. They might have seen something.'

Hamish felt sure he was being sent off to cover ground that had already been covered, but he knew it was useless to protest. He walked off.

He decided to look for the layabout youth of Braikie. There were police all over the place and they would concentrate on the residents around the shops. He wandered along the main street until he saw a group of pallid youths admiring one of their fellows' motorbikes. They showed signs of dispersing rapidly when they saw him approach, but he hailed them with, 'I just want a wee word.'

He was always amazed at how unhealthy some of the young men of the Highlands could look. In some cases it was drugs, but it was mostly a combination of bad diet and lack of exercise.

'Miss Beattie has been murdered,' he said, no longer seeing any reason to keep it quiet.

There were startled cries and they clustered around him, their eyes shining with excitement. 'Will the telly be here?' asked one. 'Will we get our pictures on the telly?'

'I should think they'll be along any minute,' said Hamish. 'Now, she was found dead last Sunday, so someone may have called on her on the Saturday evening. Were any of you passing the post office? Did any of you see anyone going up the stairs to her flat or even loitering about?'

They all shook their heads, and then a little voice from the back of the group piped up: 'I saw someone.'

They parted to reveal a small boy with a white face dotted with freckles and a mop of hair as red as Hamish's own.

'Och, Archie,' jeered the one with the motorbike. 'You're aye making things up.'

'But I did,' he protested.

'Come here, Archie,' said Hamish. He led

the boy a little away and took out his notebook. 'What is your full name?'

'Archie Brand.'

'And where do you live?'

'At 6 Glebe Street.'

'What time would this be?'

'Around nine. The night Miss Beattie was
murdered.'

'And what were you doing at that time of
night? Glebe Street is at the far end. How old
are you?'

'Ten. I was going to the chip shop.'

'Right, Archie, now think carefully. What or
who did you see?'

'It was a young fellow. I couldnae see clear,
for the street light was out. He was wearing
black clothes. He had wan o' thae baseball
caps pulled down low.'

'And what was he doing?'

'Just standing outside the post office, looking up and down, and when I came towards
him, he turned and looked in the window.'

'So you didn't see his face.'

'No, sir.'

'What age?'

'Maybe about ma brither's age. About seventeen.'

'Tall?'

'Not as tall as you.'

Hamish turned and surveyed the group. 'Is
your brother there?'

'Yes, he's the wan wi' the motorbike.'

'About his height?'

'Just about.'

Hamish wrote five foot eight in his note-book. 'Slim, fat, medium?'

'I couldnae be sure. He'd wan o' thae puffy jackets on. I walked on towards the chippy and I turned back once, but he'd gone.'

'Anyone else around?'

'No, the street was empty. There wasn't even anyone in the chip shop.'

'This could be vital evidence,' said Hamish solemnly. 'I may be calling at your home later.'

In the distance, the school bell shrilled. 'You'd best be getting back to school,' said Hamish, closing his notebook.

'Do I hafftae? I mean, this murder and all. Don't I get a day off?'

'Run along,' said Hamish. The boy reluct-antly trailed off in the direction of the school followed by the jeers of the gang headed by his brother.

Hamish walked back to the post office and studied the shops opposite. Some of them obviously used the upstairs of the premises, but above what was once a dress shop and was now an ironmonger's, he could see cur-tains at windows. He crossed the road and went up the stairs to the flats above. What had once been a dentist's surgery had the name of a law firm on the door. He remembered the murder of the dentist. There had been an old man living at the top of the stairs then. Hamish wondered whether he was still alive.

He mounted another flight of stairs and knocked at the door at the top. The door opened and Hamish thought he recognized Fred Sutherland. He was wearing a dressing gown, striped pyjamas, and a flat cap. 'Fred?'

'No, that was my cousin. I'm Jock. Fred left me the flat. Come ben. Terrible business. Two murders.'

'Who told you?'

'Joe Cromarty, the ironmonger. He came up a few minutes ago and says to me that Miss McAndrew's been murdered and that poor Miss Beattie was murdered as well.'

Hamish reflected bitterly that the whole of northern Scotland must know about the murders. Gossip in the Highlands spread as rapidly as fire in the heather after a dry summer.

'Would you like some tea?' asked Jock.

'No, I just want to ask you a few questions. Miss Beattie was killed sometime on Saturday night.' Hamish crossed to the window. 'You can get a good look across the street to the post office. Did you see anyone or anything? Might be around nine o'clock.'

'I can't remember the time. I'd been to that meeting o' yours in the community hall. Wait a bit. I did look across because Miss Beattie

71

always left her curtains drawn back and if she saw me at the window, she'd give me a wave. But the curtains were drawn tight. She did that if she was entertaining someone.'

Hamish looked at him sharply. 'A man?'

'One night I saw a man's back at the window and he disappeared into the room and Miss Beattie then drew the curtains.'

'What age of a man?'

'I couldnae right say. I just caught a wee glimpse of his back, and the window's small and cut off the top of his head.'

'But did you get an impression of his age?'

'The shoulders were pretty broad and a bit rounded. Wearing a dark suit. Couldnae tell you his age.'

'You didn't see anyone loitering in the street?'

'I didn't look down. Then I made myself a cup of tea and watched the telly.'

'Did you know Miss McAndrew?'

'I met her a few times. There's an old folks' club at the community centre. She would come there sometimes. She was promoting a reading and writing class for the elderly. Waste of time. In our day, no child in the parish left school without being able to read and write. Bossy woman. All teeth and dyed-blonde hair.'

'You didn't like her?'

'Nobody did.'

'I always got the impression she was well respected.'

'Och, you know what parents are like in Scotland. She managed to get good grades, and as long as she got good grades for the kids, the parents didn't really care what she was like.'

'I gather Mr Cromarty had a row with her.'

'Och, him? Nothing in that. He shouldn't be running a shop. He'll have a row with everyone.'

'I'd better speak to him. If you hear anything, phone me at Lochdubh.'

Hamish went out into the street and walked into the ironmonger's shop. He had expected to see a thuggish man behind the counter, but there was only a small man with thick horn-rimmed glasses and a shock of brown hair. He was wearing a brown cotton coat over his suit.

'I'm looking for Joseph Cromarty,' said Hamish.

'That's me.'

'I am Hamish Macbeth, constable at Lochdubh.'

'I heard you at the community hall. What's all this about two murders?'

Hamish told him briefly and then asked Joe if he'd seen anyone loitering around on the Saturday evening.

'I couldn't see anyone. Half day on Saturday. I spent the afternoon in my garden and then went to the pictures in Strathbane with the wife. So I've got a cast-iron alibi.'

'Nobody's accusing you of anything,' said Hamish mildly. 'Now, do you know if Miss Beattie had a gentleman friend?'

'What the hell are you implying?'

Hamish stared at the suddenly belligerent face in surprise. 'Why are you so angry? Why so defensive? Was her caller yourself?'

Joe Cromarty erupted. 'I'll phone your superiors and I'll be having you for slander.'

Hamish lost his temper. 'What the hell's the matter wi' you, you silly wee man? If there was nothing going on between you and Miss Beattie, why are you firing up?'

'I'm sick o' the gossip in this town. Everyone mumbling and whispering about everyone else's business.'

'Let's try another tack. I hear you were furious with Miss McAndrew on parents' day at the school.'

'That was legitimate. My Geordie's a bright boy and she only gave him a B in his history exam while she gave Penny Roberts, who's as dim as anything, an A. Then she wouldn't let him in the school play. I accused her of favouritism. She was aye keeping Penny in after school for a wee chat. Penny told Geordie the auld woman gave her the creeps.'

'Do you know where Penny Roberts lives?'

'Out on the shore road afore you get to Miss McAndrew's. It's a bungalow called Highland Home.'

When he left the shop, Hamish realized he was hungry. He took out his phone and called Angela Brodie, the doctor's wife, and begged her to collect Lugs and take the dog for a walk. As he put his phone back in his pocket, he felt a tap on his shoulder and turned round and saw Elspeth.

'How are you getting on?' she asked.

'Slowly. What about you?'

'I'm hungry. Let's find somewhere for lunch and I'll tell you what I've got.'

'Where's Pat?'

'He got a call from our boss, saying he must have learnt the ropes by now and there was a dried-flower show over at Lairg waiting to be covered.'

'That seems a bit odd considering there are two murders here.'

'Not to Sam. Flower shows with lots of names and pictures sell more papers in the long run, he says. The murders will be covered by the nationals anyway and television.'

'They're here already,' said Hamish, watching satellite dishes being set up and cables snaking from vans across the street outside the post office.

'Right. There's a hotel north of here with good food.'

'Which one?'

'The Clachan. My car's right here.'

Hamish looked around in case Blair was skulking about, but there were only uniformed policemen going from door to door.

They drove north out of Braikie. The coastal road became more rugged and was one-track with grass growing in the middle of it. After a couple of miles, Elspeth swung off to the right and up a winding drive bordered by thick rhododendron bushes.

'This used to be Colonel Hargreaves's place,' said Hamish.

'He got rheumatism and blamed the climate. He sold up and moved south. An English couple bought it and turned it into a hotel.'

She parked outside the hotel and they both got out. It was a Victorian building dating from the days of the nineteenth century, when the queen had made it fashionable to holiday in Scotland. They were ushered into the dining room by the new owner, John Speir. 'You've got the dining room all to yourself,' he said, showing them to a table at the window. 'But it won't be quiet for long. Press from all over have booked rooms. Terrible, these murders, but great for the hotel business. Still, I didn't expect many customers now the summer is over, so it's a set menu.' He handed them a card each. There was a choice of two dishes for each course. They both chose the same: Scotch broth, poached salmon, and sherry trifle.

'Now,' said Hamish, 'what have you got?'

Elspeth's grey eyes gleamed silver. 'Miss Beattie was having an affair.'

'I'd got that far,' said Hamish. 'Any idea who it is?'

'Billy Mackay.'

'What! The postman? But he's married.'

'Why do you think she kept it so secret?'

Hamish half rose. 'I should go and see him right away.'

'Sit down, copper. You wouldn't have found out for ages if I hadn't told you. He'll wait and I'm hungry.'

'Who told you?'

'I cannot reveal my source,' said Elspeth primly.

'All right. How did you manage to find out?'

'I'm known in Braikie more for being an astrologer than for being the local reporter, and they're a superstitious lot. Some woman asked me to read her palm. I told her the usual and then said she was holding back some secret about Miss Beattie.'

'How did you know that?'

'Just a guess.'

Mrs Harris, thought Hamish. I bet she knew.

'She got frightened and asked me not to put

77

a curse on her if she told me. I promised I wouldn't use it in the paper.'

'So Mrs Harris knew you were of gypsy blood?'

Elspeth's face fell. 'How did you know it was Mrs Harris?'

'An educated guess. And let's hope the food comes quickly. I can't wait to hear what this postman has to say for himself.'

The food was excellent and both enjoyed their meal. Elspeth drove Hamish back into Braikie. He refused to let her come with him to Billy Mackay's but promised to meet her afterwards, outside the post office in an hour, and tell her what he had found out.

By asking around, he found that Billy Mackay lived in public housing at the edge of Braikie. He knocked at the door. It was answered by a slattern of a woman wearing a stained apron and with her hair in rollers. 'Mrs Mackay?'

'Aye, that's me.'

'I would like to talk to your husband.'

'What about?'

'I'm making general inquiries, that is all.'

'He's gone fishing as usual.'

'Where?'

'Up on the Stourie. The pool below the falls. And you tell him the sink still needs fixing and he can stay away as long as he likes but he'll still have to fix it when he comes home.'

Hamish touched his cap and strode back to the Land Rover. He drove out of Braikie and up into the hills. The Falls of Stourie were a tourist attraction in the summer, but now the car park above the falls was empty except for a red post office van parked against some railings.

He made his precipitous way along a muddy path that led down the side of the falls. The sun was already going down and the cascade of water shone red in the setting rays.

Billy Mackay did not hear him approach because of the sound of the falls. He was a thickset little man in, Hamish judged, his late fifties. Hamish tapped him on the shoulder and he swung around, his face a picture of dismay.

'Up to the car park,' shouted Hamish. 'I cannae hear anything here.'

Billy reeled in his line and meekly followed Hamish up the path. He turned and faced Hamish in the car park, wearing a defeated air. He had thin brown hair, a bulbous nose, and surprisingly beautiful blue eyes.

'It's about Miss Beattie, isn't it?' he said. 'The wife'll kill me.'

'How long had your affair with Miss Beattie been going on?'

'About ten years.'

'Man, weren't you frightened of anyone finding out?'

'We kept it really quiet. I'm the postman, see,

so no one thought anything of me being around the shop. I don't know if you could really call it an affair. It was the talking, you see. The companionship. Her at home, after the children grew up and left, she let herself go and nag, nagged, nagged from morning till night.'

Hamish judged that Billy's parents had probably brought him up to speak Gaelic. He had the clear perfect English of someone who had started his life translating in his head from Gaelic to English.

'When did you last see Miss Beattie?'

'Last time was two weeks ago.'

'Why such a long gap?'

Billy hung his head. 'I got one of those filthy poison-pen letters. Whoever wrote it said he knew about the affair and if I didn't stop seeing her, the whole of Braikie would know. I told her about it and we were both frightened, so we agreed to stop seeing each other. Man, if I had known it would have driven her to take her own life, I would have risked the scandal.'

Hamish sighed. 'Billy, you're in for a shock. Miss Beattie was murdered.'

'But she hanged herself!'

'Someone drugged her first.'

'Who?'

Hamish was sure that Miss Beattie had guessed the identity of the poison-pen writer and that somehow Miss McAndrew had killed her and then someone had killed Miss McAndrew. And Billy was a prime suspect. He would need to take him in for questioning. He knew that probably someone other than Mrs Harris would know about the affair.

He said gently, 'I'm afraid I can't hush this up, Billy. I've got to take you in for questioning.'

He gave a weary shrug. 'I'm glad in a way it's out. I was proud of her friendship. She was a grand lady.' He began to sob, dry racking sobs.

Hamish went to the Land Rover and came back with a flask of brandy. 'Get some of that down you, Billy. There, man. I'm right sorry.'

It was Blair's bad luck that Daviot should still be in Braikie at the mobile unit which had been set up outside Miss McAndrew's bungalow when Hamish turned up with Billy and explained why he was taking him in.

'We'll take him down to Strathbane,' said Daviot. 'Anderson, you come with us. Detective Chief Inspector Blair will stay here to supervise the ongoing investigation. You'd better come with us, Hamish.'

Blair scowled horribly. He knew that when the boss used Hamish's first name, the constable was in high favour.

* * *

At Strathbane, it was a long interrogation. But it transpired early on in the interview that on the Saturday evening that Miss Beattie was murdered, Billy had been down in Strathbane for a reunion with some of his old army friends and had not got back to Braikie until the small hours of the morning. His alibi checked out. He was to be kept in the cells overnight, however, for further questioning. He was now a suspect in the death of Miss McAndrew. They would hold him until they discovered from the autopsy some idea of the time of her murder. Hamish was dismissed.

He left headquarters to find Elspeth waiting outside for him.

'You stood me up,' she accused.

'We'll have something to eat and I'll tell you about it,' said Hamish.

In the Italian restaurant, Jenny sat alone at one table and Pat sat alone at another. At last Pat called over, 'My date hasn't turned up.'

'Neither has mine,' said Jenny gloomily.

'So why don't we have a meal together?' suggested Pat.

Jenny gave a shrug. 'Why not?'

Chapter Four

Fear death? – to feel the fog in my throat,
The mist in my face.

— Robert Browning

Jenny lay awake for a long time. Pat had told her all about the murders in Braikie and so it was understandable that Hamish Macbeth had forgotten his date with her. Nevertheless, it rankled. If he had been meeting Priscilla, thought Jenny jealously, he would at least have phoned to apologize. Pat had been good company, and, yes, he was attractive and amusing, but he would not make Priscilla jealous. She could imagine Priscilla's cool amusement. A reporter? On a local paper? And what took you to Lochdubh and why didn't you tell me?

How quiet it was! Suffocatingly quiet. She crawled out of bed and went to the window and opened the curtains. A thick wall of mist leant against the window. She suddenly felt nervous. It looked as if the whole of the world was blanketed in thick sea fog. And out there, shrouded in the mist, was a murderer.

Jenny went back to bed. This trip had all been a dreadful mistake. She would leave in the morning.

Hamish Macbeth, too, was lying awake. He suddenly remembered he had forgotten his dinner date with Jenny. His restless thoughts turned back to the murders. People had sent him their poison-pen letters. But he shrewdly suspected that the only ones he had received were the ones without a grain of truth in the accusations. Someone, somewhere, he thought, had received a letter from Miss McAndrew which had hit on something the recipient had desperately wanted kept quiet. And there were so many suspects! Jimmy had phoned him before he went to bed to say that Miss Beattie's birth certificate had been found among her effects, proving that she was legitimate. She had also made out a will leaving everything to Billy Mackay. His thoughts turned back to Jenny Ogilvie. He had better check out her background. It was odd that such a pretty girl should choose to holiday in Lochdubh at such a time of year. He decided to question her first thing in the morning before moving on to Braikie.

* * *

Elspeth was awake as well and also thinking about Jenny. She had a shrewd suspicion that Jenny was not just an ordinary tourist. For some reason, Jenny was after Hamish Macbeth. Why? It hadn't been love at first sight. When Jenny had first set eyes on Hamish, Elspeth was sure she had been disappointed in him. Better check up on her, thought Elspeth sleepily.

A silent morning broke with every sound still muffled by the thick enveloping mist. Once more Hamish phoned Angela and begged her to look after Lugs. This time Lugs went eagerly, straining at the leash, and when the dog saw Angela, he wagged his ridiculous plume of a tail and leapt up at her, barking with joy. I cannae even keep the affections of my dog, thought Hamish gloomily after he had thanked Angela, and then he headed for Sea View to interview Jenny.

He was told Jenny was at breakfast and made his way into the small dining room.

'Good morning,' said Hamish, removing his cap and sitting down opposite her. 'I am here on official business, but first I would like to apologize for forgetting about our dinner engagement. Have you heard about the murders?'

Jenny nodded, and then said, 'What official business?'

'I have to question everyone. Have you had any connection with Lochdubh before this, or do you know anyone connected with Lochdubh?'

'No,' said Jenny quickly, and then fiddled with a piece of toast.

'So why Lochdubh for a holiday?'

'I wanted to get clear away. I stuck a pin in the map.'

Now, why is she lying? wondered Hamish, looking at her bent head, at the guilty flush rising up her neck, and at the nervous fingers now crumbling the toast.

He took out his notebook. 'May I have your address?'

'Number 7A Crimea Road, Battersea.'

'And where was it you said you worked?'

Jenny stared at him. What had she told him before?

'I – I d-don't have a j-job,' she stuttered. 'I didn't like to tell you that before. You see, Mummy and Daddy give me a generous allowance. I don't have to work and I'm a bit ashamed of being such a layabout.'

'And where do Mr and Mrs Ogilvie live?'

'Chipping Norton.'

'In the Cotswolds?'

'Yes.'

'Address?'

'Look, is all this necessary?' said Jenny desperately. 'They'll be worried sick if they know I'm up here where there have been two murders.'

'So you know about the murders?'

'Yes, I had dinner with that Pat Mallone. He told me.'

'Right. Parents' address?'

'Manor Farm, Sheep Lane, Chipping Norton.'

'Phone number?'

'I forgot to bring it with me. I can never remember it.'

Hamish closed his notebook. 'You'll be hearing from me.' He left abruptly and Jenny heaved a sigh of relief.

Her relief disappeared when Hamish came back five minutes later and sat down again. 'Now, Miss Ogilvie –' no more 'Jenny' – 'I have spoken to your parents. They do not know you are up here. Furthermore, they say you work for a computer company in the City called Camber Stein. Camber Stein confirm you are on holiday. Why did you lie to me?'

'I . . . I . . . I . . .'

'I have a friend who works at Camber Stein. Her name is Priscilla Halburton-Smythe. Do you know her? No more lies.'

'Yes,' mumbled Jenny.

'Does she know you are here?'

'No. She had talked a lot about Lochdubh. I had some holiday owing and decided to come up here at the last minute. I hadn't time to tell her.'

Hamish leant back in his chair and surveyed her. 'It would have been natural to tell her. She was brought up here, she is my ex-fiancée, her parents own the local hotel. So why not?'

'I'm telling you, I hadn't time,' shouted Jenny.

'You've been awfy interested in me since you arrived,' said Hamish slowly. 'I'm not the subject of some joke between you and Priscilla, am I?'

'No, no. Honestly, she doesn't know I'm here.'

'I'll check it out. Be back shortly. Don't move.'

Hamish went outside and took out his mobile phone, dialled the computer company, and asked to speak to Priscilla. When her cool voice came on the line, his heart gave a lurch. 'It's Hamish,' he said.

'Hamish! I haven't heard from you in ages.'

'Do you know a girl called Jenny Ogilvie?'

'Yes, of course. I work with her and she's a friend. Why?'

'She's here.'

'What! In Lochdubh?'

'Aye.'

'Good heavens. She was round at my place only about a week ago. Why didn't she tell me?'

'That's what I was wondering. First of all, she lied about where she worked. Then she said she didn't work and that her parents were supporting her. Then she said she came up on an impulse. I am not a vain man but she seemed to be setting her cap at me.'

There was a silence, and then Priscilla said slowly, 'I have been talking about you. I think she is a little bit jealous of me. Maybe she thought that if she could snare you, it might put my nose out of joint.'

Again that lurch at the heart.

'I'll get rid of her.'

There was a silence. Then Priscilla said, 'No, don't spoil her holiday. She's had bad luck with men and always chooses rotters. She's actually very kind. When I had the flu last winter, she came round and nursed me and did all my shopping.'

'I thought your fiancé, Peter, would have been on hand to do that.'

'He couldn't spare the time. He works very hard. Maybe she could help you on this case.'

'What! Her? Priscilla, the lassie's daft.'

'She's got a knack of getting people to talk to her. People on the tube end up telling her their life stories.'

'The place is crawling with police. I haff no need of herself's help,' said Hamish stiffly, the strength of his Highland accent showing he was upset. But what had he expected? That Priscilla would immediately fly up to confront Jenny? He had broken off the engagement because of Priscilla's aloofness. Why go down that road again?

'Suit yourself,' said Priscilla.

'I usually do. When's the wedding?'

'We've put it off again. Peter's awfully busy. I'll let you know.'

'Do that. I'd better get on with my work. Goodbye.' Hamish rang off and stared bleakly along the misty waterfront. The thick mist was beginning to shift and eddy like so many ghosts being called home.

He gave a sigh, then went in and sat down in front of Jenny. 'Don't ever lie to me again,' he said. 'I've just spoken to Priscilla.'

'Oh, God.' Jenny's face was scarlet and her large eyes were swimming with tears. 'I'll leave today.'

Hamish's face softened. 'No need for that. Let's forget about the whole thing. Enjoy your holiday.' He stood up and, on impulse, bent down and kissed her on the cheek.

After he had left, Jenny slowly put her hand up to the cheek he had kissed.

Mrs Dunne bustled in to clear the breakfast things away. 'What did Hamish want?' she asked.

'Just asking questions about why I was here,' said Jenny. She dabbed at her eyes with a handkerchief. 'I seem to have an allergy.'

'Morning!' Pat Mallone bounced into the breakfast room.

'I must ask you both to clear out of here,' said Mrs Dunne. 'It's past time for me cleaning the dining room.'

'It's all right,' said Pat cheerfully. 'We're just leaving. Got your coat?'

'Yes,' said Jenny, picking up her new anorak from the chair next to her. She followed him out on to the waterfront. 'Where are we going? I was thinking of leaving today.'

'You can't. We've got two murders to solve.'

'Isn't that Hamish's job?'

'What! The local bobby? In my opinion, that man's overrated. Let's go to Braikie and ask around. I've been sent to get local colour and background. The boss has a commission from the *Daily Bugle* for a feature piece. This is my chance to shine in one of the nationals.'

Hamish decided on arrival in Braikie that he should interview Penny Roberts, the headmistress's pet. He knew if he approached Arkle, he would be told that he was disrupting lessons. He entered the school and knocked at the glass door of the secretary, Freda Mather.

He heard a faint 'Come in' and opened the door. Freda turned white when she saw him and swayed in her chair. He went quickly round behind her desk and said, 'Now then, lassie, take deep breaths. That's it. There's nothing to be afraid of.'

She gulped in air and then said, 'I'm all right now. Honest. When I saw you, the first thing I thought was that there had been another murder.'

'Now, why should you think that?'

'It's silly. But there's such an atmosphere of suspicion and threat around. I'm sorry. How can I help?'

'I would like a quiet word with Penny Roberts.'

'Mr Arkle won't like that.'

'Where is Mr Arkle?'

'He's away today. He's at a board of education meeting.'

'So we don't need to bother about him,' said Hamish bracingly. 'And what he doesn't know can't upset him.'

'Won't her parents need to be present?'

'No, it's not as if she's being charged with anything. You'll do.'

Freda rose and went to the wall where class schedules were pinned up. 'Penny's in the art class at the moment and art is not her best subject. I'll go and get her.'

Hamish waited patiently. Footsteps came and went in the corridor outside.

After he had interviewed Penny, he decided, he would get the home addresses of the teachers and call on them after school. He remembered his own school report: 'brilliant but lazy'. His teachers had never really forgiven him for coming out on top in all the exams while apparently doing very little work. He wondered if Penny would turn out to be an egghead. Teachers felt comfortable with swots.

The door opened and Freda ushered in a teenager. She was a quite remarkable beauty. She had thick black hair and a perfect complexion and huge blue eyes. She was wearing the school uniform of grey sweater and grey pleated skirt with a blue shirt and striped tie. Hamish noticed that the skirt was very short and she was wearing sheer black tights and those clumpy shoes with thick soles like diving boots.

Freda produced two chairs for them and then sat down nervously behind her desk.

'I am PC Hamish Macbeth,' said Hamish.

'I know.' Penny smiled at him out of those incredible eyes and flicked a lock of glossy black hair over one shoulder. 'Word gets around.'

'Now, Penny, I'll get straight to the point. I'm trying to find out as much as I can about the character of your late headmistress.'

'Head teacher,' corrected Penny.

'Whatever. You see, sometimes the character of the deceased can give the police a clue as to why she was murdered. I believe you were something of a favourite with her.'

'Aye. She was all over me like a rash,' said Penny with an almost adult insouciance.

'So tell me about her.'

Penny shrugged. 'She was always finding excuses to invite me round to her house. Said I had a brilliant future. Always making excuses that I needed extra coaching in this and that. She said I didn't want to rot the rest of my life in a place like Braikie. Oh, I 'member. She got mad at me once. I told her I wasn't going to the university. I mean, university in Strathbane! Spotty students. Dead-alive hole.' Another flick of the hair, a crossing of long legs, a sideways glance. 'I told her I was going to be a television presenter and she went apeshit.'

'Penny!' admonished Freda.

'Sorry. But she went into full rant. Said television was full of men who would prey on me.

'I said, "What's up with that?" and she told me to get out of her house. But she sent me flowers the next day and an apology.'

'Didn't your parents find her behaviour . . . weird?'

'Oh, Ma and Da think teachers are God. They could see nothing wrong with her.'

'Did it ever cross your mind that she might be a lesbian?'

Penny's beautiful brow furrowed in thought. 'No. I mean, she didn't look Greek.'

So there *was* some innocence left in that beautiful brain, thought Hamish.

'You're bound to know sooner or later,' he said. 'Miss McAndrew appears to have been the author of those poison-pen letters. Did you have any idea she was writing them?'

For once, Penny looked shocked out of her normal composure. 'I'd never have guessed,' she said. 'I mean, who would think a head teacher would do something like that? Mind you, she always seemed to have taken a spite to someone, always complaining.'

'Did she ever complain about Miss Beattie?'

'Well, she did. Let me think. Said something about the way she was going on was disgraceful. Oh, there's something else weird.'

'What?'

'I'll tell you if you don't let on.'

'Penny, I promise to let anything you say to me stay between these four walls – unless, of course, it relates directly to the murder.'

'It's like this. Geordie Cromarty ...'

'The ironmonger's son.'

'Yes, him. He phoned me one night and said if I slipped out, he would buy me fish and chips. I'd been on this diet, see. If you're going to be on television, you have to be thin. I was fair starving so I said I'd meet him. I slipped out by the bedroom window and met him in the main street.'

'About what time of night would that have been?'

'It was just before eleven. He said to hurry up because the chippy closed at eleven. So we were going to the chippy and you know what Braikie's like at that time of night – dead as a doornail. Then I saw on the other side of the lights from the chippy's window this cloaked figure. "Someone's coming," I said. So we hid in a doorway. She passed us. She had this long black cloak with a hood right down over her face. A gust of wind blew the hood back and it was her and she looked real weird.'

'Miss McAndrew?'

'Herself. She was muttering something under her breath. I tell you, it gave us both a scare. We stayed in the doorway until we were sure she had gone, and by the time we got to the chippy, it had closed.'

'Didn't you think it odd that your former head teacher should be behaving so strangely?'

'Grown-ups are all weird, if you ask me,' said Penny with all the brutality of youth. 'I'm never going to get like that.'

'What night did you see her?'

'A few nights back. Can't remember which one.'

Hamish asked her a few more questions and then dismissed her.

He turned to Freda. 'Did you think Miss McAndrew was weird?'

'No. Like I said, I thought she was a bully. I did think she was overfond of Penny, but teachers sometimes get harmless crushes on pupils. Sometimes it's the other way round.' A smile lifted her pale lips. 'Mind you, there's no one in this school to get a crush on.'

Hamish thanked her and left. He sat on a wall outside the school and made rapid notes.

Miss McAndrew had taught many pupils in her career, seen them grow up, maybe knew their secrets. She had hit on one that meant ruin for someone. He closed his notebook with a sigh. He had better go back in again and ask to see Geordie.

Freda had regained a little bit of colour when she ushered Geordie in to speak to Hamish. If only the lassie could get another job, thought Hamish. On the other hand, maybe she would attract bullies wherever she went.

Geordie Cromarty was small and swarthy. He had hair as black as Penny's and it grew low on his forehead. His eyes were the same peculiarly silvery light grey as Elspeth's. People with such eyes were often credited with having the second sight, the ability to see the future. Hamish thought of the seer of Lochdubh, Angus Macdonald. Perhaps it might be an idea to call on him later and see if he'd heard anything. Hamish was sure most of Angus's predictions were based on gossip.

'Now, Geordie,' began Hamish, 'Penny tells me you were both out in Braikie one night and saw Miss McAndrew behaving strangely.'

'Aye, her looked like something out o' a horror film, big cloak and all.'

'Now, Penny can't remember which night it was. Can you?'

'Sure. It was the night afore that auld biddy in the post office topped herself.'

'May I remind you that Miss Beattie was murdered?'

'Was she? Cool!'

'And did Miss McAndrew go straight on down the street?'

'We didnae stop tae look, man,' said Geordie, whose speech was an odd mixture of Highland dialect and Americanisms culled from films.

'Did you experience any trouble with Miss McAndrew?'

'All the time. She told me to stay away from Penny. She said Penny was meant for better things.'

'What did you reply to that?'

Geordie looked at him with scorn. 'Lissen, copper, when the auldies are getting at ye, ye say, "Right, miss, no, miss, sure, miss."'

'Did Penny not find the attentions of Miss McAndrew embarrassing?'

'She got the best marks in her exams. I think Miss McAndrew fixed a lot of her papers.'

'Did Penny tell you that?'

'Naw, just a guess.'

'Your father was angry with Miss McAndrew, wasn't he?'

'Aye, herself gave me a bad mark in an exam. History, it was. I'm good at history. He demanded to see the exam paper and she wouldn't let him see it, so he said he'd write to the education board. My dad said she was taking her spite out on me because of Penny.'

'If you hear anything at all, Geordie, that might be relevant, let me know.'

Geordie looked as if someone had just pinned a deputy sheriff's badge on him. His face beamed. 'Sure, guv,' he said. 'You can count on me.'

After Geordie had left, Freda said, 'I thought Miss McAndrew was a bully, but I never thought she'd cheat.'

'It looks as if she might have done.' Hamish thanked her again and left. He made his way out of the school and along the quiet tree-lined street which led to the main thoroughfare. At the corner stood the community hall. He peered in the window. It was full of old people, watching television, playing cards, reading, or just chatting. He pushed open the door and went in. 'Who's in charge here?' he asked an elderly lady in a wheelchair.

'Mr Blakey, ower there.'

Mr Blakey was a thin man whose face was covered in a film of sweat. The room was not particularly warm. Hamish noticed he had a slight tic at the corner of his mouth and that his nails were bitten to the quick. The sweating, he judged, must be a nervous condition. Mr Blakey, as he was to discover, walked about in a sort of tropical rain forest.

'Mr Blakey?'

'That's me.' Mr Blakey took a damp handkerchief from his pocket and mopped his brow.

'How often do you meet here?'

'It's open every morning. Then twice a week, Mondays and Fridays, we show videos in the evening.'

'There's a Mrs Harris. She seems quite lonely. I would like to bring her along.'

'What about this Friday?' suggested Mr Blakey. 'We're showing *Green Card* at seven o'clock. I can't afford the new videos.'

'And you probably pay for them yourself,' said Hamish, recognizing one of the world's few genuine do-gooders in this thin, nervous man.

'Well, funds are not that great.'

'Is this your full-time job? You're what? In your fifties? Not old these days.'

'I worked at the bank for years. Had a bit of a nervous breakdown. This keeps me occupied.'

'I'll come on Friday,' said Hamish. 'I've got a lot of videos at home I'll never look at again. I'll bring them with me.'

Mr Blakey thanked him and Hamish made his way to Mrs Harris's flat, where he told her about the old folks' club. 'Amy – Miss Beattie – was always on at me to go, but I didn't want to be with a lot of old folk.'

'It'd be company for you. They're showing a film on Friday night. I'll take you along.'

'I don't know . . .'

'Give it a try. I'll pick you up at a quarter to seven on Friday. That way you'll not need to go yourself.'

She reluctantly agreed. Hamish's motives were not entirely altruistic. He was sure an old folks' club would be a good source of gossip.

Pat Mallone enjoyed his day with Jenny. They toured round a few beauty spots, ate lunch, and wandered around Blaikie, where he asked questions of passersby in a not very interested way. It was only when he had dropped Jenny off and returned to his office that he realized he hadn't enough for a feature piece. Sam, his boss, looked at him in irritation. Pat had started off well, but Sam had noticed he was beginning to slope off on jobs. 'You go over to

Lairg and find out how sheep prices are doing,' he said. 'Get off early in the morning.'

'But what about Braikie?'

'I'll send Elspeth.'

'But I can do it!'

'You had your chance.'

Hamish collected a reluctant Lugs at the end of a weary day when he felt he had got nowhere at all. He decided to put on his best suit and invite Jenny for dinner in the hope – although he would not admit it to himself – that Priscilla might get to hear of it.

He brushed his red hair until it shone and put on his one Savile Row suit, courtesy of a charity shop in Strathbane, knotted a silk tie over his white shirt, and was heading for the kitchen door when it opened and Elspeth stood there.

'Don't you ever knock?' asked Hamish.

'I heard you coming to the door. Goodness, you do look grand. Just as well I dressed up.'

'Why?' Elspeth was wearing a long fake fur over a filmy grey dress. Instead of her usual clumpy boots, she had on a pair of black high-heeled sandals.

Elspeth smiled. 'Because I'm taking you for dinner.'

'I was going to take Jenny.'

'Tough. She's eaten and is going to have an early night.'

'How do you know?'

The truthful answer to that was that Elspeth had met Jenny as that young lady was on her way to the police station to see Hamish. Elspeth, with true Highland aplomb, had cheerfully lied, telling Jenny that Hamish was stuck in Braikie until late, and Jenny had said that in that case she would take Mrs Dunne's offer of a meal and go to bed afterwards and read.

'Because she told me,' said Elspeth cheerfully. 'Come along.'

Hamish looked at her suspiciously as she tripped along beside him on the waterfront. The mist had come down and little pearls of moisture shone in Elspeth's hair.

Willie Lamont, who used to work in the police force and was now a waiter at the Italian restaurant, greeted them as they entered. 'The table at the window's clear,' he said. 'I'll just be giving it another clean.'

'It looks chust fine,' said Hamish, irritated as always by Willie's obsession with cleanliness and by the obscure feeling that he had somehow been hijacked by Elspeth.

Willie held a can of spray cleaner over the table. 'Just a wee scoosh,' he pleaded.

'Oh, go on,' said Hamish impatiently. 'Stand

back, Elspeth. That man's lungs must be full of Pledge.'

Willie eagerly polished the table until it shone. Finally they sat down. 'It's got worse,' said Hamish gloomily. 'When they had the checked plastic covers, he scrubbed them until they faded. Now they've got wooden tables, you can hardly taste the food for the smell o' furniture polish.'

'He used to work for you, didn't he? How was he as a policeman?'

'Awful. He couldn't get out on a case for either hanging around the restaurant courting Lucia or turning out the whole police station and scrubbing down the walls.' Lucia was a relative of the Italian owner and now married to Willie.

'Well, Lucia seems happy with him.'

'Of course, she is. She never has to do a hand's turn around the house. What are you having?'

'I don't feel adventurous tonight. I'll just have the spag bol and a salad, and some garlic bread.'

'I'll have the same.'

'And we'll have a decanter of the house wine.'

'Okay.'

'I've got to go to Braikie tomorrow,' said Elspeth after their order had been taken. 'Pat was supposed to do a colour piece on Braikie for one of the nationals, but he spent his day romancing Jenny, so I've got to do it. I'm surprised he didn't jump at the chance. He thinks he was meant for better things. Fortunately for him, although it was meant for the daily, they've decided to run it on the Sunday.'

'What sort of thing will you be writing?'

'Oh, you know, Hamish – The Village That Lives in Fear.'

'I wish you wouldn't stir things up. Behind those closed curtains at night in Braikie, people will be whispering to each other, convinced they know who did it. The whole place will soon be engulfed in malice and rumour and spite.'

'Still, I might be able to ferret something out for you.'

'Maybe you'll have another psychic experience.'

Elspeth shuddered. She had once fainted in Patel's grocery when a murderer was in the shop. She never wanted to go through anything like that again.

'Talking of psychic experiences,' Hamish went on, 'I thought of going to see Angus in the morning.'

'Why? I'm convinced our seer is an old fraud.'

'Maybe, but he hears things. I spoke to Priscilla. Jenny's a friend of hers.'

Aha, thought Elspeth. Up here to chase Hamish and put Priscilla's nose out of joint.

Their food arrived at that moment. Elspeth waited until Willie had left, then asked, 'How did that go?'

'Fine. She said Jenny had a way of getting people to open up and talk to her.'

'Isn't one Holmes good enough for you?'

'I sometimes feel I need fifty Holmeses.'

'Someone will break soon and gossip.'

'Oh, they'll gossip, and maliciously, too, as long as deep in their hearts they know their suspicions are unfounded. But what if they find out it's one of their own, so to speak, someone they like, someone they will defend from police investigation? Then the whole of Braikie will close down as tight as a drum.'

'Not necessarily. You're thinking of Miss McAndrew. A lot of people probably disliked her. Her recent crush on young Penny must have made a lot of parents feel that their own precious offspring was being passed over. You're forgetting about Miss Beattie. I did manage to find out that everyone liked her.'

'Wouldn't her affair have diminished her respectability?'

'No. Billy Mackay, the postman, is well liked. His wife is not.'

'Is there anything else you've found out about the villagers?' asked Hamish. 'I mean, anyone who was acting suspiciously? Anyone on that road to Miss McAndrew's?'

'Nothing, really. Oh, I forgot one thing. There's an old folks' club in Braikie.'

'I know,' said Hamish. 'I'm taking old Mrs Harris there on Friday, you know, the one who found Miss Beattie's body. She's lonely and needs to get out more. Also, I may pick up some gossip.'

'I'll go with you,' said Elspeth.

Hamish looked at her with a flicker of annoyance in his eyes. Couldn't she wait to be asked? But instead he said, 'What do you know about the old folks' club?'

'It's maybe not much. But when Mr Blakey was setting it up, he asked the Currie sisters for advice.'

'So?'

'Well, that means the Currie sisters will know a good bit about Braikie and the people in it.'

Hamish groaned. The Currie sisters were twin spinsters of the parish and never lost a chance to criticize him.

'I'll see them tomorrow,' he said gloomily, 'after I see Angus.'

The weather of Sutherland had made one of its mercurial changes when Hamish left the following morning, with Lugs on the leash, to walk to the seer's. The sun blazed down and the mountains soared up into a pale blue sky. He was halfway up the hill at the back of the village when he sensed someone following him and turned round. Jenny came up, her face scarlet with exertion. 'What is it?' he asked impatiently.

'I just wanted to apologize again,' said Jenny.

She looked so pretty and so distressed that Hamish said, 'That's behind us now. I'm on my way to grill our local seer. Like to come and meet him?'

'Oh, yes, please. Can he really tell the future?'

'I doubt it. But he can be a good source of gossip. I've got fish for him. He aye likes a present.'

'Oh, I haven't got anything.'

'I'll say the fish is from both of us.'

Hamish cast a calculating eye down on the top of Jenny's curls. Priscilla had said that people talked to Jenny. Once again, he thought she might come in useful.

And so it seemed. For Angus's welcome was at first sour as he ungraciously received a present of two trout from Hamish. 'Could you no' bring anything better?' he complained. 'My freezer's full of fish.'

'It's a present from both of us,' said Hamish, stepping aside and revealing Jenny.

'Come ben,' said Angus, suddenly expansive. 'So this is the wee lassie I've been hearing about. The one who's a friend o' Priscilla.'

Now, how did he hear that? wondered Hamish.

Angus's cottage parlour was as picturesque as ever with a blackened kettle hanging on a chain over a peat fire. Three high-backed Orkney chairs were grouped in front of the fireplace, and Angus waved them towards them.

'Tea?' he asked Jenny

'Yes, please,' said Jenny, looking around with interest.

Angus shuffled off to his kitchen at the back, which Hamish knew was generously furnished with the latest kitchen gadgets, including a large freezer. He also knew Angus had an electric kettle in the kitchen, but, for visitors, he preferred to go through the business of unhooking the old kettle from the fire.

When they all had cups of tea in their hands and Lugs was stretched out in front of the fire, Hamish began: 'Now, Angus, there is the question of these murders. Have you heard anything?'

Angus stroked his long grey beard. His eyes fell on Jenny, who was leaning forward eagerly. 'I do not hear. I see things,' he said portentously. Jenny let out an excited little gasp, and Angus beamed at her.

'What do you see?' asked Hamish patiently. Angus closed his eyes. The old grandfather clock in the corner gave an asthmatic cough and then chimed the hours. Jenny decided that it was worth all the humiliation of being found out to be here and witness this. Hamish, however, was becoming bored and restless. He knew Angus was putting on his usual act and wished he'd get over it and get down to what he had really heard.

Angus opened his eyes. They were staring and unfocussed. 'Oh, God,' he said in a low voice. 'Old people. Old people fainting and screaming. Something horrible. Something evil.' Lugs gave a sharp bark.

'Who? What?' demanded Hamish.

Angus's pale eyes now focussed on him. 'I think I'll go and lie down,' he said.

'That's all?' Hamish looked at him in irritation. 'Old people fainting and screaming?'

'Leave me alone, laddie, and take your young lady away.' The seer got to his feet and began to shuffle towards the back premises.

'But have you *heard* anything?' called Hamish.

Angus turned. 'You'll let that one –' he pointed at Jenny – 'get away like all the rest. You're doomed to being a lonely man, Hamish.'

'Come on, Jenny,' said Hamish. 'What a waste of time and trout.'

Outside in the sunshine, Jenny clutched his arm. 'I think he really saw something.'

'Och, he's an old fraud.'

'Where are you going now?' asked Jenny, scurrying to keep up with Hamish's long strides.

'I'm going to call on the Currie sisters. They might have heard something.'

'Can I come?' pleaded Jenny.

'I don't see why not.'

Unfortunately for Jenny, the Currie sisters had found out what thongs looked like. Dr Brodie, aware of the strait-laced sensibilities of the villagers, confined the magazines in his waiting room to conservative publications like *Horse & Hound*, *Country Life*, *Scottish Field* and *People's Friend*. But Nessie Currie had been to the dentist's in Inverness the day before and had perused the magazines in that waiting room. They were of the girlie variety, full of detailed descriptions of orgasms, how to get your man, and sexual practices which the Currie spinsters had naively believed belonged solely in the brothel. There were also advertisements of saucy underwear.

They were remarkably alike, thought Jenny as two pairs of beady eyes behind thick glasses focussed on her. She was unfortunate in that the Currie sisters never let a thought go unsaid.

'I would have thought it very uncomfortable to wear, to wear,' said Jessie, who, like Browning's thrush, had an irritating way of saying everything twice over.

'Are you talking to me?' asked Jenny.

'Who else? Who else?'

'Couldn't believe our eyes. Catapult, indeed,' said Nessie.

Jenny's face flamed red.

'We saw it illustrated in a dirty magazine,' said Nessie. 'You'll damage yourself wearing something like that. You go down to Strathbane to the draper's in the main street and get yourself some respectable knickers with elastic at the knee.'

'Could we get down to business?' said Hamish crossly. 'I have two murders to solve.'

'So why aren't you solving them?' demanded Nessie. 'Instead of going around with young lassies.'

'Young lassies,' echoed Jessie.

'I have to ask everyone if they've heard anything,' said Hamish, who was used to dealing with the Currie sisters. 'Now, did either of you know Miss McAndrew or Miss Beattie?'

'Both,' they chorused.

'So tell me about them.'

'Miss McAndrew was a bit bossy,' said Nessie. 'She had the reputation of being a

112

good schoolteacher. She came to one of our church concerts last year. Miss Beattie, well, we thought her a respectable body. We didn't know she had been ... er ... romancing the postman.'

'How did you hear that?'

'The women in Patel's were all talking about it. So Jessie and me, we decided that Miss McAndrew was in love with the postman and jealous of Miss Beattie, so she strung her up.'

Hamish's glance flicked to the new digital television set. The Currie sisters had obviously been exposed to a recent diet of American films.

'So who killed Miss McAndrew?' he asked.

'Why, postman Billy, of course. Now that we've solved your case for you, you can leave us alone.'

'That's very clever of you,' said Jenny suddenly. 'I wouldn't have thought of that.'

Both sisters beamed on her. She looked so young and pretty and respectable in her new anorak and trousers. 'The only trouble is,' said Jenny, 'that Pat Mallone told me that Billy had an alibi. He was down in Strathbane at an army reunion the night Miss Beattie was murdered.'

'So what? So what?' demanded Jessie. 'Where was he the day Miss McAndrew was murdered, when she was murdered?'

'Oh, of course you're right,' said Jenny. 'What do you think of Billy?'

'I don't hold with adultery,' said Nessie. 'But mind you, that wife of his is a fiend and Billy aye had the reputation of being a kind and decent man. If I were you, I'd be talking to Penny Roberts's parents. Now that they know Miss McAndrew was writing those dreadful letters, they might come out with something about her that they didn't realize before.'

'We'll do that. What a good idea!' enthused Jenny.

'You know Mr Blakey at the old folks' club?' said Hamish.

'Senior citizens,' corrected Jessie. 'He rightly came to us for advice. At the beginning, we vetted the videos for him in case there would be anything nasty. But we haven't been there for a while.'

Both Jenny and Hamish rose to their feet. 'You're a good lassie,' said Jessie. 'A good lassie. We hope to see you in church on Sunday, church on Sunday.'

'I'll be there,' said Jenny with a warm smile.

The Currie sisters stood at their parlour window and watched Hamish and Jenny leave. Jenny stumbled and clutched at Hamish's arm for support.

Nessie shook her head. 'It's that evil underwear. Enough to unbalance anyone. Do you think she's a virgin?'

'She'd have to be, to be,' said Jessie. 'I mean, it would be uncomfortable otherwise when you think –'

'I'd rather not, if you don't mind,' said Nessie severely. 'And you shouldn't be thinking such thoughts. But she's a brand to be saved from the burning. We'll have a go at her after church on Sunday.'

Chapter Five

I had rather take my chance that some traitors will escape detection than spread abroad a spirit of general suspicion and distrust, which accepts rumour and gossip in place of undismayed and unintimidated inquiry.

– Learned Hand

Hamish explained to Jenny that he could not take her to Braikie in a police vehicle, but she said cheerfully that she would follow behind him in her 'ridiculous little car'.

Jenny's ambition had changed. She was no longer interested in snaring Hamish Macbeth, but – remembering how much Priscilla had talked about the cases she and Hamish had solved together – in returning to London with the story about how her help had solved two murders.

Hamish just hoped Blair would not see him around with Jenny in tow. He had to admit to himself that she had a knack of getting people to warm to her.

He decided to call on Penny Roberts's parents first. He stopped in the main street and checked a computer list of addresses, then swung the Land Rover round and headed out again towards the coast end of the town and stopped outside a row of Victorian villas. The Robertses lived in a neat house, two-storeyed, with pointed gables. He knocked at the door, guiltily aware of the small figure of Jenny behind him, realizing it must look odd to bring a civilian along with him.

A dark-haired skinny woman opened the door and surveyed him. She had a thick-lipped mouth, small eyes and an incipient moustache. Must be a friend or relative, he thought. 'Police,' he said. 'I wondered if I could be having a word with Mr or Mrs Roberts.'

'Come in,' she said, stepping back. 'I'm Mrs Roberts.'

Startled, Hamish thought that Penny must surely have inherited her stunning looks from her father, but when they were ushered into a living room, Mr Roberts was introduced. He was also dark and skinny and very hairy. 'I am Hamish Macbeth.' Hamish removed his cap and tucked it under his arm. 'As this is an unofficial visit, I hope you don't mind my friend Jenny Ogilvie joining us.'

'Not at all,' said Mrs Roberts. 'Sit down. A dreadful business, all this.'

Jenny glanced around the living room. There was a two-bar electric fire, glowing orange in front of a fireplace, blocked up with newspaper. But the furniture, like the house, was dark and Victorian with two oils of Highland landscapes hanging from walls decorated in faded wallpaper.

'This house must have been in your family a long time,' said Jenny.

'Yes, it belonged to my great-grandfather,' said Mrs Roberts. 'I was lucky in a way, if you can call it luck. My mother died a week before me and Cyril –' she nodded towards her husband – 'were due to get married. Of course, we were going to stay with Mother, but the poor soul was fair gone with Alzheimer's, so it was a blessed release.'

'Housing is so difficult these days, Mrs Roberts,' said Jenny.

Hamish was about to interrupt her, but Mrs Roberts smiled on Jenny and said, 'Call me Mary. You're quite right. We could never have afforded a place like this. Not then. But Cyril is doing nicely now. He's a civil engineer with Bradley's in Strathbane. Not at work, I can see you're wondering. With all this going on, Cyril took a few days off.'

'Quite right,' said Jenny. 'You want to be with your family at a time like this.'

119

Hamish cleared his throat. 'Did you get any of the poison-pen letters?'

There was a brief silence. 'No,' said Mary Roberts. 'I mean, it turns out it was Miss McAndrew that was writing them and she was so fond of Penny that she wouldn't attack us. I mean, after all, we've no guilty secrets.'

And yet, Hamish thought, I feel you're lying. He pressed on. 'Weren't you made uneasy that the headmistress should make such a pet of your daughter?'

'We were pleased for her,' said Cyril. 'I mean, Penny's a bright girl, head and shoulders above the rest. It seemed natural to us that Miss McAndrew should take such a great interest.'

Hamish's eyes roamed briefly around the room. There were photos of Penny everywhere: Penny as a toddler, Penny as a schoolgirl, Penny on holiday in Cornwall.

'Did you know Miss Beattie well?' asked Jenny.

'We knew her the way everyone else in Braikie knew her,' said Mary. 'We chatted a bit over the counter, that sort of thing.'

'But you didn't socialize with her?'

'No, she really isn't in our class,' said Mary with all the simple snobbery of a small, remote village.

Hamish looked at them for a moment,

puzzled. There was a secret in this room – in the air.

'Didn't you have any inkling that Miss McAndrew was a poison-pen writer?'

'Oh, no,' said Mary. 'I mean, such a respectable body! How could we dream she would do such a thing?'

Jenny spoke suddenly. 'Before Penny,' she said, 'who was teacher's pet?'

'Pardon?'

'I mean, before Penny, do you know who was Miss McAndrew's favourite?'

Mary Roberts and her husband exchanged glances. 'Let me see,' said Mary. 'There was Jessie Briggs.'

'And is she still at school?'

'No, she left two years ago.'

'Where does she live?' asked Hamish.

'At the council houses. Highland Close. I don't know the number.'

'Is she working?'

'I don't know.'

Hamish asked more questions about their opinion of the late Miss McAndrew, but they did seem genuinely bewildered that the respected headmistress had been anything other than perfect.

Outside, Hamish said, 'What prompted you to ask about another favourite?'

'Just an idea,' said Jenny eagerly. 'I mean it stands to reason, if she'd made a pet of Penny, then she might have had other pets.'

'Clever idea,' said Hamish, and Jenny glowed. 'We may as well go and see this girl and hope that she and her family weren't so starry-eyed about Miss McAndrew.'

They drove in tandem to Highland Close. Hamish knocked at the first door and got Jessie Briggs's address.

Followed by Jenny, he walked up the path and knocked at a front door, noticing that the paint was peeling and the front garden behind him was full of weeds. Somewhere inside, a baby cried.

The door was opened by a thin, tired-looking girl. Her blonde hair was showing an inch of dark roots. She had startlingly green eyes and Hamish guessed that made-up and dressed up, she might still attract a lot of admiring looks.

'I am PC Hamish Macbeth,' he said. 'This is Jenny Ogilvie. Do you mind if we come in?'

'Yes, but be quiet. I've just laid the bairn down and I could do with a rest.'

She led them into a cluttered living room. Several empty bottles of Bacardi Breezer stood among film magazines on a coffee table.

'Are your parents home?' asked Hamish. The room smelled of stale cigarette smoke, stale booze and unwashed nappies.

'No, I live on my own. Unmarried mother.'

Hamish and Jenny sat down side by side on a battered sofa. Jessie picked up a wastepaper basket and shovelled empty bottles into it. 'Tea?' she asked.

'No, don't bother,' said Hamish quickly, anxious to get this interview over and get out into the fresh air.

'So is this about the murders?' asked Jessie, sitting down opposite them.

'Yes, it is,' said Hamish. 'We gather you were something of a favourite with Miss McAndrew?'

'Oh, her.' Jessie shrugged thin shoulders. She lit a cigarette and blew smoke out in their direction.

'What was your experience with her?'

'Weird.'

'In what way?'

'Well, she used to ask me home and help me with my homework. Had my ma and da all excited that I was going to be a success. I was a looker then, you wouldn't think it now.'

She rose and went over to a table by the window and shuffled through the contents of a battered shoebox and drew out a photograph. She handed it to Hamish.

'That was just after I left school.'

In the photo, Jessie's hair was thick and brown and her figure fuller. The girl in the photograph glowed with a strong sexuality.

'Do you think Miss McAndrew was attracted to you?'

'Oh, sure.' Jessie delicately picked a piece of tobacco off her tongue. 'I didnae ken about such women then. She was always stroking my hair. She said I should go to university. Then she said she was soon due to retire and she would come with me and look after me. I began to feel . . . threatened.'

'Did you tell your parents?'

'They wouldnae listen. 'You do what she says and you'll get somewhere,' they said. Ma works on the buses and Dad drives. They were fired up by her. I tried to tell them she was faking my exams and that when I sat my Highers, I'd be in trouble because the papers would go out to the examining board and I'd be exposed as not all that bright. Who knows? I may have done better if she hadn't been breathing down my neck.'

Jenny looked at her with warm sympathy. 'So you decided to rebel.'

'Aye, you can say that. Left her house one night – the old bag had tried to kiss me – and I felt mean and baffled and scunnert. I went into the pub instead o' going home. I'd never had alcohol before. There were a lot of the local lads there. They said an Alco pop wouldn't hurt and it tasted sweet, just like soda, and it felt great and I had a lot mair. The evening began to get blurry, but it was warm and free, the feeling, so I let them buy me mair booze. I can only remember the rest of the night in flashes, but at one point I was round the back o' the pub with my skirt up round my chest and wan o' them fiddling with me. And that was it.' A slow tear ran down her cheek. 'In the pudding club first time and cannae even remember who the father was. Ma and Dad hit the roof. Social security got me this place.'

Hamish cleared his throat. 'Look, Jessie, could you have any idea Miss McAndrew might have been the poison-pen writer?'

'No, but I should ha' known.'

'Why?'

'She sent me wan. I have it here.'

She rose and went back to the shoebox and drew out a letter, the writing now familiar to Hamish.

It said: 'You have ruined your life, you silly slut. Now you are prostituting yourself and you will end in the gutter where you belong. You threw away a golden chance at life.'

Hamish's mouth tightened in distaste.

'What does she mean about prostituting yourself?'

'I got a taste for the booze. It keeps me going. Costs, though. I got a fellow comes around. Nothing serious, but he pays me a bit.'

'Oh, that wicked, wicked woman,' said Jenny, bursting into tears.

Hamish looked at her impatiently, beginning to regret bringing her along.

'Let's keep to practicalities,' he said severely as Jenny blew her small nose. 'Are you addicted to the booze?'

'If you mean, can I stop? No.'

'I think there's an AA meeting in Braikie.'

'Oh, them. God botherers.'

'They're not religious. You can believe or not believe, but they've taken a lot o' people out o' the gutter. You phone them up, they'll send someone round. You can take it or leave it. No one will force you.'

Jenny had dried her eyes and had found a phone book and was looking it up. 'I'll just phone Strathbane and they'll put me in touch with someone here,' she said eagerly.

'Jenny!' admonished Hamish. 'Chust leave it. The lassie has to do it for herself.'

Undeterred, Jenny wrote down the number and handed it to Jessie.

'Jessie,' said Hamish, 'here's my card. Phone me if you hear anything or think of anything.'

Outside, he said to Jenny, 'This is not going to work. I admit you ask some good questions and people take to you, but you cannot let your feelings get involved in a police case.'

'It's very hard,' said Jenny.

'Furthermore, if Blair gets wind of you going around with me, I'll be in deep trouble.'

'Where do we go now?'

'I'm thinking. So many suspects. It's nearly lunchtime. I'd like to go to the school and see if any of the teachers have thought of anything. Why don't you wait outside and have a chat with anyone around?'

Jenny pouted. 'Can't I come in with you?'

'No, leave this one to me.'

The playground was full of noisy children. Hamish noticed that a woman he guessed to be a volunteer was supervising them. With any hope he would find all the teachers in the staff room. He had decided it would be better to interview them all together than separately in their homes.

By dint of opening several doors, he found the staff room. They were all there: Maisie Hart, Henrietta McNicol, Jamie Burns and Matthew Eskdale, all puffing on cigarettes.

Four dismayed faces looked up through the haze of cigarette smoke as Hamish entered the dingy room with its institution-green walls and scarred and chipped furniture.

'Chust continuing my inquiries,' said Hamish, made nervous by the sight of teachers, reminding him of his own schooldays.

He found an empty chair and sat down and took out his notebook. Four wary pairs of eyes stared at him.

'Now, to begin, I need more of your

impressions of Miss McAndrew. Were you aware that she might have been faking the results of exam papers?'

'I thought once that she might,' said Maisie cautiously. 'I mean, what was that girl – Jessie – that's it.' She looked round at the others. 'She had brilliant results in the school exams, but when it came to the ones that were sent out to the examining board, she barely scraped through.'

'I thought that was exam nerves,' protested Henrietta. 'That's what Miss McAndrew said.'

'She was a bit of a bully,' said Matthew Eskdale. 'Made Jamie's life hell. Didn't she, Jamie?'

'I've already told this policeman that,' said Jamie, 'so there's no use trying to move the focus off yourself. You sucked up to her something awful.'

'No, I didn't!'

'You did.'

'Gentlemen,' protested Hamish, 'we're getting nowhere.'

Outside the school, Jenny was approached by a swarthy boy. 'You come here with that copper?' he asked.

'Yes,' said Jenny. 'I'm helping him.'

'My name's Geordie Cromarty and I'm helping him as well.'

'How clever of you,' said Jenny, batting her eyelashes at him.

Geordie eyed her speculatively. He and his pals had often discussed the charms and experience of older women, each one dreaming of a Mrs Robinson who would deftly remove their unwanted virginity, but the ladies of Braikie were built on formidable lines and some still wore corsets and so they had given up hope. But here in front of him in the school playground, sitting on the wall and showing lengths of black-stockinged leg, was a beauty. He puffed out his chest. 'I could tell him a few things.'

'Like what?' breathed Jenny, gazing at him with well-feigned admiration.

'Like Miss Beattie was seen going to Miss McAndrew's house three days afore she was killed.'

'Heavens! Are you sure? Who told you?'

'I have my sources. But it's true.'

'If I were the police,' said Jenny cautiously, 'I would insist you named your source.'

'Aye, but I promised not to tell.'

'Say you told me. I wouldn't tell Hamish.' Jenny crossed her fingers behind her back.

The school bell shrilled out. 'Break's over,' shouted the volunteer. 'Form orderly lines. You over there, Geordie, get in line.'

'Gotta go,' he said. 'Meet me after school.'

'Where?'

129

'Out o' town. Just past Miss McAndrew's house, there's a big rock on the shore. See you there.'

He swaggered off to join the others.

Jenny saw Hamish emerge and decided quickly to keep Geordie's news to herself.

'Nothing,' said Hamish, coming up to her. 'Nothing new. She was a bully who had favourites and who forged exam papers for them.'

'I think I saw that inspector of yours,' lied Jenny. 'Thickset man in plain clothes came past in a police car. It slowed down and he glared out the window at me.'

'Blair. You'd better make yourself scarce,' said Hamish. 'I'll tell you later if I've found anything.'

To his relief, Jenny just grinned and swung down from the wall. 'I'll check with you later,' she said.

Hamish decided to have a look at the post office. Although Billy Mackay had inherited the business, they would need to send someone in to cope with the pensions and deliver the mail.

To his surprise, he found the whole shop open for business and old Mrs Harris behind the shop counter while a stranger manned the post office section.

'What's going on?' he asked her.

'The lawyers phoned me and said that Billy

had asked me to run the shop until they released him. I used to work in a grocery when I was young, so it isnae that difficult. It's fun.' Her elderly eyes sparkled. 'They've got a mannie to cope wi' the letters and pensions and stuff. I've to get paid. Imagine that! Me earning at my age.'

'Great,' said Hamish. 'You still on for Friday night?'

'Looking forward to it. Oh, more customers.'

Hamish retreated to the street, where he bumped into Elspeth. 'So what have you dug up?' he asked.

'I'll tell you over a drink. I don't come cheap.'

When they sat down at a corner table in the dingy pub with their drinks, Hamish found himself wishing that Elspeth would dress better, and then he instantly chastised himself for being one of those men who couldn't accept people just as they were.

Elspeth was wearing her favourite battered tweed fishing hat, a man's anorak and corduroy trousers, and a black T-shirt which had been washed so many times it was almost grey.

Still, what did he expect her to wear while reporting around a Highland village? Stilettos and a frock?

'What have you found out?' he asked.

'Rumour and counter-rumour. Nothing concrete.'

'I suppose they still think Billy did it.'

'No, as a matter of fact. They say if he'd killed his nagging wife, they could understand that. He always was a popular figure. Help anyone.'

'So what are you going to write?'

'As it's for a national, a colour piece about the drama of murders invading a respectable Highland village. The dark-shadow-of-suspicion yackety-yak. Mrs Harris is working in the post office shop. Is she still going to see that film with us?'

'Yes.'

'You've been seen going around with Jenny tailing you in that ridiculous car of hers. Why do you put up with her?'

'She's got a knack of making people open up.'

'Oh, really? I thought her interest was in you, although Pat Mallone seems quite keen.'

'Elspeth, I will use anyone who might help me solve this case. We could take her along with us to this movie. I think she would be good with the old people.'

Elspeth's silver eyes narrowed a fraction. 'I thought we were going together.'

'Come on, Elspeth. You invited yourself and I am taking Mrs Harris. Hardly a hot date.'

'I wasn't competing, copper. I feel in my bones something is going to happen there and I don't want bouncy, wide-eyed Jenny around.'

'Oh, have it your way,' said Hamish.

'Anyway, you really are only taking her around in the hope it gets back to Priscilla,' said Elspeth.

'I am not! I'm going back on my beat.'

Hamish stood up, stiff with outrage.

Elspeth looked amused. 'See you tomorrow.'

Jenny waited in the shadow of the rock on the beach. The sky had clouded over and a thin drizzle was starting to fall. Great sluggish waves rose and fell and fanned out on the pebbles of the beach. A seagull cried mournfully overhead.

'Psst!'

Jenny jumped nervously. Geordie appeared around the other side of the rock.

'You startled me. So what have you got to tell me?'

Geordie swaggered. 'It'll cost ye.'

'How much?'

'A kiss.'

'Oh, go on with you. You're only a kid.'

He looked at her stubbornly.

Jenny sighed. She thought briefly of London, red buses, restaurants, crowds. Civilization. What was she doing on a draughty Highland beach with an amorous schoolboy?

'Oh, all right,' she said. 'Pucker up.'

Geordie planted a kiss on her mouth, grinding his lips against her own. 'There!' he said, releasing her. 'I bet you've never been kissed like that before.'

And I hope never again, thought Jenny, longing to take out a handkerchief and scrub her lips. 'So what do you know?' she asked.

'Someone I know saw herself . . .'

'Miss Beattie?'

'Aye, her. Three days afore the murder. She went into Miss McAndrew's house.'

'You told me that. What more?'

'After half an hour, she came out and she was crying sore. Fair broken up, she was.'

'Can't you tell me the name of the witness?'

'I cannae. Mair than my life's worth,' said Geordie dramatically.

They could hear the sound of a car coming along the road. It screeched to a halt. 'I've left my car out on the road,' said Jenny, and then found she was talking to the empty air. Geordie had disappeared.

'Jenny!' called Hamish's voice.

She walked round the rock and back up to the road.

'What were you doing down there?' asked Hamish.

'I just stopped to look at the sea.'

'Aye, a grand day for it,' said Hamish sarcastically. He walked down to the rock and round to where Jenny had been standing. She followed him reluctantly. Hamish stooped and picked something up off the ground and held it to his nose. He stared down at her. 'This is a cannabis roach. Not smoked today. There are several others lying about. So, Jenny Ogilvie, what were you doing hanging around what looks like the local lads' cannabis smoking area?'

'I was meeting someone who had information.'

'Who?'

'I promised not to say.'

'Your lipstick's smeared.'

Jenny blushed and took out a handkerchief and scrubbed her mouth. Hamish surveyed her. 'I think you've been kissing someone. Pat Mallone isn't around today and as far as I know, you don't know anyone else. Now, who would want a kiss for information? A randy schoolboy? Come on, Jenny. Out wi' it.'

'It was Geordie Cromarty.'

'And what did he have to say?'

'Oh, very well. He said someone he knows, and he won't say who, saw Miss Beattie going into Miss McAndrew's house three days before the murder.'

'Which murder?'

'Oh, I didn't ask. Her own, I guess. Anyway, Miss Beattie came out half an hour later and she was crying.'

Hamish frowned. 'I thought maybe Miss Beattie was murdered because she had something on Miss McAndrew. But it looks the other way round. I'll get back to Lochdubh and phone Jimmy Anderson and see what they've dug up on Miss Beattie's past. Are you going to stay here and romance the local talent?'

'No, I'll follow you.'

Once back at the police station after collecting Lugs, Hamish phoned up Strathbane and asked to speak to Jimmy Anderson. He was told that the detective was out on duty. He had just replaced the receiver when there was a knock at the kitchen door. He opened it to find Jimmy himself standing there.

'Any whisky in the cupboard?' asked Jimmy.

'Some, but don't drink it all.'

Jimmy sat down at the kitchen table as Hamish lifted a bottle of whisky and a glass down from the kitchen cupboard. 'It's cold in here,' complained Jimmy.

'I'm just back. I'll light the fire.'

Lugs rattled his empty water bowl on the floor. Hamish filled it up with water, shoved logs and paper and firelighter into the stove, and threw in a match. It lit with a roar.

'Now we've got you comfortable, I want information out of you.'

'Not drinking?' asked Jimmy, pouring himself a hefty measure.

'Don't feel like it. I'll have coffee.' Hamish

filled up a kettle and put it on top of the stove and sat down opposite Jimmy.

'What do you want to know?' asked Jimmy. 'I'm sure you've ferreted out more than us.'

'I want to know about Miss Beattie. Was she born in Braikie, or did she live here all her life?'

'She was born in 1966 in Perth of middle-class parents. Father owned a garage and did well in a modest way. His wife was a house-keeper. Both staunch Free Presbyterians.'

'Wait a bit. When she was murdered, she must have only been thirty-six. Man, I thought she was older. I mean, all that grey hair. Mind you, the last time I saw her, she was hanging. So when did she come to Braikie?'

'She came about sixteen years ago, as a young woman. Did cleaning jobs at first and then heard the old postmistress was about to retire and went and trained for the job and got it. She must have had some private money because she bought the place. At first it was just a post office, but then she expanded it into a shop and got various locals to help out.'

'I cannae understand it,' complained Hamish. 'Here I was thinking she was an older woman. In fact, I think that's what most of them believed, and yet the older ones must have known her age if she came here as a young woman.'

Hamish began to feel irritated with himself.

He should have asked questions about Miss Beattie himself.

'What's Billy been saying?'

'They've released him.'

'Does no one tell me anything?'

Jimmy looked amused. 'They don't usually have to.'

'It's chust that I've got the long, long list of suspects. I have something for you. Someone saw Miss Beattie visit Miss McAndrew's cottage three days afore she was murdered. She stayed half an hour and came out crying.'

'Who told you that?'

But Hamish wanted to keep Jenny's name out of it. He didn't want the police to know he had been taking an amateur round with him.

Miss Beattie's unexpectedly younger age raised a lot of questions. Billy would know. He glanced at the clock. Eight in the evening.

'Finish your whisky, Jimmy, and shut the door behind you. Come on, Lugs.'

'Where are you going?'

'I've got to see Billy.'

Jimmy leant back comfortably in his chair. 'Run along. I'm off duty.'

'And don't drink too much and drive.'

Jimmy gave him a limpid look from his bloodshot blue eyes. 'Wouldnae dream o' it.'

Hamish, with his dog beside him on the passenger seat, sped off to Braikie again.

* * *

Billy answered the door. 'Where the missus?' asked Hamish cautiously.

'Out at her sewing circle, thank God. Come in. I thought they were going to keep me there for ages, for I'd had enough o' that bad-tempered cheil, Blair. So I asked for a lawyer, which is what I should have done in the first place. Got a smart woman. She pointed out that they had no evidence and she really went for Blair. I think he'd met his match.'

'Billy, I didn't know poor Miss Beattie was only in her thirties.'

'Aye, folk forgot all the same. The cancer aged her a lot.'

'Cancer?'

'Yes, she told me. It was shortly after she came to Braikie. She got cancer of the fallopian tubes. She said she was frightened to death. Her hair turned almost white. She told me she always lived in fear of it coming back. She'd had one hell of a religious upbringing, and she thought God was punishing her.'

'Yes, I just learned her parents were strong Free Presbyterians. I think I'd better try to see them.'

'You can't. The father died ten years ago of cancer of the lung, and two years after, a heart attack took the mother off. That's when me and Amy got together. I would stay on in the evenings to console her. She blamed herself for leaving home, I think. There had been some breach, and after she left, she never went to see them.'

'Can you think of anything in her past that Miss McAndrew could have found out to upset her?'

'Me and Amy were that close.' A tear ran down Billy's cheek. 'She would have told me.'

'Even if Miss McAndrew had found out about her affair with you? Wouldn't that have been enough?'

'Aye, but she would ha' told me.'

'Did she ever talk about her?'

'Let me see. She used to say things like, "I cannae thole that woman. There's something creepy and nasty about her."'

'Anything more concrete?'

'Hamish, I'm so glad to be out. Look, she'll be back in a moment. I'll phone you if I remember anything.'

Hamish left and drove slowly back, with Lugs asleep on the seat beside him. When he entered the police station, it was to find the bottle of whisky, which, he thought, had thankfully only been a quarter full, standing empty on the table.

Tomorrow, he decided, he would see what the old folks had to say about Miss Beattie's past.

He was just drifting off to sleep when he suddenly opened his eyes with a start. That small boy, what was his name? Archie Brand, that was it. He must call on him.

Chapter Six

Mordre wol out, certeyn, it wol nat faille.
— Geoffrey Chaucer

Hamish felt himself reluctant the next day to call at the school and demand to see Archie Brand. He did not like Mr Arkle and felt sure the head teacher would find some obstacle to put in his way.

But to his relief, Mr Arkle was out somewhere and the meek secretary, Freda, went off and collected Archie and brought him into her office.

'Now, Archie,' said Hamish, 'can we go over again what you told me?'

'It was the night her at the post office was murdered. I was going to the chippy . . .'

'What time would that be?'

'About nine. There was this fellow standing outside the post office. He was looking up, you know, at the upstairs windows.'

'Right. Now tell me as much as you can remember.'

'He was all in black,' said Archie, red-faced and squirming in his seat. 'He had a baseball cap pulled down over his eyes and his clothes were black. He had wan o' thae down-filled jackets and a pair o' black trousers and black sneakers.'

'Did you see his face?'

'Naw. Thon cap was pulled right down.'

Hamish stifled a sigh. Nothing more there.

'Thanks, Archie. If you remember anything more, phone me at the police station in Lochdubh.'

'Right, boss,' said Archie proudly.

Hamish returned to Lochdubh and phoned Jimmy. 'Have you got a time of death for Miss McAndrew?' he asked.

'Sometime during the night, Hamish. You know how it is. They can never pinpoint the exact time. But she was killed in her bed and she hadn't yet eaten any breakfast, and from the contents of her stomach, they guess it must have been somewhere in the small hours.'

'No sign of forced entry?'

'None.'

'That's odd. I don't see her getting out of bed and letting her killer in and then going back to bed and waiting to be stabbed. I'd swear whoever it was got her when she was asleep. What kind of lock on the front door?'

'Just a Yale. Easily picked.'

'Footprints, fingerprints?'

'No fingerprints. No footprints. This is one cold-blooded murderer. He'd vacuumed his way out of the house. The vacuum was lying just inside the door.'

'Anything in the bag?'

'Our murderer took the vacuum bag with him. Not a fibre, not a hair.'

'Anyone been down to Perth to check on Miss Beattie's background?'

'Perth police did that. An old neighbour remembered she had some sort o' falling-out with her parents and left. They were a close-mouthed religious pair and never spoke about it.'

'I'm not getting anywhere with my inquiries. How about you lot?'

'Blair's got another case down here which leaves me in charge. You know what he's like. When a case seems impossible to solve, he dumps it on some other sucker, said sucker being me.'

'I'm going to the old folks' club tonight. Maybe some of them will remember something.'

'My, my. The excitement of living in the Highlands. Have fun.'

* * *

143

Pat Mallone walked along the waterfront, filled with unease. He had a great deal on his conscience. The day before, Elspeth had said, 'Thank goodness that's finished. I'll get a cup of coffee and send it off.'

Pat had stopped by her desk. 'Your colour piece?' he had asked.

'That's the one. Be a lamb and have a look at it. Won't be long.'

Pat had sat down at Elspeth's computer. He quickly read the piece. It was brilliant. A wild impulse seized him. It was all ready to be sent off to the *Bugle*. He erased Elspeth's byline, put his own on, and sent the article off. Then he erased his byline and typed Elspeth's back in.

'What do you think?' asked Elspeth, appearing behind him.

'Great,' said Pat. 'I sent it off for you.'

'That's a bit high-handed of you. I might have wanted to make changes.'

Pat twinkled up at her, turning on the full force of his Irish charm. 'I'm sure you thought it was perfect.'

Elspeth grinned. 'As a matter of fact, I did.'

What Pat now hoped was that because the article was not written by a member of their own staff, the *Bugle* would not use the byline on the piece, but if they were pleased with it, they might offer him a job. He would need to sweat it out until Sunday when the paper appeared.

144

He saw Jenny walking towards the police station. He hurried to waylay her.

'Where are you off to?' he asked.

'I was just going to see if Hamish was at home.'

'I think I saw him driving off earlier,' lied Pat. 'I've got to cover an amateur dramatic show at Cnothan this afternoon. A children's affair. Feel like coming?'

'Yes, all right,' said Jenny.

'How long are you staying?'

'I don't know,' said Jenny. 'I've got a lot of leave owing.' As a matter of fact, she had phoned her office that morning and claimed that she had caught the flu. The only trouble was they had asked for a doctor's certificate.

Pat looked down at her guilty, flushed face.

'Is that the truth?'

'No,' said Jenny, turning even redder. 'I said I had the flu and now they want a doctor's certificate.'

'So we'll pinch one.'

'How do we do that?'

'I'll tell this local doctor I've got back pain, you create a diversion, and I'll nick one.'

'Could you?' breathed Jenny.

'It's worth a try. Come on. The surgery's open.'

They walked into the surgery. Pat explained his problem to the receptionist, glad he had taken the precaution of signing on when he'd

145

first arrived in Lochdubh and therefore was saved the business of filling out forms. 'After I go in,' he whispered to Jenny, 'create a diversion in the waiting room, something to get him running out.'

'I'll try,' Jenny whispered back.

There were only two elderly patients before Pat was due to be called. Jenny tried to read a romantic story in the *People's Friend*. But the print jumped before her nervous eyes.

At last it was Pat's turn. He breezed in. 'Sit down,' said Dr Brodie. 'What's up with you?'

'It's my back,' said Pat, his eyes roving over the doctor's desk.

'That's unusual,' said Dr Brodie.

'Why?'

'People usually complain of bad backs on a Monday so they get a week off work.'

'I'm not trying to get off work,' said Pat. 'I just want something to ease the pain.'

'Did you do anything to strain it?'

'As a matter of fact, I did. Sam wanted me to lift the photocopier to another part of the office. It was heavier than I expected.'

'I should think it's nothing more than a temporary strain. I'd better examine you just the same. Go behind the screen and strip to the waist.'

Why wasn't Jenny doing something? wondered Pat.

Then he heard the sound of a heavy fall from

the waiting room, and the receptionist came running in, shouting. 'Doctor, come quick. There's a lassie's fainted.'

Pat peered over the screen. The minute Dr Brodie was out of the room, he ran round the screen, his eyes scanning the desk. There it was, the book of forms. He quickly tore one off the top and put it in his jacket pocket and then went into the waiting room, where Jenny was being helped into a chair.

'I'm all right,' she was saying. 'Just a dizzy turn.'

The doctor saw Pat. 'I'd better examine this young lady first. You wait here.'

'Right,' said Pat. 'Actually, I'm probably making a fuss about nothing. A couple of painkillers'll probably put me right.'

Jenny was helped into the consulting room. Pat waited anxiously. She was gone for ages. Jenny had to have a full examination. At the end of it, Dr Brodie studied her rosy cheeks and bright eyes and said slowly, 'I would say you are one remarkably healthy lady. Have these murders made you nervous?'

'Oh, yes,' said Jenny, seizing on the excuse. 'I was helping Hamish with his inquiries yesterday and it was all very exciting. I think the horror of it all got to me today.'

'I don't know what Hamish was thinking of to involve you in two nasty murder cases,' said Dr Brodie. 'I'll be having a word with him.'

'Oh, don't do that,' pleaded Jenny. 'I wouldn't want to get him into any trouble.'

'Nonetheless, I'll be speaking to him. If you get another fainting fit, come and see me. The receptionist will give you the necessary forms to fill in with the name of your London doctor. Send that young man in.'

After examining Pat thoroughly, Dr Brodie felt he was wasting his time. Both Pat and Jenny seemed to be in perfect health.

After they had gone, he phoned the police station. Hamish was out, so he left him a message and then walked to his home – to find Hamish sitting in his kitchen, drinking coffee.

Hamish listened patiently to Dr Brodie's lecture and then said cynically, 'Did you check your prescription pad?'

'No, why?'

'A healthy young man like Pat Mallone claims to have a bad back. Then a healthy young woman has a fainting fit, which means you have to run out, leaving Pat alone. Didn't that make you suspicious?'

'I'd better go back and check.'

'I'll come with you.'

They walked together to the surgery. Once there, Dr Brodie checked his prescription pad. 'Nothing missing,' he said.

'And everything looks the same?' asked Hamish. 'Nothing's been moved?'

'Not that I can see.'

A doctor's line to say she was sick, thought Hamish. He opened his mouth to say something and then decided to remain quiet. He had a feeling that such as Jenny might find out something if she stayed, and he was willing to turn a blind eye to a small crime in the hope of solving the bigger ones.

Hamish returned to the police station to find a grey-haired woman waiting outside. 'Constable Macbeth?' she asked doubtfully, looking up at Hamish and then down to the peculiar-looking dog at his heels.

'The same. And you are?'

'Mrs Dinwiddie. Miss Beattie's sister.'

'Come into the station,' said Hamish.

In the kitchen, she sat down primly on the edge of a chair and crossed her ankles. She wore her grey hair in an old-fashioned bun. Her face looked tight and her mouth was a thin line. Hamish wondered briefly if it had got that way after years of clamping down on emotions. Then he reminded himself that her sister had recently been murdered and she may have just been holding grief at bay.

He made two mugs of tea and then said gently, 'How can I help you?'

'I heard about you,' she said, 'from Amy, my sister. She always said you were so clever. I've had enough of that Detective Blair. I want to know if you are any further forward in finding out who killed Amy.'

'At the moment, no,' said Hamish. 'But I will,' he added, with a confidence he did not feel. 'Depend on that. Tell me about your sister. Why did she leave home?'

'It happened when I was away at the university in Edinburgh,' said Mrs Dinwiddie. 'She wrote to me and said she couldn't stand living at home any longer. Our parents were very religious, very strict. It was easier for me because they were proud of me getting to university. Anyway, I wasn't a rebel like Amy. Amy wanted to wear make-up and go out with the boys, and they kept locking her in her room. Then they would get members of the congregation round to read the Bible to her and lecture her. One day, she just took off. Father said her name was never to be mentioned again.'

'What did she work at before she came up to Braikie?'

'She worked in a supermarket as a checkout girl. Actually, she was pretty bright at school, but fell to pieces just before the final exams. I think Father was harder on her than he ever was on me. I used to worry that she might have a breakdown. I wrote to her about their deaths, but she didn't bother to come to the funerals.'

'What about boyfriends?'

'She would be allowed those but only if it was some fellow from the church. She was seen out with a bunch of bikers and locked in her room for two weeks after that. I never knew if there was anyone special. She didn't tell me.'

Perth, thought Hamish. Perhaps the secret lies somewhere in her past.

'Did the police give you her papers? Old photographs? Things like that?' he asked.

'Not yet. They are going to release them to me soon.'

'I would like to see them. You see, Mrs Dinwiddie, sometimes if I can form a picture of a person and their background, I can get an idea of why they might have been killed.'

'I'll send them to you.'

'When's the funeral?'

'Tomorrow, in Perth. I've made the arrangements.'

'I would be grateful if you could let me have your address. You live in Perth, don't you?'

'Yes, here's the address.' She produced a card from her handbag.

'I might call on you soon.'

'Let me know when. Because if I have any photos or papers that might interest you, I'll keep them instead of sending them up here.'

Hamish thanked her and saw her out.

He returned to the kitchen and fed Lugs, forgetting in his preoccupation with the case that the animal had already been fed.

151

He sat down at the table and stared into space. 'The problem is, Lugs,' he said to the dog's uncaring head, which was buried in his food bowl, 'there's too many damn suspects. Was it one of the parents? Or the schoolteachers? That might account for Miss McAndrew's murder but not Miss Beattie's. Are there two murderers here? Maybe I'll pick up something at the old folks' film show.'

Lugs ambled away from his now empty food bowl, keeled over, and fell asleep.

Early that evening, Hamish put a selection of videos in a bag and went out with Elspeth to her car. There were still too many police in Braikie and he did not want to be spotted giving a civilian a lift in a police car. He was almost relieved to see Elspeth wearing one of her usual grunge outfits: old anorak, jeans and tweed fishing hat. There was always something unsettlingly attractive about Elspeth when she dressed up. He was wearing a suit, collar and tie and maliciously hoped he was making Elspeth feel inferior.

'Why are you all dressed up?' asked Elspeth as she drove out of Lochdubh under a black and windy sky.

'As a courtesy to old Mrs Harris. I see you haven't bothered.'

'Wasn't time,' said Elspeth cheerfully. 'I was

out reporting. A wee boy got stuck up on the top of the falls.'

'Which one?'

'Diarmuid Patel. He was standing in the middle of the top of the falls, too scared to move one way or the other.'

'Not much of a story.'

'Not compared to murder and mayhem, but you forget, we're a local Highland paper.'

'How's your astrology piece doing? Haven't read it lately.'

'Sam says it's what sells the most papers. I'm good at it.'

Hamish snorted. 'You're good at making things up.'

A buffet of wind shook Elspeth's small car as she moved along the coast road. 'Another Sutherland gale,' said Elspeth. 'When I see one of those nature films on television and they speed up the sky scenes so that the clouds race from horizon to horizon, I think they should come up here and find it doesn't need any tricky camera work to make the sky look like that.'

Mrs Harris came downstairs to meet them when they parked outside her building. In honour of the occasion, she had put a sort of 1940s make-up on her face: white powder and dark red lipstick.

Elspeth drove to the community hall and parked the car.

The hall was full, but Mr Blakey had reserved them seats at the front. He thanked Hamish for his present of videos.

'I'm looking forward to this,' said Elspeth. 'I didn't see *Green Card* when it was first released.'

The elderly audience were rustling sweetie papers: The local shop nearby still sold sweets from large glass jars and put them in paper bags. An elderly woman next to Elspeth offered her a jelly baby from a large crumpled bag. Elspeth took one and murmured her thanks.

Elspeth turned to Hamish. 'That's a very small screen for a movie,' she said. 'Actually, it's not a screen. It's just a telly.'

'All our Mr Blakey could afford,' murmured Hamish. 'Shh, it's about to start.' Hamish wondered why so many should turn out on a cold windy night to watch a video on a television set when they could have rented one and watched it in the comfort of their homes, but then he reflected that the show was free and they obviously enjoyed each other's company.

Elspeth settled back to enjoy the film but soon found her enjoyment impaired by the voices all around her. Some had seen it before and insisted on telling their neighbours what was going to happen next, and the deaf had companions who bellowed scraps of dialogue into their ears.

When the film was over, noisy and appreciative applause rang out. Mr Blakey walked to the front of the room and held up his hands. 'Before you all go,' he said, mopping his forehead with a large white handkerchief, 'a video was delivered to me this morning from Help the Aged, suggesting you all might like to see it before you go home. It is only fifteen minutes long.'

He slotted the video in, pressed Play, and then signalled to someone at the back of the room to turn out the lights again.

At first there was nothing but white dots on black. 'Must be broken,' someone shouted.

And then, suddenly, there was a picture of a room and the camera swung round to focus on a figure in a chair.

'That's Miss Beattie!' came a chorus of horrified voices. There was another shot of a black screen with dancing lights and then a picture of Miss Beattie's lifeless body, swinging this way and that.

Pandemonium erupted. The elderly screamed. Chairs were overturned. Some women fainted.

The screen went blank.

Hamish ran to the door and locked it and took out his phone and called for backup.

He turned and shouted, 'Sit down, everybody. Nobody is to leave until statements are taken.'

Mr Blakey confronted him. 'But some of the women have fainted.'

'See they're all right, and if there's any sign of anything more serious than a fainting fit, let me know. How did you get that tape?'

'It was put through the hall letter box, I don't know when. I found it when I came to open up. There was a letter with it.'

'I'll need to see that. But first let's get this lot calmed down.'

Hamish went up and stood in front of the now blank screen. Mr Blakey switched on the lights. Elderly women were being helped back to their seats. The air was redolent with the scent of urine. Poor things, thought Hamish.

'Listen,' he said. 'The police are going to need your help. We'll not keep you any longer than possible. When backup arrives, leave your names and addresses and then you will be allowed to go home. If any of you can think of anything that's of use, stay behind. Now, this tape, supposed to have come from Help the Aged, was put through the letter box of the hall. Anyone who saw anyone near the letter box, please let me know. Aren't there usually refreshments served after the movie? I think a lot of you could do with a cup of tea.'

Six women got up meekly and headed to the kitchen off the hall. Hamish surveyed the audience.

The panic was slowly being replaced with a

buzz of excitement. The ones who had fainted appeared to have recovered.

Mr Blakey handed Hamish a letter. Hamish took out a pair of thin plastic gloves and took the letter from him and read it. It was type-written. He read: 'Dear Mr Blakey: As a member of Help the Aged, I thought this fifteen-minute documentary might interest your members.' It was unsigned.

'What was I to think?' pleaded Mr Blakey. 'It had a label on the video, "Help the Aged".'

'You left it in the machine?'

'Yes, I just switched the machine off.'

There came a thumping at the door and a cry of 'Police! Open up.'

Hamish went to the door and opened it. Jimmy Anderson stood there flanked by six policemen.

'We were doing door-to-door inquiries when we got your call,' said Jimmy. 'What the hell's going on?'

Hamish explained. Jimmy ordered the policemen to go around and take names and addresses and told them to keep back anyone who had something of interest to say.

'Where's the video?' he asked.

'In the machine. I thought it had better be left there for the forensic boys. This is the letter that came with it.'

Jimmy put on gloves, took the letter from Hamish, and put it in a glassine envelope.

Where's Elspeth? wondered Hamish suddenly, looking around. Police were moving among the crowd, while women served tea and cakes and sandwiches. No Elspeth.

'Type up your statement when you get back to Lochdubh and then send it over,' said Jimmy. 'In fact, you'd best be off and do that now.'

'I'd better talk to Mrs Harris first. I brought her along with me.'

Hamish made his way to where she was sitting. 'I know your name and address, Mrs Harris,' he said, 'so I can take you home.'

'Where's that girl, Elspeth?'

'I don't know,' replied Hamish. How was he to get back to Lochdubh if Elspeth had disappeared? Elderly people were gradually making their way out of the hall, now nervous and subdued. Hamish suppressed a groan. Of course, Elspeth would have run off to file a story, which Sam would send out to the news agencies and nationals. Braikie would be swarming with more press than ever before by the morning. And the pressure of the media would mean Blair back on the job, ranting and raving.

Hamish escorted Mrs Harris outside. To his relief, Elspeth was sitting in her car, her mobile phone at her ear, talking busily. He rapped on the window. She said something into the phone and rang off.

Hamish and Mrs Harris got into the car. 'Are you all right?' Elspeth asked her.

'I cannae take it in yet,' said Mrs Harris. 'Was that really Amy in that fillum or was it some awful joke?'

'We'll find out,' said Hamish. 'Are you going to be all right on your own?'

'Aye, I'll be fine once I get into my flat and have my things around me.'

'People will be talking about nothing else in the morning,' said Hamish. 'If you hear anything you think might interest me, phone me.'

'I'll do that,' said Mrs Harris.

When they dropped her off, Hamish got into the front seat of Elspeth's small car. 'Home,' he said.

'I thought the whole point of this was to talk to some of the old people and find out if they knew anything,' said Elspeth. 'And what about the letter that came with the video? Mr Blakey said something about a letter.'

'I've got to file a statement, and they can all wait. What was the point of the video? It didn't show the murders.'

'It could be a warning.' Elspeth expertly swung the car round a startled sheep in the middle of the road. 'Maybe someone tried to blackmail the murderer or murderers, someone who was in on it. He or they didn't pay up. Maybe it was a warning that next time they'd show more.'

'This is the Highlands of Scotland!' shouted Hamish, exasperated. 'Not some damn horror film. Wait a bit. Horror films. There's something there. A child. What if a young child found that video and sent it to the community hall as a joke, not knowing that it was showing part of a real murder?'

'And typed the letter to go with it? Not likely,' said Elspeth.

'You're right.'

'You know what this means?'

'What exactly are you getting at?'

'It means,' said Elspeth patiently, 'that if whoever sent the video to the community hall was in on the murders but did not perform them, then that person is liable to find himself murdered.'

'Won't wash. Whoever filmed the murder was as much a part of it as the man or men who strung Miss Beattie up. Someone's looking at a long jail sentence.'

Elspeth suddenly swung the car to the side of the road and stopped. She darted out and was violently sick. Hamish climbed out and handed her a rather grubby handkerchief. 'There, now,' he said gently. 'It's the shock.'

Elspeth choked and gasped and then handed Hamish back his handkerchief, unused. She took a small packet of tissues out of her pocket, extracted one, and dabbed her mouth. 'Sorry, Hamish, it's a nightmare.'

'It is that,' he said grimly. 'Get back in the car, lassie, and I'll drive.'

Jenny and Pat Mallone were just finishing a meal at the Italian restaurant when Iain Chisholm entered. He bent his head over a table of diners and whispered urgently. There were cries and shocked exclamations. Iain left. The diners he had spoken to leant over to the next table and began to whisper. More cries of shock and alarm.

'Something's up.' Pat got to his feet. 'And I'm going to find out.'

He walked over to the diners Iain had first spoken to. Jenny watched. She couldn't hear what they were saying because they were whispering. Finally, Pat came back. 'I'd better get to the office,' he said. 'You'll never believe what's happened now.'

'What?

'A video was shown at the community hall in Braikie tonight. Someone had delivered it and said it was a short documentary from Help the Aged. It showed Miss Beattie hanging.'

'Gosh!'

'I'd better see Sam and get over to Braikie.'

'Can I come with you?'

'No, I'll need to take a photographer with me.'

* * *

When Pat got to the newspaper office, it was to find that Elspeth had already phoned over the story, and it had been sent off to the nationals along with library pictures of the community hall.

Pat chewed his thumb in vexation. At least the nationals would send their own reporters. Most of those reporters would rewrite Elspeth's story and put their own names on it. He didn't want Elspeth to get an offer of a job on a national newspaper before he did.

Hamish worked late filing his report. Blair phoned back at two in the morning and told him to go to Braikie as early as possible and do door-to-door inquiries. Hamish set the alarm and tried to compose himself for sleep, envying Lugs, who was snoring at the end of his bed. But sleep would not come. He felt sure that somewhere amongst all the people he had interviewed lay a clue to the murders, a clue he had missed.

Chapter Seven

O waly, waly, gin love be bonnie,
A little time, while it is new!
But when 'tis auld it waxeth cauld,
And fades awa' like morning dew.
                    – Anonymous

The following morning, Jenny, wrapped in a rosy dream, ate her breakfast. Pat had told her his ambitions of being an ace reporter on a national newspaper and then moving on to television. Jenny was determined to return to London engaged to be married. Hamish Macbeth was proving too difficult and she obscurely blamed him for having caught her lying. But now, if she was married to a top reporter, that would be something to brag about. And it would mean no more disappointing affairs, no more going out on dates. She would be Mrs Mallone. They would have a trim London house, somewhere fashionable, and she would see him off in the morning and then have nothing else to do but leave instructions for the cleaning woman. No more work. No more going to the office. Wouldn't it be wonderful to be married *before* Priscilla! I'll make her my bridesmaid, thought Jenny. I'll make her wear a yellow dress. Yellow was never Priscilla's colour.

Now, what should she do with the day? Pat had phoned to say he would be spending the whole day in Braikie. She could go there herself and see if she could find out anything. Yes, that might be a good idea. If she was going to be Mrs Mallone, then she should help her future husband in getting his first break. She could see it now. He would become a foreign correspondent for the BBC and she would go with him everywhere and become something of a celebrity. Of course, that notion rather spoiled the dream of having a lazy married existence at home. Suddenly, she remembered the seer's prediction. He had been right! She would go and see him first.

Wasn't one supposed to take a present?

She walked along to Patel's store and bought a large box of chocolates and then set off up the hill to where Angus lived. The day was windy, with great gusts of wind that sent her staggering up the hillside. Seagulls were dotted about the sheep-cropped grass like the work of so many taxidermists, standing still, their tail feathers to the wind. Jenny did not know that this was a sign of worse weather to come.

She ploughed on upwards and arrived panting on the seer's doorstep. She was raising her hand to knock when Angus opened the door. His eyes gleamed with delight when he saw the large box of chocolates. Angus loved sweets. 'Come in, lassie,' he said. 'I was expecting you.'

'You were?' Jenny felt a shiver of delighted apprehension.

She walked in, handing him the box of chocolates. Jenny was very fond of chocolates and hoped he would open the box and offer her one, but Angus asked her to be seated and bore the box off to the kitchen.

'Tea?' he asked on his return.

'Nothing for me,' said Jenny. 'Did you hear what happened last night at the community hall?'

'Of course.'

'And you saw it all?'

For a moment, Angus looked startled. He remembered that something weird had happened when this girl had visited him with Hamish but could not remember what it was he had said. 'Aye,' he said portentously, 'I see in the future.'

Jenny wriggled with excitement. 'So do you know who committed these murders?'

'I'm working on it,' said Angus. 'I said I could see the *future*.'

'Yes, but if you can see the future, then you will know who it is Hamish is going to arrest.'

'Hamish Macbeth has had a lot of luck, but this could be the time his luck will run out. He may never find out who murdered those two people.'

'I would like to help him, you see,' said Jenny eagerly.

'Then you're wasting your time. Macbeth has no interest in you.'

Jenny flushed to the roots of her hair. She rose to her feet and said crossly, 'You're not half as clever as you think you are. I have no romantic interest in Hamish Macbeth. You've really nothing to tell me that's worth a large box of chocolates. I'll just take them back.'

For one brief moment, Angus was speechless. No one had ever demanded a present back. 'Get out of here, lassie,' he roared, 'and don't come back again. A bad thing's going to happen to you, but because of your rudeness and meanness, I am not going to tell you. Shove off!'

He loomed over her. Jenny, suddenly terrified, shot to her feet and ran round him to the door. She jerked it open and hurtled out. Clouds were racing across the sky. She reflected that surely nowhere else in Britain could you get four changes of climate in one day. A rainbow arched over the black and stormy waters of the loch and she found herself wondering, ridiculously, why it did not bend under the ferocity of the wind.

Would something bad happen to her? Or had he just been mad because she'd asked for her chocolates back?

Mentally trying to shrug off a feeling of foreboding, she gained the waterfront and got into her car. Now for Braikie. She was just moving slowly along the waterfront when Iain Chisholm came running out of his garage, waving his arms for her to stop. Jenny jerked to a halt and wound down the window.

'Going far?' asked Iain.

'Just over to Braikie.'

'There's a bad storm coming up. That car's only a three-wheeler. It could be blown over when you reach the shore road. I could put something heavy in her as ballast.'

But Jenny, still frightened by the seer, was anxious to get away. 'I'll be all right,' she said crossly. 'If the wind gets too strong, I'll just pull over.'

She let in the clutch and drove off before Iain could say anything else.

As she drove up out of Lochdubh, at the top of the first hill, a great gust of wind and rain made her hang on grimly to the steering wheel as the car bucked and rocked, but soon she was down the hill on the other side, driving between great banks of gorse. I'll be all right when I get to Braikie, she told herself. As she drove slowly now towards the coast road, the sky was black and the thin single-track road in front of her twisted and glistened like a giant eel. She negotiated a hairpin bend and cruised down on to the shore road. Monstrous waves were pounding the beach. I'll be all right, I'll be all right, she told herself fiercely. Just a little way to go and I'll be in the shelter of the houses. She was halfway along the road when with a great roar, the wind hit the car and blew it over on its side. Struggling to unfasten her seat belt, she realized her arm was broken. Helplessly, she lay there against the door of the car, praying for help to come along. Then she realized she was listening not only to the roar of the wind but to the roar of the waves. A huge wave struck the little car and drove it into a ditch. She screamed from the pain in her arm and fainted.

From his croft high up above the shore road, a crofter, Duncan Moray, saw what was happening and picked up the phone and called the police. He was old, in his eighties, and did not feel strong enough to go to the rescue himself.

Jenny came out of her faint. Another wave pounded down on the car. The sea was coming right across the road. She could only hope the tide would turn and leave her, miraculously, still alive. Oh, God, she was going to die here in this ridiculous car in the wilds of the northernmost part of the British Isles, and all because she had been jealous of Priscilla.

And then she thought she was hallucinating because through the window of the passenger side, above her head, she saw the face of Hamish Macbeth. But he turned out to be real, because he wrenched open the passenger door. 'There's another big wave coming,' he said. 'Come on, take my hand.'

'My arm's broken,' said Jenny. 'My right arm.'

'Give me your left hand. Quick!'

But another wave struck, drenching Hamish and flooding the car. 'Do you want to die?' roared Hamish as the wave retreated. He leant in and put his arms round her waist and began to pull her upwards. 'Here's the ambulance,' he said. He shouted over his shoulder, 'Come on, boys, or she'll have us all drowned.' He let Jenny go, and she fell backwards with a moan. She felt the car rock and then it was pushed upright. Another wave struck it and she could hear yells and curses from outside. Then the door was opened and two ambulance men eased her out. They lifted her bodily into the ambulance and slammed the door.

The ambulance moved off, the driver swearing as a wave struck his vehicle. The ambulance man inside with Jenny said, 'I would put a splint on that arm now, but it isn't safe with us rocking like this. Didn't you hear the warnings not to go out?'

But Jenny had fainted again.

Jenny recovered consciousness as she was being lifted down into a wheelchair. She was soaked to the skin and shivering with cold and shock. In the hospital, an admissions clerk said sourly, 'It's a shame to give up a bed for a mere broken arm. But we'd better get these wet clothes off her and take her along to X-ray.'

Jenny could not possibly feel like a heroine. She felt like a badly behaved child and she also, superstitiously, felt that Angus had put a curse on her.

Fortunately for Jenny, by the time she was put into a hospital nightgown and robe after a nurse had sponged her down and administered strong painkillers, she looked remarkably pretty again, and a susceptible doctor insisted that, after her arm was set, she be kept in for the night and allowed to go home in the morning.

Her first visitor was Elspeth. 'I'd like to put a piece in the paper about your accident,' said Elspeth.

'I feel such a fool,' said Jenny. 'Everyone will think I'm a fool.'

'No, they won't. Everyone knows you aren't used to the weather up here,' said Elspeth soothingly, although she was thinking of how tired she was of idiots who would not respect the dangers of Highland weather – climbers who had to be rescued at great expense and who then sold the stories of their ordeals to the tabloids and never thought of giving any money to Highland Rescue, whose members had risked their own necks to save them.

'I'll send a photographer round to take a picture of you when I can find him. You'll look really pretty.'

Jenny told her story, omitting the fact that Iain had tried to warn her, not guessing that Elspeth would hear of Iain's warning before the day was out.

Jenny also omitted the fact that Hamish Macbeth had been first on the scene.

'You haven't mentioned Hamish,' said Elspeth.

Somehow Jenny resented Hamish for having caught her out in her lies and having not found her attractive enough.

'Oh, well,' she said sulkily, 'it didn't seem necessary. The ambulance men got me out.'

'I met Hamish before I came here,' said Elspeth. 'The poor man was sitting in the mobile police unit with only a small towel to cover his modesty while he tried to dry his clothes at a two-bar electric heater.'

'I must get the names of the ambulance men,' said Jenny, deliberately ignoring the subject of Hamish Macbeth. 'I must thank them.'

Elspeth closed her notebook. 'Well, that about wraps it up. There are more exciting stories up here than you'd get on the streets of London.'

'I thought Pat would be covering this.' Jenny took out a small mirror from her handbag on the bed and studied her appearance.

'I'm sure he would have. He wasn't in the office when I left. Sam was phoning him. He had slept in.'

'But he should be here soon?'

'I don't see why,' said Elspeth. 'I've got the story.'

After she had left, Jenny applied some make-up and brushed her hair. It was awkward with the plaster cast on her arm. Her next visitor was Hamish Macbeth, wearing an old pair of trousers, short in the leg, and a long Fair Isle sweater.

'Sorry about my appearance,' he said. 'I had to borrow some clothes. My uniform dried but it was so encrusted with salt I had to take it to the dry cleaner's.'

'What about Iain's car? Was anyone able to rescue it?'

'We didn't even try. It's insured. I phoned Iain and he said it would be a write-off anyway so to let the sea do its worst. I see you've got the screens around your bed. You're not that ill, are you?'

'It's a good way of not having to talk to the other patients.'

'Oh, you should try, lassie. You might hear some gossip.'

'I've given you enough help,' said Jenny pettishly.

'Suit yourself. I chust called round to see you were okay,' said Hamish, turning to leave, the sudden sibilance of his accent showing he was annoyed with her.

But after he had gone, Jenny thought that perhaps she was being silly. She had risked life and limb to see if she could find out anything about the murders. She stretched out her good arm and drew aside the curtain. She stared in surprise at the girl in the bed next to her. It was Jessie Briggs, the former favourite of Miss McAndrew.

'What are you doing here?' asked Jenny.

'Got pumped out,' said Jessie in a weak voice.

'Drugs?'

'Naw, he left me. The boyfriend. Told him to give me a bottle of whisky as a farewell present and I drank it along with a lot of aspirin. Didn't want to live.' Large tears ran down her pallid face. She wiped them away with the back of her hand. 'I would ha' succeeded in killing myself if that interfering auld biddy from next door hadn't peered in the window and seen me lying on the floor and called the ambulance.'

'You should be grateful to her. She saved your life.'

'So what!'

'Listen, did you phone AA?'

'Oh, them. I phoned them the once. I told them it was all Miss McAndrew's fault I was in this state and some woman says to me, she says, "Nobody makes you drink. It's not as if she held you down and poured it down your throat." I said it was because she'd ruined my life. She says she used to suffer from self-pity as well and used to blame everyone for her drinking. I told her to go and shove her head up her arse.'

'Try them again and go along. What have you got to lose'

'Maybe.'

'Who do you think murdered her?'

'How should I know? One o' the teachers. She made their life hell. Joseph Cromarty, the ironmonger. He hated her. I passed them in the street not long afore she was killed and he was shouting at her that she was a disgrace and he was glad she had retired. He said if she'd stayed on, he would have murdered her.'

'Joseph's a decent man,' said an old lady in the bed opposite.

'Shut up and mind your own business,' snapped Jessie.

Jenny gave the old lady a weak smile.

Jessie lay back on her pillows and closed her eyes, just as Jenny's next visitor came in – Iain Chisholm.

'How's your car?' asked Jenny.

'Och, I'll be getting herself out at low tide. I did try to warn you.'

'I'm awfully sorry,' said Jenny. 'Hamish said you're insured.'

Iain silently cursed Hamish Macbeth. He'd come to the hospital hoping to get a cheque from Jenny.

'Well,' he said huffily, 'so she is. But that was a rare car. Not many of those around nowadays.'

He looked so angry that Jenny said quickly, 'Maybe I can rent something else from you. I should still be able to drive.'

'I have a wee Morris Minor. But I will need to be charging you more for the rental, seeing as how you are the bad risk.'

'Like how much?'

'A hundred and twenty-five pounds a week.'

'I'll think about it.' Jenny copied Jessie and lay back on her pillows and closed her eyes while she privately resolved to go down to Strathbane and rent something modern.

She kept her eyes firmly closed until she heard Iain leave.

Elspeth met up with Pat Mallone in the main street of Braikie. A savage gale was whipping rubbish down the street from overturned dustbins. Her face was soaked with rain and flying salt spray blown in from the sea. 'Let's get inside somewhere,' shouted Pat, 'and compare notes.'

They went into the dingy pub. Most pubs now supplied coffee but not this one. They ordered soft drinks and went to a corner table. 'I was up at the school,' said Pat, 'trying to get a word with the teachers, but that head teacher, Arkle, turned me away before I could speak to anyone. What about you?'

'I've been interviewing Jenny. Quite a good local story.'

'What's this about?' asked Pat.

Elspeth knew the town had been buzzing with the rescue of Jenny Ogilvie and wondered, not for the first time, how a reporter like Pat Mallone could miss stories that were right under his nose. As usual he had slept late, and she guessed that he had rushed up to Braikie, gone to the school and been turned away, and had not tried to do anything else but look for her to see if he could save himself some work. She told him about Jenny's rescue.

'I'd better go up to the hospital and see her.'

'Why? I've already phoned over the story.'

'We're pals. I'd better go now.'

Elspeth glared after his retreating back. Pat had been quite keen on her, she thought sourly, before Jenny came along. Still, as far as Hamish Macbeth was concerned, Jenny wasn't a threat. It had been mean of Jenny not to give Hamish any credit for her rescue. Elspeth grinned as she thought of the story she had phoned over, which would go out in the weekly paper under Sam's headline: LOCAL HERO.

She decided to make her way to the community centre to see if Mr Blakey was available. As she went out of the pub, the wind seized her old fishing hat and sent it bowling down the street. Elspeth scampered after it, but another greater gust of wind sent it flying up over the rooftops.

When she gained the shelter of the community centre, water was streaming down her face from her rain-soaked hair. Mr Blakey was mopping the floor. 'A leak in the roof,' he said mournfully. 'I saw you last night.'

'Before I speak to you, have you a towel or something I could use on my hair?'

'Sorry, there's just the hand drier in the toilet.'

'That'll need to do.' Elspeth made her way across the hall and into the ladies' toilet. She banged on the hand drier and crouched under it, occasionally reaching up to switch it on again after it had automatically switched off. At last she straightened up and fished in her capacious handbag for a brush and dragged it through her frizzy hair before going back into the hall.

'I tried to see you earlier,' she said. 'I'm from the local paper. I thought this place would be full of reporters.'

'I think it would have been, but there's a landslide on the road. Two of them tried to climb over the hill and had to be rescued. But the tide's turned and they think they'll get the blockage cleared soon.'

'You must have been very shocked by that video.'

Mr Blakey sat down suddenly on a chair. 'I'm frightened,' he said. 'It was such an evil thing to do, and why pick on the old folks?'

'Has anyone told you or the police if anyone was seen in or around the community centre when the package was delivered?'

'The problem is that I just found the package when I opened up. That would be around five o'clock. It could have been delivered anytime during the day.'

'I saw you handing Hamish a note.'

'Yes, that came with it. I told you about that. It simply said it was a video from Help the Aged.'

'Typewritten?'

'Yes.'

'Oh, well, the police will be searching everywhere in Braikie for the typewriter that was used.'

'What worries me, too,' said Mr Blakey, 'is that they'll be too frightened to come back for another film show. They used to love them.'

'I'll see what I can do.' Elspeth's busy mind was already forming an appeal. Maybe raise money for a proper screen and cinematography equipment. She asked him some more questions and then said she had to file a story. She went back out into the storm and located her car, stopping on the way to buy a rain hat and a towel.

In the car, she once more dried herself and then took out her laptop, pushed back the driving seat to its limit to give herself more room, and began to type busily. When it was finished, she sent it over and then phoned Sam, the owner and editor. She told him about her idea of an appeal to help the community centre. 'Great,' said Sam. 'Where's Mallone?'

'I think he's up at the hospital seeing Jenny.'

'Didn't you tell him you'd already done that story? And have you a camera? Harry can't get through. There's a landslide.' Harry was the photographer.

'Yes, I've got a camera.'

'Then get a photo of Jenny and one of Hamish. Get as many photos of the locals as you can. That's what sells this paper. And get Pat to take photos as well.'

'I doubt if he'll have a camera.'

'I'm seriously thinking of sacking him, Elspeth.'

'Give him a talking-to first.'

'I already have. Doesn't seem to make a damn bit of difference.'

Elspeth rang off and located her camera. She drove up to the hospital. Pat was sitting on the end of Jenny's bed, laughing and joking and eating most of the chocolates he had brought her.

'Look what the cat dragged in!' cried Pat.

'Harry can't get through, so I'm here to take a pic of Jenny,' said Elspeth. 'Have you a camera, Pat?'

'No.'

'Well, after I take Jenny's picture, you'd better come with me. Sam's orders are that we're to take as many pictures of the locals as possible and get their comments.'

'Can't you do that?'

'It would be nice to have some help.'

Elspeth took several photographs of Jenny and then said, 'Come along, Pat.'

'I don't take orders from you,' he muttered, but he bent and kissed Jenny on the cheek and reluctantly followed Elspeth out of the hospital. 'I'll follow you down into the town,' he shouted above the roar of the wind.

Elspeth set off and parked in the main street. But when she got out of her car, there was no sign of Pat Mallone. Wearily, she set off in the direction of the post office.

To Elspeth's delight, there were six elderly ladies clustered around the counter in front of Mrs Harris, all chattering and exclaiming about the events of the night before. Elspeth interviewed them and then photographed them.

As Elspeth was taking the used film out of her camera and searching in her pockets for another roll, Mrs Harris exclaimed, 'Would you look at that!'

Everyone swung round in alarm. Mrs Harris was pointing at the window. 'Sunshine,' she said.

The weather of Sutherland had gone in for one of its mercurial changes. Pale yellow sunlight was flooding the street outside.

Elspeth left the shop. The wind was dropping rapidly and the clouds were rolling back. Elspeth strolled around the streets and shops, photographing and interviewing the locals, enjoying the now friendly, blustery wind and the feel of warm sun on her cheek, and all the time looking for Hamish Macbeth. At last she caught up with him as he came out of the dry cleaner's. He was wearing the old sweater and trousers he had borrowed and carrying his cleaned and pressed uniform. Elspeth raised her camera and took his picture.

'Och, Elspeth,' said Hamish angrily. 'Could ye no' wait until I got my uniform on?'

'It's better like this,' she said. 'Have you seen Pat Mallone?'

'Not a sign.'

Elspeth sighed. 'Tell you what, Hamish, my expenses aren't that great, but they would certainly run to taking a policeman for lunch.'

'You're on. Where?'

'What about that hotel outside Braikie where we went before?'

'Right.'

'My car's just along there.'

'If Blair sees me,' said Hamish, glancing around, 'I won't be able to go.'

'Then hurry up!'

They were just sitting down in the dining room when Elspeth's mobile phone rang. 'Excuse me,' she said to Hamish, and answered it.

'I'll go and change into my uniform,' said Hamish. 'Thank goodness I didn't wear my cap for the rescue or I'd never have been able to get it back into shape.'

Elspeth heard Sam's voice on the phone. 'Mallone's turned up trumps,' he said. 'He's got marvellous quotes. Better than yours. But no photos. If I give you the addresses, could you get round there and take pictures?'

'Wait till I get my notebook.' Elspeth took it out of her handbag and opened it on the table. 'Fire away.'

She wrote down the names and addresses and then said cautiously, 'Sam, are you sure these people exist? I mean, Mrs McHaggis of Tavistock Street? Apart from the daft name, I don't remember a Tavistock Street in Braikie. Tell you what, I'm having lunch with Hamish Macbeth. I'll show him the names and addresses and get back to you.'

When Hamish returned, now in his uniform, Elspeth explained about Pat Mallone's quotes, names and addresses.

'Let me see,' said Hamish.

He carefully read the list and then leant back in his chair, looking amused. 'The man should be writing fiction.'

'Are you sure?'

'I know every street in Braikie and I don't see one genuine address on this list. He's made the lot up.'

'I suppose I'll need to tell Sam.'

'You'll have to. If he publishes any of that, people from Braikie will soon put him wise.'

Elspeth phoned Sam and told him that Pat had made the lot up. 'That's it,' said Sam angrily. 'I'll give him a month's notice. That's more than he deserves.'

Pat was back seated on the end of Jenny's bed, regaling her with some highly embroidered stories of his life in Dublin, when his mobile phone rang.

Sam's angry voice came down the line. 'You're fired.'

Pat said airily to Jenny, 'Office business.' He walked rapidly outside the ward.

'Why?' he asked.

'Because you made up all these people and quotes and addresses, that's why. You're on a month's notice.' Sam rang off.

'Bugger!' said Pat loudly, startling a passing nurse.

Jenny looked up as he walked back into the ward. 'What's up?' she asked.

He pulled a chair up to the bed and drew the screens around it. 'I made up some quotes,' he said, 'and Sam found out. He's fired me.'

'Oh, poor Pat,' said Jenny. 'What are we going to do?'

Warmed by that 'we', Pat drew his chair closer. 'I wonder,' he said, turning the full blast of his Irish charm on her, 'whether you might be prepared to put me up in London for a week? I'm sure to get a job on one of the nationals.'

Jenny looked at him cautiously, wondering how he hoped to get a job on a national when he had been fired by a local paper. The only boyfriends Jenny had ever been able to keep were the few that had scrounged off her. Not only did she earn a good wage but she had a modest income as well from a family trust.

'I've a better idea,' said Jenny. 'You've got a month. If we could find out who the murderer is, you would have a great story and could send it direct to the nationals. Then you would be sure of getting a job. I'll help you.'

'What can we find out that the police can't?' demanded Pat sulkily.

'I've got a lead.'

'What?'

She told him about Joseph Cromarty threatening to kill Miss McAndrew. 'You could start there. Look! The sun's shining now.'

Pat's mind worked quickly. He would appear to go along with her plan, casually ask for her home address before she left, and then just turn up on her doorstep. Better look enthusiastic.

'That's a grand idea.' He stood up. 'I'll get to work right away.'

But when he drove down from the hospital and entered the main street, it was to find it swarming with press. The landslide must have been cleared quickly. He went to the pub instead where he knew some of the other reporters would be. Perhaps he could pick their brains and find out how to get a job on a national.

Hamish was weary by the time the day was over. Blair had ordered him home, his superior anxious to get rid of this policeman who had a nasty knack of taking any glory away from him.

He fed Lugs and then made his own supper. He wanted permission to go to Perth but was sure he would not get it. Miss Beattie was the key to all this. Of that he felt sure. His shoulder ached from the effort of righting Jenny's car and fighting with the force of the waves. He could persuade Dr Brodie that he needed a day off.

'Lugs,' he said.

The dog cocked his heavy head on one side and looked up at him with those odd blue eyes.

'Fancy a trip to Perth?'

Chapter Eight

What's gone, and what's past help
Should be past grief.
                    – William Shakespeare

Hamish called on Dr Brodie at breakfast time the following day and secured a note to say he was suffering from exhaustion. He had debated whether to leave Lugs with Angela, but that would be a way of telling the good doctor that he was lying and wanted an excuse to go off somewhere.

'I'd planned to take you anyway, I suppose,' said Hamish as Lugs sat proudly beside him on the passenger seat. 'But behave yourself! No wanting to stop for a walk every fifteen minutes.'

He heard a rap on the window and rolled it down to face the gimlet eyes of the Currie sisters. 'Aren't you coming to the kirk this morning?' asked Jessie.

'Not today.'

He began to roll up the window but heard Jessie shout, 'You could do wi' some spiritual help. You've begun talking to yourself. We saw you!' Hamish motored off.

As he drove over the humpback bridge, he noticed that the River Anstey was in full spate from the storm, although the weather had calmed down considerably. The sky above had a fresh-scrubbed look. He rolled down the window again and breathed in the scents of pine and wild thyme. He felt his spirits lift. It was good to be getting away.

He was halfway on the road south to Perth when he suddenly thought of that poison-pen letter, the one found lying on the floor under Miss Beattie's body. They had all assumed it came from Miss McAndrew. But why would Miss McAndrew accuse Miss Beattie of being a bastard when it was plainly not true? He swore under his breath. What if, for some reason, someone wanted them to think it came from the usual source? Someone had definitely wanted them to think Miss Beattie had committed suicide. He decided to phone the hand-writing expert when he got back.

Perth lay dreaming in the sunset, south of the craggy peaks of the Highland line. The River Tay curved through the town, gleaming silver. He stopped the police Land Rover on the outskirts and let Lugs out for a run while he consulted a map of the town that he kept with a pile of others in a cardboard box in the back. Mrs Dinwiddie lived on a new housing estate, just outside the town and just off the A9. As he headed in that direction, he now wished he had phoned her first. She might be away for the day.

But Mrs Dinwiddie was at home and she welcomed him warmly. 'My husband's gone to visit his elderly father,' she said, 'so we should have some peace and quiet. The police returned my sister's papers to me yesterday and I was just going to get in touch with you.'

She led Hamish into the kitchen. 'Tea?'

'Grand. Thanks.'

'Is that your dog out in the car? I don't mind dogs.'

'I'll bring him in,' said Hamish gratefully. 'I forgot his water bowl and he'll be thirsty.'

When they were all settled, Hamish with a mug of tea and Lugs with a bowl of water, Mrs Dinwiddie left the kitchen and came back with a pile of papers. 'I've been through them myself,' she said. 'Nothing much but bills and bank statements. No letters at all.'

'What about photographs?'

'She had some of those.'

'May I see them, please?'

She left and came back with a battered-looking photo album. Hamish opened it up. There were photos of Highland games and photographs of the post office and one of Billy fishing. Nothing exciting. Ever hopeful, he turned over the last blank pages of the album. In the back was a dusty plastic envelope of photos.

He opened it and began to look through them. There was a photo of two little girls. He held it out to Mrs Dinwiddie. 'That's me and Amy when we were small,' she said.

Then a photo of a severe-looking couple. 'Our parents,' said Mrs Dinwiddie.

There were more photos of Amy and her sister, some when they were older, some in high school uniform.

And then there was one of Amy Beattie with a group of bikers. At that stage of her life, she had thick black hair and a roguish expression. She was wearing tight jeans and a leather jacket. 'I wonder they let her out of the house dressed like that,' said Hamish, showing the photograph to Mrs Dinwiddie.

'Oh, she used to buy clothes she liked and hide them under the bed. She would change into them somewhere outside. Then Mother found out about her wearing them and the house was searched. My parents had a ceremonial burning of them in the garden. Poor Amy cried and cried.'

'The fellows in this picture, do you recognize any of them?'

Mrs Dinwiddie pointed to a handsome young man who was sitting astride a motorbike, smiling at Amy Beattie. 'That's Graham Simpson. He was at school with Amy. I think they used to be close, he and Amy – well, as close as we could get to any boy with our parents always watching us.'

'Do you know if he's still in Perth?'

'Yes, someone told me about him. He's manager of the Scottish & Regional Bank in Turret Street. But what can he have to do with Amy's death?'

'I don't know. Maybe someone found out something about her background she didn't want anyone to find out.'

'That would explain suicide, but not murder.'

'I'd like to see him just the same. Can I keep this photograph? I'll give you a receipt and send it back to you.'

'Keep it as long as you like.'

'Where is the church you used to go to?'

'Down by the river. Harris Street.'

Hamish left with Lugs and got into the Land Rover and looked up Turret Street on his map of Perth. Once there, he went into the bank and asked to speak to the manager. The cashier gave him an anxious look. Hamish was in uniform. 'Nothing wrong, is there?' she asked.

'No, no,' said Hamish soothingly. 'I just want a wee word with him.'

He waited. The cashier returned and said, 'Follow me,' and ushered him in through a heavy mahogany door.

The man who rose to meet Hamish bore little resemblance to the carefree, handsome biker in the photograph. He was tall with thinning hair, a heavy red face and a thick body.

'Sit down,' he said. 'What's this about? No one been fiddling the accounts, have they?'

'No, nothing like that. I am Police Constable Hamish Macbeth from Lochdubh. You will have read about the murder of Miss Beattie.'

'Yes, indeed. Dreadful business, but what's that got to do with me?'

'Sometimes if I can find out more about the murder victim, I can sometimes find the murderer,' said Hamish. He drew out the photograph and handed it over. 'This is you, isn't it?'

'Michty me, so it is. And Amy.'

'Were you Miss Beattie's boyfriend at one time?'

'Hadn't a chance. Her parents were that strict. We were able to see each other for a bit and then they started locking her up at home, and Mr and Mrs Beattie came round one evening to see my parents. They called me a limb of Satan and my father threw them out of the house.'

'She left Perth suddenly, I believe. Do you know the reason for it?'

'The reason was her parents. I guess she couldn't stand them any more.'

'But time heals wounds, and yet Miss Beattie did not even attend their funerals.'

'You'd have to have known them. Right pair of scunners. Now, if you'll excuse me . . .' He half rose.

Hamish surveyed him. 'You seem in a hurry to get rid of me.'

'It's not that. I have an appointment with someone. They should be here any moment.'

'One more thing. The other young men in the photograph. There are three of them. Can you tell me if I can contact them?'

'I shouldn't think so. I only remember one of them and that's Peter Stoddart and he went to Australia.'

'Why can't you remember the names of the others? I find one can usually remember the names of friends of one's youth.'

'Peter was my friend. The others, as I mind, were just visiting the town from down south.'

Hamish left with an uneasy feeling that the man had been lying to him. But he drove to Harris Street and parked outside the church. The congregation were just leaving and the minister was standing on the church porch. He was an elderly man. Hamish could only hope he had been minister at the time Mr and Mrs Beattie were alive.

'Might I be having a word with you?' he asked. 'I'm investigating the murder of Miss Beattie. Do you remember her parents?'

'I became minister here after Miss Beattie left home. But, yes, I remember Mr and Mrs Beattie. Come along to the manse. It's a bit chilly here.'

Hamish followed him to the manse next door. The minister led him into a gloomy Victorian kitchen. 'Sit yourself down and I'll make some tea. My wife died last year and I'm still not very domesticated but I do my best.' Hamish waited patiently while the minister made tea and put the teapot, milk and sugar, cups, and a plate of digestive biscuits on the table.

'Did you ever hear any talk of why Miss Beattie left home?' asked Hamish.

He shook his head. 'I am not surprised she left home. However, I heard some talk from some parishioners that she was a wild girl and from others that she was disgracefully bullied. The Beatties were very strict, very strict indeed. They saw sin everywhere. They were even having their doubts about me. They considered me too lenient with the youth of the parish. They did not seem to understand that life had moved on since the days of *their* youth. I am afraid it is only the middle-aged and elderly that attend my church these days. I cannot go out and terrorize young people into attending, which is what the Beatties wanted me to do.

'I am sure Miss Beattie left home because she could not stand the harsh discipline any more.'

Hamish asked him some more questions, but it all seemed very simple. There had been nothing more dramatic in Amy Beattie's past than a pair of insufferably bullying parents.

As he drove back north, he reflected that the handwriting expert would hardly be available on a Sunday, so he went to police head-quarters. He hoped Jimmy Anderson was not still up in Braikie, but he found him in the detectives' room typing up reports.

'Hamish!' said Jimmy with a grin. 'Heard you were sick.'

'Between ourselves,' said Hamish, 'I've been down to Perth. I had a hope that there might have been something in Miss Beattie's back-ground that might give me a clue, but I can't seem to think of anything. But an idea occurred to me: What about that letter that was found with Miss Beattie's body? I mean, the poison-pen letter.'

'What about it?'

'I mean, it turned out to be a load of rubbish. She wasn't a bastard. Was it the same hand-writing as the others?'

'Cost you a double whisky.'

'Och, all right. If a gannet could drink whisky, it would be just like you.'

Jimmy booted up his computer. Hamish sat down next to him, obscurely thankful that

Jimmy did not smoke. Hamish had given up smoking a while ago, but the occasional yearning for a cigarette never seemed to go away.

At last Jimmy said, 'Here it is. The letter was sent to Roger Glass, thon handwriting expert. He said it was the same handwriting as the others.'

'Now, that's odd.' Hamish leant back in his chair. 'I have a feeling that the murders were committed by lucky amateurs. I mean, we're not dealing with hit men here. But why leave a letter they were sure we would find out didn't contain anything like the truth?'

'Don't ask me, Sherlock,' Jimmy was beginning, when Hamish disappeared under the desk.

Jimmy swung round just as Detective Chief Inspector Blair lumbered into the room. 'I'm off to Braikie,' he said, 'and you're coming with me.'

'Just finishing up here,' said Jimmy. 'I'll be right behind you.'

'Get a move on, then.'

'I thought you didn't work on Sundays.'

'The boss is terrified by all the press coverage and says we've got to work until we find someone. Hurry up!'

Jimmy nodded. He waited until Blair had left and then said, 'You can come out now.'

Hamish groaned as he unwound his lanky form from under Jimmy's desk. 'I'd better wait until I'm sure the old scunner is on the road. Then I'll get to Lochdubh fast in case he decides to drop in.'

'Don't forget you owe me a whisky.'

At the *Highland Times*, Elspeth was starting to read through a pile of national Sunday papers. She turned to the Sunday edition of the *Bugle*, wondering if they had used her colour piece. She flipped over the pages and then she found it. She stared at the large byline as if she could not believe her eyes. 'Pat Mallone,' it said.

She remembered Pat telling her he had taken the liberty of sending off her article. He must have erased her name and put his own on, and once the article had gone he had put her name back on it.

Sam was having a day off and had gone to visit relatives in Alness. She picked up the phone and dialled the *Bugle* and asked to speak to the editor of the Sunday paper, only to be told he was never at work on Sundays. Elspeth then got through to the news desk of the daily and told them that the article featured under Pat Mallone's byline was actually her own and her editor could confirm it. 'Don't worry,' said a voice from the news desk. 'We'll let him know.'

'What was that about?' a colleague asked when he put the phone down.

'Oh, some girl up in the Highlands claiming another reporter stole her article,' he said. 'Nothing interesting.' Then he promptly forgot about it.

Still thirsting for blood, Elspeth went out to look for Pat Mallone.

At that moment, Pat Mallone was sitting in the Italian restaurant with Jenny. Jenny had been telling him about her dreadful experience after the church service when she had been waylaid by the Currie sisters and given a lecture on sin.

Pat then whipped out a copy of the *Sunday Bugle*. 'I've been saving this to show you,' he said. He proudly opened the page at 'his' article.

'How wonderful!' cried Jenny. 'May I read it?'

'Go ahead.'

As Jenny was reading the article, Pat suddenly saw Elspeth's face peering in at the restaurant window. 'I'll be back in a minute.' Pat shot out of the restaurant door. Jenny could see Elspeth shouting at him and Pat shrugging his shoulders. She turned back to the article. It was very good. She had just been beginning to think that Pat was not a very dedicated reporter. But this article proved not only that he was a dedicated reporter but that he could write as well. Oblivious to the angry voices outside the restaurant, she fell into a rosy dream where Pat would become a famous writer.

He was just accepting the Booker Prize when the real-life Pat came back into the restaurant. Jenny blinked the rosy dream away. 'What was all that about?' she asked. 'Elspeth seemed angry.'

'Oh, office squabble.' He sat down and smiled at her. 'To tell you the truth, I think Elspeth's jealous of you.'

'I think Elspeth's keen on Hamish Macbeth.'

He took her hand. 'You're so pretty, all the women are jealous of you.'

Jenny looked into his blue eyes and caught a flicker of something at the back of them, something like fear.

'Did she threaten you?'

'That wee girl! Don't make me laugh.'

'You're afraid of something, aren't you?'

Pat thought quickly. He planned to go south and try his luck, and he wanted free lodgings.

He gave a shrug. 'You're a sharp girl. I think Elspeth knows that the colour piece might get me a job on a national. She knows my ambitions. I need this month's notice to look around. I'm frightened she puts in a bad word about me with Sam and he might tell me to leave this week.'

Privately, Jenny, although she had originally sympathized with him, thought there was surely little more he could do to make Sam even more furious with him.

'If you could dig up a really good story about this murder,' she said, 'then Sam might relent.'

'I've tried to best I can,' he said moodily. Then those blue eyes of his looked at her speculatively. 'But if you could get close to Hamish Macbeth, he might let something drop. Could you do that for me?'

'Hamish Macbeth is not interested in me!'

'But you haven't really tried,' wheedled Pat. 'I feel you and I are destined to be together for a long time.'

Jenny gave a little gasp. 'Do you mean marriage? You and me?'

Oh, well, why not? thought Pat. He could always wriggle out of it later. 'I'll get you the ring as soon as I get a job on a national,' he said. 'Gosh, I feel like ordering champagne, but I haven't enough with me.'

'I'll order it,' said Jenny, flushed and happy. She made to raise an arm to call Willie, the waiter, but Pat stopped her. He had visions of Willie asking what the celebration was about and Jenny telling him.

'Let's keep it our secret for the moment,' he said. 'It would be difficult for you to get anything out of Hamish Macbeth if he knew you were engaged to me.'

'All right,' said Jenny. Then she gave him a

wicked grin. 'But I know a better way to cele-
brate. Let's go back to your place.'

'Think of your reputation! My landlady
would have it all over the village and the
Currie sisters would be making you spend
every day with the minister to cleanse your
soul.'

'I suppose you're right.'

When they walked outside, it was a cold
moonlit night. 'A braw bricht nicht, the nicht,'
said Jenny, although all her *ch*'s were pronounced as *k*'s and came out as 'a braw brick
nick, the nick.' 'Let's go for a stroll.'

'It's early yet. Tell you what, run along to
that police station and get to work on Hamish.'
He gave her a little shove. 'It's our future
you're working for.'

But he did not kiss her good night. Jenny
walked off forlornly in the direction of the
police station. She had received her first proposal of marriage, and yet it all felt wrong.
He's just using you, screamed a voice in her
head.

Hamish Macbeth opened the kitchen door and
looked down at the forlorn figure of Jenny.

'What?' he demanded.

'I just came to say hello.'

'Oh, come in. Don't be long. I want to get to
bed early. Tea? Coffee? Something stronger?'

'Nothing for me.'

Jenny sat down at the kitchen table and shrugged off her anorak. Under it, she was wearing a shimmering grey dress with a low neckline and long filmy sleeves to hide the plaster cast on one arm.

'Been out somewhere grand?' asked Hamish.

'Just the local restaurant.'

'With Pat Mallone?'

'Yes.'

'I hear he's been fired.'

'It's so unfair!'

'I think making up all those names and addresses was the last straw as far as Sam was concerned.'

'I suppose.'

Hamish sat down opposite her. 'So what's eating you? You look miserable.'

'It's these dreadful murders.'

'Then you should head south and get out of it.'

'Doesn't seem much point. I've got more time off because of this arm.'

'But you could go back to your parents and rest up and be looked after.'

'Never mind that,' said Jenny. 'Are you any further forward in finding out who did it?'

'Not a clue.' Hamish leant back in his chair and studied her. 'Pat must be desperate for a story to stop him getting sacked.'

'That's nothing to do with me.'

'And yet you have dinner with him at the restaurant. I saw both of you when I was walking Lugs. Immediately after dinner you're here on your own.'

Jenny flushed and rose to her feet. 'It was just a friendly call.'

The telephone in the office shrilled. 'Wait,' ordered Hamish. He went through to the office and picked up the receiver.

It was Jimmy Anderson. 'Get on your uniform, laddie, and head for Braikie. There's been another death.'

'Who?'

'Thon wee secretary, Freda Mather. Overdose o' sleeping tablets was helped down with vodka.'

'Suicide or murder?'

'Looks like suicide. Left a note saying, "I can't go on. I'm sorry I did it." Blair thinks that wraps things up.'

'Is he daft? And even if she had the strength to hoist up Miss Beattie, who took the video?'

'Stop talking and get over here.'

Hamish went back into the kitchen. 'I've got to go,' he said. 'Another death in Braikie.'

'Who?'

'You'll find out soon enough. Off with you.'

Jenny took out her mobile phone and dialled Pat's number, but he had his mobile switched off. She called at his digs and was told by his landlady that he hadn't come home.

He's obviously heard about this death and gone straight to Braikie, she thought.

Elspeth came shooting out of her place and got in her car and drove off. Well, at least Pat will be there first this time, thought Jenny.

Pat Mallone sat in the bar of the Tommel Castle Hotel, wondering why it was so quiet. He had come up to join the crowd of national reporters who were staying at the hotel and who usually crowded the bar in the evenings.

Had Pat had the instincts of a real reporter, he would have guessed that something else must have happened to cause this mass exodus.

Instead, he sat sipping his drink and hoping that Jenny was finding out something useful from Hamish Macbeth.

Hamish Macbeth rarely lost his temper, but he found rage boiling up when he reached Braikie. Blair was determined that Freda had murdered both Miss Beattie and Miss McAndrew and that was that. The note saying 'I did it,' was proof positive. In vain did Hamish argue that she probably meant that she was about to commit suicide and did not want anyone else blamed. How could such a wee lassie, he shouted, have the strength to hoist up Miss Beattie, take that video, and frenziedly stab Miss McAndrew to death?

Blair's eyes gleamed with malice. 'How dare ye speak to your senior officer in such a way?' he shouted. 'You're suspended until further notice. I'll be having a word wi' Daviot.'

Hamish drove back to Lochdubh, cursing himself. He should have let it go. On the other hand, why should poor Freda Mather's name be blackened?

He let himself into the police station, feeling weary. At least he would get a good long night's sleep.

Hamish was awakened at nine the following morning by a banging on the front door. The villagers only ever came to the kitchen door. He wrapped himself in a dressing gown and wrenched open the front door. The hinges were stiff with disuse.

Superintendent Peter Daviot stood there. 'Sir!' said Hamish.

'I would like a word with you, Constable,' said Daviot.

'Come ben,' said Hamish. 'I'll put on a pot of coffee.'

Daviot shrugged off his dark cashmere coat and hung it on the back of a chair while Hamish busied himself making coffee. Lugs was still asleep, lying on the end of Hamish's bed.

'I take milk and two sugars,' said Daviot. Hamish carried two mugs of coffee over to the table.

'I hear from Mr Blair that he has suspended you,' said Daviot. 'What prompted you to shout at a senior officer?'

'Freda Mather was an unfortunate girl,' said Hamish wearily. 'She had been bullied by Miss McAndrew and now I am sure she was recently being bullied by Mr Arkle, Miss McAndrew's successor. I am perfectly sure the "I did it" on the suicide note simply meant she wanted people to know she had committed suicide and no one was responsible for her death. She was looking after her mother, who is not well and will probably now have to go into a home. I know the press have been hounding you, sir, for a result, but I cannot believe that such as Freda was responsible for these murders. Has a statement been issued to the press?'

'Only that she committed suicide. We are awaiting forensic reports and pathology reports.'

Daviot studied Hamish. He had been relieved and delighted when Blair had given him the news that both murder cases had been solved. But the news that Hamish Macbeth had been so furious that he had verbally attacked a senior officer worried him. The superintendent felt comfortable with Blair, who was a member of the same Freemasons' lodge as himself and who never forgot to send Mrs Daviot flowers on her birthday. He was not so sure of Hamish, who had sidestepped promotion several times and had unorthodox ways.

But Hamish Macbeth had a knack of solving crimes, a knack that seemed to elude Blair.

Sunlight was streaming in the kitchen window and an early frost was melting from the grass outside. He felt he suddenly understood, and not for the first time, why this odd policeman was so attached to his police station.

'If not Freda,' he said, 'who?'

Hamish ran his long fingers through his fiery red hair. 'There's someone in Braikie with a secret, a secret so important to them that they would kill rather than let it come out. I think Miss Beattie knew that secret and I think Miss McAndrew did as well. One or other of them, or both, decided to speak about it and that's why they were killed.'

'Could this Freda Mather not have at least been part of it?'

'I chust cannae believe it.' The sudden sibilance of Hamish's accent showed how upset he was.

'I tell you what I am going to do,' said Daviot, 'because we need every man on this case. I will wait here while you get your uniform on and then you will follow me to

Braikie. You will apologize to Mr Blair for your insolence and then you will go to the school. I gather from your reports that you have already interviewed the schoolteachers. I want you to talk to them again.'

'Right you are, sir.'

Hamish went through to the bathroom and hurriedly washed and shaved before getting into his uniform. An apology to Blair was worth keeping the case open and stopping the detective chief inspector from blackening Freda's name. He went into the office and phoned Angela Brodie and asked her if she would come and collect Lugs and look after the dog.

Then he set off for Braikie, following the superintendent.

As he drove along the coast road, he marvelled that the sea should be so calm, with only bits of flotsam and jetsam strewn across the road as a reminder of the ferocious storm.

Blair was standing outside Freda's house. He looked tired and unshaven. His heavy face darkened when he saw Hamish Macbeth arriving.

'I think we should keep Macbeth on the case,' said Daviot. 'He knows the locals better than anyone. You have something to say, do you not, Constable?'

Hamish stood before Blair, his face the very picture of contrition. 'I am right sorry I shouted at you, sir,' he said. 'Please accept my apology.'

Blair opened his mouth to blast Hamish, but Daviot said quickly, 'Good, that's settled. Get off to the school, Macbeth.'

Suppressing a grin, Hamish drove off to the school. To his surprise, he saw Pat Mallone driving away from the school with Jenny beside him and wondered what they had been doing.

Pat Mallone was elated. He had a decent story at last. He forgot that the whole thing had been Jenny's idea. Jenny had said that maybe Freda had committed suicide because she had been bullied. There was a lot of bullying that went on in schools. To humour her, he had gone along with her idea and had struck gold. They had caught the teachers as they were arriving at the school and they had talked freely about how Freda's mother was a demanding tyrant and how Mr Arkle had made the girl's life hell. Pat and Jenny had tried to interview Mr Arkle, but he had snarled at them and rushed off into the school.

Pat also ignored the fact that it was Jenny's sympathetic manner which had elicited the quotes. Bullied to death. What a story!

Back at the *Highland Times*, Sam listened to his account. 'Great stuff,' he said. 'Write up a piece for us and get it off as well to the nationals and the agencies.'

Jenny sat down beside Pat at his desk. When she saw what a bad typist he was, she said, 'I'll type. You dictate.'

By altering a lot of Pat's clumsier sentences, she felt it was a good article. It only showed what Pat could do with a strong woman to help him. Jenny's spirits had risen and she dreamt of a great and successful future for both of them.

Hamish guessed that Pat and Jenny had spiked his guns. A furious Mr Arkle refused to let him speak to the teachers. When Hamish told him that he would arrest him and charge him with obstructing the police, Arkle relented. But when Hamish interviewed the teachers, all were wishing they had not criticized their head teacher, so they did not mention his treatment of Freda but confined themselves to comments that they believed Freda's mother to be demanding and difficult.

For want of a better idea, he decided to have another go at Joseph Cromarty. He found the truculent ironmonger in his dark shop. The sun now only shone on the other side of the street. The nights were drawing in fast. Soon the sun would rise at ten in the morning and set at two in the afternoon. Winter was one long dark tunnel in northern Scotland.

'What d'ye want?' demanded Joseph. 'I'm busy.'

'Aye, I can see that,' said Hamish sarcastically, looking around the empty shop. 'Now, you were once overheard saying you felt like killing Miss McAndrew . . .'

'So what? Me and a lot o' other people.'

'What other people?'

Joseph scowled horribly. 'I cannae bring them to mind. Leave me alone.'

'Think, man. I'm not accusing you of anything. Haven't you heard anything, seen anything?'

'I thought the murders were solved,' said Joseph. 'That wee girl, Freda, did them.'

'No, she didn't. That was a suicide, pure and simple.'

'Come on! There was a polis in here earlier saying as how everything was wrapped up.'

'He made a mistake,' said Hamish wearily.

He tried a few more questions without getting anywhere. Hamish wandered over to the post office. He hoped it might be quiet and that he might have a chance to have a word with Mrs Harris, but it was full of chattering women, all exclaiming and gossiping about Freda's death.

They fell silent when they saw him. He asked them all if they could think of anything,

211

any small thing, that might help to solve the murders. Startled faces looked at him. Shocked voices exclaimed that they had heard Freda Mather was a murderess. Hamish's news that Freda had nothing to do with the murders sent them all scurrying off.

'Are you sure Miss Beattie never said anything to you about why she left Perth?' Hamish asked Mrs Harris.

'Just that she had been unhappy at home and that her parents were awfy strict. Maybe you should try Billy again. He's still out on his rounds but he should be back any minute. He starts around six in the morning with his deliveries. He drives his van in round the back.'

Hamish left and went up a lane at the side of the post office and waited patiently in the yard at the rear.

After a ten-minute wait, the post office van came into the yard. Billy climbed out and greeted Hamish with, 'I shouldn't feel happy about that wee lassie's death, but to tell the truth, it's a weight off my mind. I thought that bastard Blair would never give up suspecting me.'

'I'm afraid whatever policeman has been gossiping around Braikie is wrong, Billy. Freda took her own life and I'm willing to bet anything she had nothing at all to do with the murders.'

Billy sat down suddenly on an upturned crate. 'Will this all never end, Hamish? It's a misery at home with herself nagging me from morn till night. Now Amy's gone, life looks awfy bleak.'

Hamish pulled up another crate and sat down next to the postman. 'Are you sure, Billy, she never gave you a hint of why she left Perth?'

'Well, she would talk a lot about how strict her parents were. Things like that.'

'What about old boyfriends?'

'No, never.'

'Was she frightened of anyone?'

'She was frightened of the poison-pen writer.'

'Why frightened, Billy? People were angry and upset, but frightened?'

'Our affair meant a lot to her, as it did to me. She said, "If she takes this away from me, there'll be nothing left."'

'Wait a bit. When she was talking about the poison-pen writer, she said "she"?'

'I never gave it much thought. I mean, we all thought it must be some woman. I mean, it's hardly the thing a man would do.'

'But there was a case recently of a man in England who was exposed as a poison-pen writer and the story was in the Scottish papers.'

'I don't remember that.'

213

'Billy, I want you to think and think hard. Go over all the conversations you had, and if you can remember the slightest thing, let me know.'

'But what would that have to do with the death of Miss McAndrew?'

'Some way they're tied together.'

'I'll do my best.'

Chapter Nine

*Man is neither angel nor beast; and the
misfortune is that he who would act
the angel acts the beast.*
                                    – Blaise Pascal

At the end of a long day, Hamish returned to
his police station. He checked on his sheep and
locked his hens up for the night. There was a
fox roaming around and Hamish knew if he
saw it, he would take his shotgun and blast the
animal to kingdom come. He was always
amazed at the bleeding hearts of townspeople
who would step on a cockroach but went all
sentimental over Mr Foxy. Had they ever been
at the receiving end of the cruelty of a fox, who
would kill lambs and hens and leave them
bleeding, not killing for food but for the sheer
hell of it, perhaps it would have changed their
minds – although he doubted it. There existed
in the British Isles a large body of people who
neither knew much about nor understood wild

animals, the sort of people who would shake their heads and say, 'Animals are better than people any day,' by which they meant that they demanded unconditional love from dogs and cats but found humans too difficult.

He had been turned off animal documentaries on television because they always gave animals pet names, saying, 'Here comes Betty,' and on the screen limps an antelope, say, which has been rejected by the herd, and ten to one it is going to be eaten before the end by some other creature that Hamish cynically thought the film makers let out of a cage to speed up the process. Then there is little Jimmy, the baby turtle, just hatched and struggling towards the ocean, and Hamish always knew that little Jimmy was not going to make it. Some marauding seagull would get him. So all in all, he found an animal documentary as much fun as a porno film.

He went indoors and made himself some supper and was emotionally blackmailed into sharing it with Lugs, who whined and rattled his bowl, although he was sure Angela had fed the dog earlier.

He then went through to the office and switched on the computer and began to go through his reports. Archie had said he had seen someone possibly aged seventeen lurking near the post office. But he had not seen the person's face and seventeen would seem old to Archie, so it could have been anyone.

There was a knock at the kitchen door and he heard Elspeth's voice calling out, 'Hamish, are you there?'

'I'm in the office,' he shouted back, 'but I'm busy.'

Undeterred, Elspeth strolled into the office. 'Hard at work, copper?'

'Aye, I'm going over my notes, so I haven't time to talk.'

'Why don't we go over them together? I might see something you've missed.'

'I doubt it,' said Hamish crossly.

'Come on, Hamish. Even if I make a stupid suggestion, it might spark an intelligent one.'

'Oh, all right. Sit down and keep quiet.'

Elspeth pulled up a chair beside him and sat quietly while he scrolled through the notes on the computer screen. He reached the notes he had typed in after his visit to Perth. 'I haven't sent this stuff over,' he said, 'because I didn't get anywhere and I wasn't even supposed to be there.'

'Wait a minute,' said Elspeth. 'This Graham Simpson said that Peter Stoddart was in Australia. Now, that name rings a bell. Let me think.'

Hamish waited patiently.

'I know. Moy Hall, outside Inverness. I was covering the fair there a year ago. I'm sure a chap called Peter Stoddart won the clay pigeon shoot.'

'Could be lots of Peter Stoddarts.'

'But we got a photo of him.'

'Let's go along to that office of yours and see if you've still got the photo in the files.'

As they walked into the newspaper office, Sam waylaid Elspeth, saying, 'Don't you think I should give Pat another chance? He did a good story on the bullying.'

'I haven't had time to tell you,' said Elspeth, 'but that colour piece in the *Sunday Bugle* was mine. He put his byline on it instead of mine.'

Sam sighed. 'Oh, well, in that case he can leave at the end of the month. What are you doing here, Hamish?'

'Detecting.'

'If you come up with anything that would make a story, let me know.'

Elspeth went to the filing cabinets where the photographs were stored. 'We've had so many dizzy village girls helping out with the filing, God knows what it'll be under.'

She tried under 'Moy Hall'. Then under 'Clay pigeon shooting'. No success.

'Can you remember the headline?' asked Hamish.

'It was something daft. Sam does the headlines. Oh, I remember: FASTEST GUN IN THE NORTH.'

'Try under "F".'

'Really, Hamish!'

'You ought to know how the locals think.'

'Okay, Sherlock. Here are the F's. Gosh, you're right. I've got it.'

Elspeth pulled out a photograph.

'Let's take it over to the light,' said Hamish. He fished in his inside pocket and pulled out the photograph of Amy Beattie with the bikers.

In Elspeth's photograph, a burly man stood holding up a silver cup. His hair was white. Hamish looked from Elspeth's photograph to the one in his hand.

'I swear they're one and the same person,' he said. 'Can you fish out the article? There would be a caption under the photograph.'

'We still keep back copies of the paper in bound volumes. You'll need to help me. They're through in the storeroom.'

Hamish walked with her through to a room at the back of the building where the bound volumes of the paper were stored. Elspeth scanned the spines. 'It's that one. Up on the top shelf,' she said.

Hamish reached up and lifted it down. They carried it to a table. Elspeth opened it and flipped through the August editions of the newspaper until she found the right one. 'Here we are! Right on page one.'

They both bent over the paper, their heads together. The caption under the photograph read: 'Winner of the clay pigeon shoot at Moy Hall, Mr Peter Stoddart of Perth.'

'Where in Perth?' demanded Hamish.

'I might have put it in the article,' said Elspeth. 'Ah, here it is. Peter Stoddart, plumber, of 58 Herrich Road, Perth.'

Hamish closed the book, lifted it up, and put it back on the shelf. 'I've got to get to Perth tomorrow,' he said. 'That bank manager said this Stoddart was in Australia. Why would he lie?'

'You'll maybe find out he went to Australia and came back again. Go and see him first before you start accusing the bank manager of anything.'

'I've got to get to Perth without Blair knowing anything. If I tell him, he'll tell me I'm wasting my time and if I've got any suspicions, to tell the Perth police. Och. I'll chust go. With luck he'll think I'm somewhere around Braikie making inquiries.'

'But what's so important about all this, Hamish?'

'I've got to find out what drove Miss Beattie away from her home.'

'That's easy. Her parents.'

'Maybe. I've got to try anyway.'

Hamish set off with Lugs beside him early the next morning. It was a dismal day with a fine drizzle smearing the windscreen. This time, he was not wearing his uniform. He shouldn't have been wearing it the last time, he thought. He could have been spotted by some Perth policeman. Of course, some Perth policeman could easily spot the Land Rover, but he felt less conspicuous walking around in civilian clothes. He decided to try to find Peter Stoddart and tackle him first.

Again, outside Perth, he stopped by the road, walked Lugs and consulted his map of Perth. Then he set off again, hoping that Stoddart worked from home.

Herrich Road was in a fairly new housing development on the outside of the town. He located Stoddart's house and went up and knocked at the door, which was answered by a tired, faded-looking woman.

'I am Police Constable Macbeth,' said Hamish. 'Is your man at home?'

'Aye, come in. What's the matter?'

'Nothing to worry about. I just wanted a wee talk with him.'

She ushered him into what she called the lounge. Hamish sat down on a cream wool-covered sofa and looked around. The room smelled of disuse. How odd, he mused, that in this modern day and age so many houses in Scotland kept a room for 'best'. What a waste of living space.

The door opened and the man from the

photograph walked in. 'What's up?' he said. 'You lot were round last month to check the guns and the gun cabinet.'

'Nothing to do with that,' said Hamish soothingly. He took out the photograph he had got from Mrs Dinwiddie. 'Is that you?'

'Aye, so it is. I loved that bike.'

'You'll have read about the murder of Miss Amy Beattie?'

'I did that. Bad business. But what's it got to do with me?'

'I'm trying to find out why Miss Beattie left Perth.'

'Oh, that's easy. I remember it fine. It was those parents of hers. They found she'd been sneaking out to meet us and locked her up in her room after they'd burnt her clothes.'

'Was she your girlfriend?'

'Not me, laddie. She and Graham were pretty thick. But it didnae last long.'

'Have you ever been to Australia?'

Stoddart looked puzzled. 'No, why?'

'Someone said you had.'

'Who was it?'

'Oh, just someone. I'll maybe let you know later. Nothing to worry about. What was your impression of Miss Beattie?'

'She was a wild one. Up for anything. I 'member when Graham's folks were away for a week. Graham was on his own so he threw a party. We all got awfy drunk and Amy was dancing on the coffee table. It was a glass one and it broke. Graham was in such a state. He and Amy started shouting at each other and it got a bit nasty, so we all left them to it.'

'Who were the others?'

'Some bikers from down south and the local girls they'd picked up.'

'Thank you,' said Hamish. 'I would appreciate it if you did not tell anyone of this visit.'

'Why?'

'I'm working undercover,' said Hamish desperately. But his lie appeared to satisfy the plumber.

As Hamish was driving towards the bank, his radio crackled and he heard a voice hailing him. He cursed and switched it off. His absence had been noted, but he did not want to turn back now.

'I want that bastard found ... now!' Blair howled to Jimmy Anderson. 'He's probably still in his bed. He's not answering his radio. Get over to Lochdubh and see if you can find him.'

'Why me? Can't you send one of the policemen?'

'No, you're so pally with him, you can go.'

Cursing Hamish under his breath, Jimmy drove to Lochdubh. He knocked at the kitchen door of the police station and shouted at the windows.

'It's no use raising a fuss.' Jimmy swung round. He recognized the minister's wife, Mrs Wellington.

'Where's he gone?' he asked.

'I don't know,' said Mrs Wellington. 'But I was up early and saw him driving out of Lochdubh.'

No point in asking in which direction, thought Jimmy. There was only one road out of Lochdubh.

'You're not the only one looking for him,' said Mrs Wellington. 'Sergeant MacGregor over at Cnothan is in bed with the cold. His wife phoned me. She said there's been a burglary at the grocer's and Hamish has got to cover for him.'

Annoyed as he was with Hamish, Jimmy saw a way of getting his friend off the hook. He thanked Mrs Wellington and phoned Blair.

'Macbeth has been dragged off to cover a burglary at Cnothan. MacGregor's sick.'

'Oh, all right. But he should have reported to me first.'

Now, thought Jimmy, all I have to do is to keep phoning Hamish and hope he answers. He'd better get to Cnothan fast before that grocer calls headquarters. Then he thought, Cnothan isn't far. I could nip over there myself to soothe them down. But, by God, Hamish had better pay me in whisky for this.

When Hamish presented himself at the bank, the cashier who had gone in to see the manager reappeared, looking flustered.

'I'm afraid Mr Simpson isn't in today.'

'Is that a fact?'

'Where are you going?' she shrieked.

Hamish went straight to the bank manager's door and opened it. Graham Simpson leapt to his feet. 'You've got no right to barge your way in here.'

'And you have no right to lie to the police. Sit down. I've a few questions for you regarding Amy Beattie. You lied to me.'

'I did not,' blustered the bank manager.

'You said that Peter Stoddart went to Australia when he's right here in Perth.'

'Is he? Someone must have told me he had gone to Australia.'

'Havers. You had an affair with Amy Beattie, didn't you?'

'Oh, well, it isn't a crime. I had a party one night at my house. We all got a bit drunk and Amy damaged a table. We had a row and then made up. We were both very drunk.'

Hamish sat down and surveyed him. He suddenly remembered that poison-pen letter that had been found by Miss Beattie's body,

225

which read: 'I have proof that you're a bastard. Your father never married your mother and I'll tell everyone.'

He had never been able to see the point of that letter. Miss Beattie's parents were married. But what if that letter had been sent to some-one else, and that someone else had been so frightened that it had led to murder.

In a level voice, he asked, 'So when did she tell you she was pregnant?'

'I'm a respectable man,' he began.

'Forget it. You can stay a respectable man unless you go on blocking my inquiries.'

Graham Simpson bowed his head. Hamish thought he wasn't going to say anything, but at last he said in a low voice, 'What a mess. She somehow managed to get a note to me three months later. She said she'd been missing her periods. She said her parents would kill her. I thought about it for a week and worried about it. Then I told my parents. They said I had to marry Amy, do the decent thing. I was going to go round there, but her parents arrived at our home and started shouting that Amy had run away and where was she? We couldn't help them. Another week went by and I plucked up courage to go and call on them. They said they had a letter from Amy saying she never wanted to see either of them again. Her parents said they had struck her name from the family Bible and she was no longer any daughter of theirs. I never heard from Amy again.'

'Are you telling me the truth this time?'

'I swear to God. This could ruin me if it gets out.'

'If you didn't kill anyone, it's certainly not going to ruin you. How could an affair with a girl all those years ago ruin you?'

Hamish left the bank and climbed into the Land Rover. He took out his mobile phone to check for messages. There was a text message from Jimmy Anderson. It read: 'Get your arse over to Cnothan fast. There's been a break-in at the grocer's.'

Like Jimmy, Hamish saw a way of covering up his visit to Perth. He switched on the blue light and the siren, no longer caring if the Perth police saw him, and broke the speed limit all the way north to Cnothan.

Although Jimmy had called before him, he had made only a cursory inspection before speeding off. Hamish found that the shop had a security camera and after studying the film was able to make out the features of two of the local youth. He arrested them and drove them down to Strathbane, where they were formally charged and told to appear in the sheriff's court in a month's time.

By the time he got to Lochdubh, he realized he hadn't eaten all day and neither had Lugs. As usual, he fed the dog first before scrambling some eggs for himself. He was just sitting down at his computer when Elspeth walked in.

'Do you never knock?' he asked angrily.

'Come on. Out with it. I helped you, remember?'

'Oh, all right. Sit down and be quiet.'

'Wait a bit,' said Elspeth. 'What's that about Archie seeing a seventeen-year-old lurking near the post office?'

'I've thought about that. It could have been someone much older. All Archie could really describe were the clothes.'

'Where were you today?'

'Down in Perth.'

'Find out anything?'

'Keep it to yourself. I found out why Amy Beattie ran away from home.'

'Why?'

'She was pregnant.'

'Goodness,' said Elspeth. 'Was it Stoddart?'

'No, it was the bank manager, Graham Simpson.'

'So where's the child?'

'Elspeth,' said Hamish angrily, 'if I knew that, I'd . . .' He suddenly gazed blankly at the computer screen.

'What?' demanded Elspeth.

'I'm thinking about that letter, the one found with Miss Beattie's body. It said: "I have proof that you're a bastard. Your father never married your mother and I'll tell everyone." What if that was a letter sent to someone else? Let me think. Chust suppose for a minute Miss Beattie's child is alive and well in Braikie. Adopted, maybe. The adopted parents are desperate to protect the child and intercept that letter sent to the child.'

'But if they adopted the child, they had nothing to fear. Doesn't add up, Hamish.'

'You're right. Shut up and let me go back over my notes.'

'When did Miss Beattie arrive in Braikie?'

'Folks say about sixteen years ago. I said shut up, Elspeth.'

Elspeth sat quietly and impatiently. Then Hamish said, 'Why did you ask when she arrived in Braikie?'

'I was thinking of the one person who seems to have caused strong emotions and she's sixteen.'

They looked at each other and both said at the same time, 'Penny Roberts!'

'Miss Beattie had changed a lot in appearance,' said Hamish. 'Billy said she had survived cancer. But in the early photographs she's attractive, and Graham Simpson used to be a good-looking young man. Now, Mr and Mrs Roberts are far from lookers. I remember wondering how they had managed to produce such a beauty. What if Miss Beattie wanted to claim her daughter? What if Miss Beattie wanted Penelope to know that she was her real mother? What if Miss McAndrew had found out the secret of Penelope's birth?'

'That would certainly tie the two murders together,' said Elspeth slowly. 'Miss McAndrew may have guessed the truth. She wanted Penny to go to university. Just suppose she threatened to tell Penny the name of her real mother unless they helped her get Penny to university?'

'The problem is how to go about it,' said Hamish. 'If I tell all my suppositions to Blair, he'll demand evidence and I haven't got any.'

'Someone must have known Miss Beattie was pregnant when she arrived.'

'Not necessarily. She did some cleaning work when she first arrived. What if she cleaned for the Robertses and blurted out her secret? Maybe Mary Roberts had always wanted a child. Maybe she arranged that she would masquerade as the pregnant one while Miss Beattie went away somewhere arranged by her. The baby is born. Mary Roberts discards the cushion she's been wearing and produces the newborn baby. I'd better start by going to see them in the morning.'

Elspeth heard a sound. She held up a hand. 'Did you hear something?'

They listened but could only hear the sound of the wind.

* * *

230

Jenny crept away from the police station, her heart beating hard. She had entered the police station hoping for a word with Hamish. Elspeth had left the door open. Jenny heard the sound of voices coming from the office and decided to listen.

Here was a story! What if she could find out the truth herself and tell Pat? She looked at her watch. Nearly eleven o' clock.

She had caved in and rented the Morris Minor from Iain after having beaten the price down. It was a sad rust bucket of a car, but it went all right. She went to it, got in, and drove in the direction of Braikie. The cast on her arm itched and was beginning to look dirty. Jenny decided to confront the Robertses, tell Pat what she had found out, and then go back with him in the morning. He could then see the Robertses himself and she would go to the hospital and ask them when the cast could be removed.

To her relief, when she parked outside the Roberts house, she saw a light burning in a downstairs window. They had not yet gone to bed.

Mary Roberts answered the door. 'Oh, it's you,' she said. 'What on earth brings you calling at this time of night?'

'I've found out something important that may interest you.'

'Come in, then. But don't stay long. We were just about to go to bed.'

'Where's Penny?' asked Jenny as she was ushered into their living room and Cyril Roberts rose to meet her.

'It's half-term. She's gone to stay with my sister and her family in Lochinver,' said Mary. 'So what brings you?'

Jenny sat down. Now she was here, she felt embarrassed and awkward. 'I was thinking about that poison-pen letter that was found with Miss Beattie's body. What if that letter had originally been meant for someone else? And someone didn't want anyone to know their child was not their own?'

Mary Roberts looked puzzled. 'But what's that got to do with us?'

Jenny braced herself. 'I thought Penny might not be your daughter.'

The Robertses exchanged glances and then burst out laughing. Mary said, 'You think because we're a right ugly pair that we couldn't have had a beauty like Penny? Oh, don't blush. We've heard that one before. Have you told anyone about this daft idea of yours?'

Jenny did not want to admit she had been eavesdropping in the police station. 'I haven't told anyone. It just came to me. You see, that reporter, Pat Mallone, and I are thinking of getting married and I wanted to give him a story. I hope you're not offended.'

'Och, you're young and the young can be silly. I'll get you a cup of tea and then you can be on your way.' Mary stood up and went behind the sofa.

'I don't really need anything,' said Jenny. Then a savage blow struck her on the back of her head and she lost consciousness.

'What did you do that for?' cried Cyril as Jenny's body slumped across the sofa.

'She's a chatterbox,' said Mary. 'She'll go chattering to that reporter. We can't risk it.' She fished in Jenny's pocket and drew out the car keys. 'Go and drive that car of hers up in the hills and lose it. I'll see to her.'

Hamish was driving towards Braikie the following morning, wishing the case were closed, so that he could go fishing and enjoy this rare fake spring day. A warm wind was blowing in off the Gulf Stream and great white clouds scudded across a pale blue sky. He had almost reached the outskirts when a small figure hurtled in front of the police Land Rover and held up its arms.

Hamish swore and screeched to a halt and looked down at the excited features of Archie Brand.

He got down from the Land Rover and said severely, 'I could have run you over. Don't ever do that again.'

'But I saw something awfy weird last night.'

'What?'

'I sometimes sneak out at night and go for a walk. Don't tell my ma.'

'What's this got to do with anything?'

'Up on the cliffs, the other side o' Braikie, I was up there last night. I like lying on the top of the cliffs and looking down at the waves. So I was lying in the heather when I hear this car. It drives offa the road and right to the edge o' the cliff. Then this man gets out and he gets behind the car and gies it a God Almighty shove and it goes right o'er the cliff and down into the sea, just like in the films. I hid right down in the heather until he had gone.'

'Get in,' said Hamish. 'Show me where.' Archie clambered in beside Hamish. 'What did this man look like?'

'Couldnae tell. It was right dark and I was feart. There wasnae any moon.'

What now? wondered Hamish grimly. He drove through Braikie and out and up on the cliff road until Archie shouted, 'Right here!'

Hamish stopped and he and Archie got out. 'Tide's out,' said Archie, tugging Hamish along by his sleeve. 'We might see something.'

Hamish went to the edge and then lay down on his stomach and peered over. Large glassy waves were crashing on the rocks below and pouring over a shattered Morris Minor.

'Och, it didnae burst into flames,' said Archie's disappointed voice at his ear. 'In the fillums, they aye burst into flames.'

Hamish recognized Iain's Morris Minor. He went to the Land Rover and radioed for help. Then he phoned Iain and asked him if he'd rented the car to Jenny. 'Yes, I rented it to the lassie yesterday,' said Iain.

'You'd best get out here fast and identify it because it looks as if it's your car that's in the sea.'

Hamish gave him instructions and sat down to wait. 'Will I have to say I was out here at midnight?' said Archie.

'I'm afraid so,' said Hamish. 'You saw the man. You may remember something about him. Your mother will forgive you. It's not a crime.'

'You don't know my ma,' mumbled Archie miserably.

'Does she have a car?'

'Yes.'

'Okay, what's your phone number? We'd better have her up here while they interview you.'

Hamish phoned Mrs Brand, who said she would be with him as fast as she could.

It was as well she arrived the same time as Blair, or Hamish was sure the bad-tempered detective chief inspector would have tried to shake information out of the boy.

It was a long morning. Policemen in climbing gear went down the cliff and reported that there was no body inside the car but that the driver's window was open and that Jenny might have tried to swim to safety. Hamish was then sent back to Lochdubh to see if Jenny had been seen in the car.

Her landlady said her bed had not been slept in, Pat Mallone was nowhere to be found, and Hamish drew a blank right, left and centre until he met the minister's wife, Mrs Wellington.

'I thought you would have been the last person to see her,' she boomed, fixing Hamish with a gimlet eye.

'Why's that?'

'I saw her in the distance late last night. She was leaving the police station and she got straight into her car and drove off.'

Hamish stood staring down at her, deaf to Mrs Wellington's lecture about the seduction of innocent maids from London. Elspeth thought she had heard something. What if Jenny had been listening to their conversation? What if Jenny had decided to go and see the Robertses?

He should phone Blair. But Blair would go crashing around to the Roberts house and they would deny it and that would be that.

Hamish jumped into the Land Rover and sped off back in the direction of Braikie.

Jenny recovered consciousness. She was bound and gagged. She felt terribly sick and was terrified of vomiting into the gag and choking. All around was blackness. Where was she?

Memory came flooding back. She had been talking to the Robertses and then she had received a blow on the head. She kicked out with her feet, which met a wooden door. She kicked again.

Cyril Roberts's voice came from the other side, low and menacing. 'I've a shotgun here. If you make a sound, I'll blast you through the door.'

Jenny slumped back in terror.

Then she heard Mary Roberts's voice. 'We cannae keep her in that cupboard forever. When are you getting rid o' her?'

'When it's dark.'

'Why didnae ye just shove her over the cliff in her car?'

'I don't know. I don't want another killing.'

'Too late for that,' came Mary's grim voice.

'Well, it was your idea to get rid of the car. You said you'd see to her.'

Their grumbling voices faded away.

Jenny began to pray. If only God would get her out of this, she vowed, she would go back to the safety of London, work hard at her job, and forget about men.

Pat Mallone arrived at the office, late as usual. The phone on his desk was ringing. He picked up the receiver. 'Jack Pelting here,' said a voice at the other end. 'I'm the news editor of the *Bugle*. Can you come down to London for an interview?'

Pat's heart beat hard with excitement. 'Yes, I could,' he said eagerly. 'In fact, if I leave now, I could put up somewhere in London overnight and be ready for an interview in the morning.'

'We'll book you in at the Jessop Hotel near St Katherine's Dock. Know it?'

'I'll find it.'

'Right. I'll see you tomorrow at eleven in the morning.'

Pat thanked him and rang off. He punched the air. Sam came in and glared at him. 'Get yourself over to Braikie. Jenny Ogilvie's car has been found at the bottom of a cliff and she may have drowned.'

Pat hesitated for only a moment. Jenny could take care of herself if she was alive, and if she was dead, there was nothing he could do about it.

'Right,' he said cheerfully. 'On my way.'

He went straight to his digs and packed up. He left a note for his landlady to say he would not be back, packed a suitcase, slung it in his car, and drove off whistling, taking the long road south.

Chapter Ten

I passed through the lonely street.
The wind did sing and blow;
I could hear the policeman's feet
Clapping to and fro.
 – William Makepeace Thackeray

Hamish parked outside the Roberts house. What had seemed so clear-cut now began to seem like nonsense. They were a respectable couple who doted on their daughter. They were not serial killers. And how should he approach the subject? But concern for Jenny gnawed at him. He climbed down from the Land Rover, went up to the front door, squared his shoulders and rang the bell.

Mary Roberts answered the door. 'Oh, it's you,' she said. 'We were just going out.'

'Husband not working?'

'He had time owing, so he's having a bit of a holiday.'

'May I come in?'

She looked reluctant. 'I haven't got round to cleaning up. Oh, well, just for a minute.'

Hamish followed her into the living room. Cyril Roberts rose to meet him, putting down the morning paper as he did so. 'What brings you here, Officer?'

'Jenny Ogilvie's gone missing and her car's been found at the foot of the cliffs.'

'That's terrible,' said Cyril. 'Was the poor lassie drowned?'

'We're still searching. The passenger window of the car was open and she might have escaped that way and the body taken out to sea. Have you seen her recently?'

Upstairs in her cupboard prison on the landing, Jenny heard the sound of voices. She tried to summon up courage to scream, but she was feeling weak and sick. And what if whoever was visiting the Robertses was in on the plot?

'No, we haven't seen her since she was last here with you,' Cyril was saying. 'Do you need any help in the search?'

'No, we have enough men on it. Where is Penny?'

'Half-term. She's over at my sister's in Lochinver,' Mary said.

'When Miss Beattie first came to Braikie, she did house cleaning. Did she clean for you?'

'Yes, she did, for a bit, and then she found they needed a postmistress and took the exams and got the job. She was lucky, although, mind you, no one in Braikie wanted the job and folks from Strathbane usually don't want to live anywhere so remote.'

Hamish's confidence in his theory was ebbing by the minute. They both seemed so relaxed.

'Did you hear a car round about midnight last night?'

'Not a sound,' said Mary.

Hamish gave up. 'Well, if you hear anything, let me know.'

Mary Roberts showed him to the door.

Upstairs, Jenny slumped in the cupboard, weak tears running down her face.

Hamish called at the villas next door and asked if they had heard a car around midnight. But no one seemed to have heard anything. Yes, said one, he might have heard a car, but he took no notice of cars passing on the road.

Hamish leant against the Land Rover and thought hard. Surely, the Robertses could not be guilty. It would be a mad risk to drive Jenny's car off when any of the neighbours might just have been looking out of the window. But the neighbours were all elderly and could be guaranteed to go to bed early.

And yet he had a feeling that the murders had been committed by rank amateurs, and amateurs with an amazing amount of luck;

amateurs who barely stopped to think what they were doing. And Jenny had last been seen hurrying away from the police station. If she had heard what he was discussing with Elspeth, then maybe she had decided to play detective herself.

'What's he doing?' hissed Cyril Roberts. Mary turned away from the window where she had been keeping watch. 'He's just standing there.'

'I don't like it.'

'They've got no proof.'

'Och, why didnae ye just have the girl in the car when you pushed it over the cliff?'

'Stop saying that. You were the one who told me to get rid of the car. You were the one who said you would see to her.'

'He cannae stand there all day,' said Mary. 'He's been to the neighbours and thank God they don't seem to have seen anything. We'd best get her out and kill her and that way there'll be no danger of her making a noise in case Macbeth or anyone else calls.'

'Is there any way we can get out of this without killing her?'

'Don't be daft. Are you going soft?'

'It's getting like a nightmare. I can't just go up there and kill her in cold blood. If I shoot her with the shotgun, the police will call in every registered shotgun in Braikie. I can't thole the idea of bashing in her head in cold blood. You do it.'

'Might make too much of a noise. That call from the police will have alerted the neighbours to something. We'll need to wait until dark. We'll drive her up in the hills to that old quarry and throw her in. The sides are so steep, no one could get out of there.'

Hamish's mobile phone rang. It was Priscilla, phoning from London. 'Hamish, what's happened to Jenny? She has sent a sick note but I'd swear Jenny was never sick.'

Hamish told her briefly about Jenny's car. 'Oh, Hamish,' cried Priscilla. 'What's become of her?'

'I hope to find out before it's too late,' said Hamish. 'I'll call you back as soon as I hear anything.'

'He's still there,' said Mary Roberts, 'and we'll need to go out.'

'Why?'

'I told him we were on our way out, and if we don't go, he might get suspicious.'

Hamish's mobile rang again. It was Elspeth. 'Hamish, Pat Mallone has done a bunk. He was supposed to go to Braikie, but he left a note for his landlady to say he wouldn't be coming back, and all his stuff has gone. Do you think Jenny's gone with him?'

'Let's hope so. Have you got a note of his car registration number?'

'Yes, I got it out of the records.' She gave it to him. 'What about the Robertses?'

'Cool as cucumbers. I'll get back to you.'

Hamish phoned Jimmy Anderson and explained about Pat Mallone and that Jenny might be with him. Then he said, 'I'd better check if her stuff's been packed up as well. But I still think it might be worth pulling Mallone in for questioning. Why should he run off today of all days?'

'I'll get on to it,' said Jimmy.

Hamish phoned Jenny's landlady and asked if her clothes were still in her room. 'Aye, I've just been up there to clean,' said Mrs Dunne. 'Everything's there.'

Hamish's heart sank. For one wild moment, he had hoped Jenny had gone off with Pat and that they had shoved Iain's car over the cliff out of mischief.

He turned round as the door of the villa opened and the Robertses came out. 'Do you mind moving?' shouted Cyril. 'You're blocking the drive and I have to reverse out.'

Hamish moved the Land Rover and

watched as the couple got into their car and drove off. He began to follow them.

Pat Mallone was cruising along the A9, whistling to the radio. The tall Grampian mountains soared up on either side of the car. A golden future stretched out in front of him. He realized he was glad to be leaving the Highlands behind, glad to be returning to civilization. He was just debating whether to go into Aviemore and have a late breakfast when he heard the sound of a police siren behind him. He slowed down to let the police car past, when to his horror, it swung in in front of him and a police hand flapped out of the window indicating that he should stop.

Pat stared at the speedometer as he stopped the car. He hadn't been going over the limit.

He rolled down the window.

'Yes, Officer? Is it important?' he said to the policeman who was staring down at him.

'Are you Patrick Mallone?'

'Yes, but . . .'

'You are to accompany us back to Strathbane for questioning.'

'Why?'

'Miss Ogilvie has gone missing.'

'Well, that's her problem,' said Pat furiously. 'Look, I've got to get to London.'

'That will not be possible.'

Rage and frustration boiled up in Pat. This Highland idiot of a copper was standing between him and a beautiful future, between this savage world of the north of Scotland and the glitter of London.

In a red mist of rage, he rolled up the window and accelerated off round the police car in front and straight down the A9. Up went the speedometer to 100 mph and then to 115. Logical thought had left his brain. On he flew, zipping past car after car, several times narrowly missing a crash with a car coming the other way.

He glanced in his rear-view mirror. The blue light was now nowhere in sight. Get off the road, screamed his brain. But his emotions had taken control and they were telling him that he would be all right if only he could leave the Highlands of Scotland behind.

He eased his speed down a little and then gave a gasp of fright. A policeman on a motorbike had crept up on one side and was flagging him down.

Up went Pat's speed again. He rounded a bend and jammed his foot on the brakes as hard as he could, stopping himself in time from running into several stationary cars in front.

The policeman on the motorbike stopped beside him and rapped on the window. Other policemen were appearing round the cars in front. A roadblock, thought Pat. Of course, they would put up a roadblock. He got out of the car.

'Over the bonnet o' yer car, and pit yer hands ahint yer back,' roared the policeman. Feeling limp with fright and dismay, Pat meekly did as he was told. He was handcuffed and led to a police van and thrust inside while charges of speeding, not stopping when asked, obstructing police in their inquiries rang in his ears.

Pat sat miserably in the police van. Surely, they would question him and then let him go. He could then drive down to Inverness and get a flight to London.

Sam received a phone call later that day from the police asking him to confirm that Pat had been on his way south for an interview with the *Daily Bugle*. Sam said grimly he knew nothing about it and suggested they phone the news editor of the *Bugle*. When the police rang off, Sam phoned the news editor, Jack Pelting, of the *Bugle*. Jack confirmed that Pat was due for an interview the following morning.

'He's been taken in by the police for questioning,' said Sam. 'His girlfriend's disappeared. If I were you, I wouldn't bother about him.'

'Why? He seems a good journalist. That colour piece on Braikie was excellent.'

'That wasn't his. That was written by Elspeth Grant and he put his own name on it.'

Jack Pelting sighed. 'Do me a favour and get a message to him and tell him the interview's off. What about this Elspeth Grant?'

'Don't you dare,' said Sam. 'I need her.'

Sam then phoned police headquarters in Strathbane and told them to tell Pat Mallone that he was no longer wanted in London.

Pat was being grilled by Detective Chief Inspector Blair. In vain did he keep repeating that he did not know what had happened to Jenny.

Why, then, Blair roared, did he take off like that without even informing his boss on the *Highland Times* that he was going? The questioning went on and on and Pat's miserable eyes occasionally strayed to the large clock on the wall in the interview room as the hand went slowly round, eating up the precious minutes.

At last it was over and he was bailed to appear at the sheriff's court in Strathbane. He was told his car was outside in the car park. Just as he was turning away, the duty sergeant handed him a note. 'Message for you.'

Pat grabbed it and went out to his car. He was about to drive off when he thought he'd better read the message. It was from Sam. 'Jack Pelting has cancelled your interview.'

He thumped the steering wheel in a fury. Then he looked at his watch. Six o'clock. Maybe he could just catch Jack. He phoned the *Bugle* and asked to speak to the news editor. He waited impatiently, chewing his knuckles. When Jack came on the phone, he sighed with relief. 'It's Pat Mallone,' he said. 'Look, I can still make it. I was taken in by the police because a girl I know has gone missing. But I've just been released because it's got nothing to do with me, so if I get down to Inverness for the plane, I can still make it.'

'Your boss up there tells me that you pinched another reporter's copy for that piece on Braikie.'

'That was a mix-up.'

'Not the impression I got. Anyway, the interview's off.'

'But . . .'

The phone went dead.

Pat sat there for a long time, and then he slowly drove off. To hell with the lot of them. He was going back to Ireland.

Hamish had kept a discreet eye on the Robertses all day. They had gone out twice to the shops and were now inside their villa. He drove back to Lochdubh and changed out of his uniform. He phoned Angela, with whom he had left Lugs earlier, and begged her to keep the dog overnight. Then he phoned Elspeth and asked if he could borrow her car.

'Why?' she asked.

'Because I want to keep an eye on the Roberts house without being seen.'

'Only if I can come with you.'

'All right,' said Hamish reluctantly. 'If they've really got Jenny, they'll probably make a move to get rid of her during the night.'

He walked along to the newspaper office. Elspeth was just emerging. 'You work late,' commented Hamish.

'Well, Pat did do some work, and now that he's gone, I'm stuck with double the amount of stories as well as the astrology column. Then Mrs Glennon over in Alness who does the cookery recipes is sick, so I had to do them as well.'

'Wasn't that difficult? All the measures of stuff and so on?'

'I found an old Scottish cookery book in the office and pinched stuff out of that.'

'Plagiarism, Elspeth?'

'I suppose. It's an awfully old book. I just hope I don't get found out.'

Hamish got into Elspeth's small car and they drove off. It was a cold, blustery evening with great clouds racing across a half moon.

'Do you really think the Robertses are the culprits?' asked Elspeth.

'I can't think of anyone else. I mean, Jenny was seen leaving the police station.'

'If it was them, they were taking an awful risk, driving her car to the cliffs and sending it over. Any of the neighbours could have seen them driving off.'

'Most of the neighbours would have been asleep. Nobody heard anything, except for one who thought – just thought – he might have heard a car.'

'Let's say it is them,' said Elspeth. 'I wonder who sent that video to the community centre?'

'Aye, that's the odd part of it.'

They drove on for a bit in silence.

'If I'm wrong about them,' said Hamish at last, 'I won't know where to begin.'

'I checked before I left the office,' said Elspeth. 'They haven't found any body in the sea. Heard from Priscilla?'

'Yes, she was worried because Jenny was claiming to be sick and she said that Jenny is never ill.'

'That's hit one of my hopes on the head.'

'Which was?'

'That Jenny had got so scared with the murders or that someone had scared her and that she had simply taken off, leaving everything behind.'

'First pushing a car over a cliff?'

'Yes, it does sound stupid. But maybe she abandoned the car with the keys in it and some youths took it for a joyride.'

'Far-fetched.'

'Maybe, but I'm beginning to think our suspicions of the Robertses are far-fetched. To commit two, possibly three, murders and all because you don't want anyone to know your child isn't your own!'

'I sometimes think the land up here and the long black winters and the isolation twist people's minds,' said Hamish. 'The soil is thin and the rock is old and there are parts up here where something bad has happened, oh, maybe long ago, and you can feel a malignancy seeping out of the very ground.'

Elspeth gave a nervous laugh. 'The old folks would say it's the little people and give them an offering of iron and salt.'

They reached the coast road, drove past the row of villas where the Robertses lived, and parked at the end.

'What now?' asked Elspeth.

'We wait and hope.'

Jenny blinked in the light as the cupboard door swung open. Cyril Roberts reached in with powerful arms and pulled her out on to the landing. He raised a sharp knife and Jenny's eyes dilated with terror. But he stooped and cut the rope round her ankles and hoisted her to her feet. 'Walk!' he ordered.

Jenny took a few steps, but she was so weak with hunger and from the blow to her head that she would have fallen if he had not held her up.

Mary Roberts appeared. 'Help me down the stairs with her,' said Cyril.

'All this effort,' grumbled Mary. 'Why are we keeping her alive?'

'Because when we drop her in the quarry, I want her found with water in her lungs from drowning. Then they can maybe think she committed suicide.'

'She smells.'

'She hasn't been to the toilet. What do you expect?'

Jenny was dragged down to the living room and dumped on a chair, but not before Mary, with housewifely concern for her furniture, had put newspapers down on it first.

'When do we move?' she asked.

'Another hour yet.'

'Look out of the front door and make sure that copper isn't lurking about.'

Cyril went to the front door, opened it and looked up and down the road. Elspeth's small black car was parked under the shadow of a drooping laburnum tree and he did not see it.

He went back in. 'All clear,' he said.

* * *

Elspeth's eyes began to droop. Her head slowly fell sideways and rested on Hamish's shoulder and soon she was asleep. Hamish felt tired himself. The warm weight of Elspeth resting against him was making him feel drowsy. For once there was no wind and the night was quiet.

In his mind, Hamish was suddenly up on the River Anstey on a clear sunny day. Priscilla was walking along beside him, the sunlight glinting on her blonde hair. He felt warm and happy. They were together at last. He heard the sound of a car and frowned in his sleep at the idea of intruders. And then he was awake as the Robertses' car drove past him.

Hamish shook Elspeth awake. 'They're off and I missed them. I fell asleep. Follow them at a distance, and you'll need to drive without lights. The minute they stop, cut your engine so they don't hear ours.'

Elspeth let in the clutch and moved off, praying that whichever one of the Robertses was driving would not look in the driving mirror and spot them. The car in front headed out of Braikie on the Lochdubh Road.

'It's all twists and turns now,' said Hamish, 'so we can keep fairly close without them spotting us.'

'Where do you think they're going?' asked Elspeth.

'I'm trying to think. If they've got Jenny and want rid of her, you'd think the sensible thing would be to take her to the cliffs where the car went over and drop her body in the sea. Then it would be assumed she was in it when it went over.'

'But forensics would surely discover she had been killed later.'

'They're not magicians. Once a body's been in the sea for a bit, battered by rocks and eaten by fish, there wouldn't be much left to say when she was killed.'

Hamish took out his mobile phone. 'I'm calling for backup,' he said. 'If they haven't got Jenny, I'll look a fool, but it's worth the risk.'

He phoned Strathbane and explained his suspicions and why he was following the Robertses on the Lochdubh Road. Elspeth turned a bend in the road. 'Hamish,' she said, 'I've a feeling they've gone.'

'Stop the car!' Hamish peered out into the darkness. He rolled down the window and listened. 'There's the sound of a car up on the hill to the left. That's the old quarry, the one that's filled with water. That's where they've gone.'

'How do I get there?'

'Turn round, then back round the next bend, and you'll see a road covered with heather on the right.'

Hamish phoned Strathbane again and gave instructions as to how to get to the quarry.

Elspeth found the road and her small car began to bump over the ruts. 'Not far now,' said Hamish. 'We'll go the rest of the way on foot. On second thoughts, you stay here. It'll be dangerous.'

'I want the story,' said Elspeth. 'I'm coming.'

'Then keep behind me and don't do anything daft.'

They walked quickly up the old overgrown road, their feet making no sound on the grass and heather that covered it.

Cyril switched off the engine. 'Here we are,' he said.

'Are you going to give her another dunt on the head afore you throw her over?' asked Mary.

'No. Don't want things to look too suspicious. I told you, the sides of the quarry are so steep that even if she had the strength to swim, she'd never have the strength to climb out.'

They both got out of the car. Cyril lifted out his shotgun. 'What's that for?' asked Mary.

'We've come this far. Got to make sure no one surprises us. Hold the gun and I'll open the boot and get her out.'

Hamish and Elspeth crouched down in the heather. The moon raced out from behind the clouds. 'He's got a gun,' said Hamish, his mouth against Elspeth's ear. 'Damn.'

'He wouldn't be idiotic enough to shoot a policeman, would he?' asked Elspeth.

'That pair are mad enough to do anything.'

'Did you hear something?' asked Mary sharply.

Cyril froze and listened hard. 'Nothing,' he said.

Mary shivered. 'This place gives me the creeps. It's haunted, you know.'

'Havers.' Cyril opened the boot. 'Help me get her out.'

There was a rustling in the heather beside Hamish. He felt Elspeth moving away and shot out an arm to stop her, but she had gone. He swore under his breath. He would need to confront the Robertses, but he wished he could get to that shotgun first.

He thought the Robertses had really gone mad. He was sure Cyril Roberts would shoot them both and get rid of their bodies even if he told him that reinforcements were on their way.

The Robertses dragged Jenny out and laid her on the heather. 'Now, the thing is,' said Cyril, 'we roll her to the edge, cut off the ropes, rip off the gag, and push her over. Right?'

'Right,' said Mary. 'Hurry up. I feel something here.'

And then they both froze as a silvery, unearthly voice whispered across the heather. 'You are wicked and I have come to take you away.' Then there was an eerie laugh.

Mary's face, already bleached by the moonlight, was now as white as paper. 'It's the wee folk,' she said through dry lips.

'Pull yourself together, woman.' Cyril picked up the shotgun and swung it to the left and the right.

'You will suffer unbelievable torture,' mocked the unearthly voice. Cyril fired to the right. Silence.

Then from the left came the whispering, jeering voice again. 'Bullets cannot hurt us.'

Mary slumped down against the side of the car and began to cry with fright. Beside himself with rage and fear, Cyril stood straddling Jenny's body where she lay on the heather, glaring around him.

'Let her go,' called the voice, and to the terrified Cyril it seemed to be coming from the sky above his head.

He left Jenny and ran desperately this way and that, trying to find the source of the voice.

'You are going to die,' mocked the eldritch voice.

'Mary,' shouted Cyril, 'come here and grab her and let's get this over with.'

Mary continued to sob, shivering and wrapping her arms around her body.

Jenny summoned up all her energy and began to roll down the slope of the hill when Cyril went to his wife to try to get her to her feet.

Despite the tussocks of heather, it was a steep slope away from the lip of the quarry, and she slowly gathered momentum until she bumped up against a rock and lost consciousness.

Damn, he's loading the shotgun again. I should have taken him, thought Hamish. I could even have chanced it while he was dealing with Mary.

'Now untie her and ungag her,' Cyril was ordering his wife. 'She can scream all she likes. No one will hear her up here.'

'What about the fairies?' screeched Mary.

'There's no such damn thing as fairies. When we get rid of her, I'll blast whoever that is playing tricks. Now get on with it!'

Mary moved round to the back of the car and let out a scream. 'She's gone!'

'What!' The moon shone bravely down. Cyril joined her and stared down at where Jenny had so recently lain. Then he looked wildly around, swinging the shotgun this way and that.

'We've taken her where you'll never get her,' cackled the unearthly voice.

Mary Roberts said in a dull voice, 'God have mercy on me.' She ran to the edge of the quarry and jumped over.

'Mary!' shouted Cyril. He dropped the shotgun and ran to the edge of the cliff.

Hamish rose to his feet and sprinted up behind him. He seized Cyril, threw him to the ground, and handcuffed him. In the distance came the wail of police sirens.

'Elspeth!' he shouted. 'Where are you?'

'Down here,' shouted Elspeth from somewhere behind him. 'I've got Jenny. You keep an eye on him and I'll look after her. Are you going after Mary?'

'I'll need to wait for help. If I went down there after her, there's no way I could get both of us out again.'

Hamish cautioned Cyril, who was crying so hard that he did not seem to hear him.

Hamish took out his mobile phone and said he would need ropes, divers and an ambulance.

Police cars with sirens wailing and blue lights flashing bumped up towards them.

Jimmy Anderson was the first out. 'What's happening, Hamish?'

'This is Cyril Roberts, who is guilty of kidnapping Jenny Ogilvie and trying to kill her. He is guilty of the other murders. His wife, Mary, has jumped into the quarry. See if you can get men down there. I don't have any rope.'

'You're lucky,' said Jimmy. 'We still had the men in Braikie who were looking for Jenny's body down the cliffs, so they have all the equipment.' He walked away from Hamish and began to bark out orders.

Hamish saw Elspeth and Jenny in the light from the police cars. 'How is she?' he asked.

'Very weak. Don't wait for the ambulance. Get someone to take her to hospital immediately.'

'Right!' Hamish arranged for a policeman and policewoman to drive Jenny to the hospital and to stay with her.

When Jenny had been ushered into a police car, Hamish said to Elspeth, 'You could have got yourself shot. What on earth possessed you to pretend you were a fairy?'

'Anything to stop them throwing her over. And it worked.'

'What if Mary Roberts didn't believe in fairies?'

'Most people up here will believe in fairies if their mind's a bit overturned. Do you think Mary Roberts will still be alive?'

'I doubt it. I think she wanted to die when she went over.'

Cyril Roberts was being put into a police car just as Detective Chief Inspector Blair came roaring up.

Hamish had to go through the whole story of how he had come to suspect the Robertses. When he had finished, Blair said, 'You wait here to see if they get Mrs Roberts out alive. I'll go with Cyril Roberts to Strathbane and question him.'

'Sir,' said Hamish, 'I think as I solved the case, I should be there when he is questioned.'

'You'll stay here and do as you're told,' snarled Blair, already wondering how he could take all the credit himself.

As Blair marched off, Jimmy whispered, 'Don't worry, Hamish, I'll drop over tomorrow if I can manage and give you a full report of what Roberts said. And by the time that lassie of yours has finished her reports for the papers, everyone will know it was you and not Blair who solved the mystery.'

The night had turned chilly. Hamish waited patiently until the lifeless body of Mary Roberts was brought up from the quarry.

Then he wearily went back to join Elspeth, who was sitting in her car with the engine on and the heater blasting.

'Get me to the office,' she urged Hamish when he told her Mary Roberts was dead.

'I've got to send a lot of stories over to the nationals and the agencies.'

'Won't it be locked?'

'Sam gave me a set of keys.'

'How are you feeling?'

'A bit sick. I was very frightened.'

Hamish hugged her and then, involuntarily, he kissed her full on the lips. He emerged from the kiss with his pulse racing. 'Sorry about that,' he said hurriedly.

'For what?' demanded Elspeth crossly, and set off down the track.

Before he went to bed, Hamish sat down at his computer and filed his report. He felt bone weary. He carefully skirted around his visits to Perth. After he had finished, he sat and scowled at the screen. The one piece of the jigsaw that was missing was why the Robertses had sent that video of the murder of Miss Beattie to the community centre film show. It just didn't make sense. The trouble with dealing with amateurs, he thought, was that it was like dealing with madmen. It made them so hard to catch. He yawned and stretched. He wished now he hadn't kissed Elspeth. It was time he had another girlfriend, but preferably someone outside the village, away from the gossiping tongues of Lochdubh.

* * *

Jenny recovered quickly from her ordeal and, despite protests from hospital staff, insisted the press be allowed to interview her.

And so, although Elspeth had gamely sent out stories praising the acumen of Hamish Macbeth in solving the mystery, all that went by the board as far as the press were concerned. Jenny with her black curls and big brown eyes claimed to have worked out who the murderers were all by herself.

She only felt a little pang of conscience as she described how by sheer female intuition she had arrived at the solution and then followed that up with a colourful description of her ordeal. She did not mention Elspeth's 'haunting'. Jenny had learned from the minister's wife, Mrs Wellington, who had called to visit her, that Pat Mallone had simply taken off, even though he knew she was missing. So, feeling rebuffed and diminished, she had decided to get as much glory out of her kidnapping as possible.

One reporter, less seduced by Jenny's attractions than the rest, asked her, 'Is it true that you were listening at the police station door whilst Hamish Macbeth was discussing the case and that's how you found out about the Robertses?'

Jenny blushed but said, 'I went to see Hamish, yes, but all I heard was someone with him, so I went away. You see, I had already worked things out for myself and I had been going to tell him. But when I heard he had someone with him, I decided to investigate for myself.' She fluttered her eyelashes at the reporter. 'It was silly of me, I know, but at that time it was just an idea.'

Chapter Eleven

In winter, when the dismal rain
Came down in slanting lines,
And Wind, that grand old harper, smote
His thunder-harp of pines.
                    – Alexander Smith

The following day, Hamish received a phone call from Priscilla. 'What's all this?' asked Priscilla. 'Jenny's over the front page of every newspaper saying she solved the murders.'

'She was listening at the kitchen door when I was discussing the case with Elspeth. That's how she found out.'

'Elspeth? Oh, that little reporter. That your latest squeeze?'

'Elspeth Grant is a friend of mine and has been a great help to me.'

There was a silence and then Priscilla said, 'So can't Elspeth put the papers right?'

'The papers have got their heroine and they are not going to change their story and say it was some boring Highland copper. Are you coming up soon?'

'I thought of flying up to see Jenny, but I am too cross with her to bother now. She shouldn't have snatched the glory from you.'

'Well, the lassie's probably done me a favour. Anytime I have even a wee bit of success, Peter Daviot starts mumbling about moving me to Strathbane.'

'But he surely knows it was you who solved the murders?'

'Aye, but he's driven by the press. What gets in the press is only what interests Daviot. Another thing: I am perfectly sure Blair backed up Jenny's story so that I would get as little credit as possible.'

'Jenny's parents phoned me today,' said Priscilla. 'They are now speeding north to take their daughter home, so she'll soon be out of your hair.'

Hamish wanted to ask her how her love life was getting on and whether she was about to get married soon, but he dreaded what the answer might be. So instead, he talked about the locals, about how he had to woo back his dog's affections because Lugs had spent so much time with Angela that he seemed to prefer going there, and how pleasant it was to settle back down to a less demanding life.

'Why did the Robertses do it?' asked Priscilla.

'Because their child wasn't their own.'

'I know that. But to commit two murders!'

'I'll find out and let you know,' said Hamish. 'Jimmy Anderson is going to call and let me see a transcript of the interview.'

When she rang off, Hamish went out to feed his hens and check on his sheep. The air was cold and damp and the wind had shifted round to the northeast. The long Highland winter was howling on the threshold.

By faking references, Pat Mallone had managed to get a job on the *Dublin Mercury* as a junior reporter. On his way to work, he stopped by a shop to buy cigarettes, a habit he had taken up after his flight from the Highlands. Although he was perfectly sure the Scottish police would not go to the trouble to extradite anyone on such a minor charge, he still felt uneasy. The shop sold the British newspapers, and there was Jenny's face smiling up at him from the front pages. He bought several and then, after buying his cigarettes as well, stood on Grafton Street and read the stories.

If only he had stayed, he thought bitterly, he could have basked in some reflected glory. Of course, none of what had happened to him was really his fault. It had all been just bad luck.

* * *

After another two days, Hamish was just beginning to think that Jimmy had forgotten about him when the man himself appeared in the evening, carrying a bottle of whisky.

'Come ben,' said Hamish. 'It is not like you to be providing the whisky.'

'I feel you deserve it, laddie. I was getting damn sick o' Braikie. How you can bear living up here fair beats me.' As if in answer to him, the wind howled around the police station like an Irish banshee.

'Sit yourself down,' said Hamish, putting two glasses on the kitchen table. 'Did Cyril Roberts confess?'

'Aye,' said Jimmy, pouring a large whisky for himself and a small one for Hamish. He tugged several pieces of paper out of his jacket pocket. 'Read that.'

Hamish spread the papers on the table and began to read.

'Amy Beattie,' Cyril Roberts had written, 'came to us as a cleaner sixteen years ago. My wife, Mary, found her crying in the kitchen one day and asked her what was troubling her. Amy said she was pregnant. She said she would have to have the child and then give it up for adoption. Now, Mary and I couldn't have children. We'd always longed for one. We'd thought of adoption, but the adoption societies are so difficult. So when Mary told me, we hit upon a plan. We've got a holiday cottage over in Caithness, just north of Helmsdale. Amy would go and live there when her time was near. Meanwhile, Mary would tell everyone she was pregnant. Then when Amy was due, we'd go over there. Mary used to be a nurse so she would deliver the baby. She would come back with it as our own.

'We doted on Penny as she grew up. Have you seen her? Have you ever seen anything more beautiful? Amy seemed to have started a new life for herself. We'd given her a large sum of money and she bought the post office. We'd inherited a lot of money after Mary pushed her own mother down the stairs.'

'I remember,' said Hamish, 'that Mary said her mother had Alzheimer's and died a week before she married Cyril.' He went back to reading.

'And then one day Amy Beattie turned up. She said she wanted Penny to know the identity of her real mother. We couldn't be having that. We threatened her and we thought that would keep her quiet. But she went to Miss McAndrew. Miss McAndrew was hot for Penny to go to university and Penny wanted a career in television. Miss McAndrew told us that if we did not make sure Penny went to the university, then she would tell everyone in Braikie that Penny was not our child. Then the anonymous letter arrived, addressed to Penny. The post was late that morning and it arrived

271

after Penny had left for school. We opened and read it and we were pretty sure it was from Miss McAndrew.

'Mary said no one was going to take our precious child away. We told Amy that we had decided to let her tell Penny but we would like to discuss it with her first. We went round to her flat. Mary put a strong sleeping draught in her tea and when she was unconscious, we hanged her and left that anonymous letter, knowing that Miss McAndrew would read about it in the papers and take it as a warning. Just to be sure, we took a bit of video film and sent it to her as a further warning. No, I don't know who sent it to the community centre. We thought that was an end to it. Then Miss McAndrew phoned up soon afterwards and said she had been wrestling with her conscience. She said she would have to go to the police and tell them everything. It was late at night and Mary said she wouldn't go to the police that night and had to be silenced. I said that one killing was enough and Mary said she would kill *me* if I didn't help her. She said she would do it. Now, Penny had keys to Miss McAndrew's house. I begged Mary not to do it, just to frighten Miss McAndrew, and Mary said all right. We let ourselves in and crept up to the bedroom and then Mary produced this knife and began to stab and stab and stab.

'And we thought for a while we'd got clean

away with both murders. We were even able to go on as normal. We adore Penny. And then that girl Jenny called. Mary hit her on the head. I wish we had just bluffed our way out of it because she didn't really know anything. But once it was done, we shut her up in a cupboard bound and gagged. I got rid of the car. If only I had put Jenny in it. That was a big mistake. So it had to be the quarry.'

Hamish looked up from his reading. 'It doesn't make sense.'

'What doesn't make sense?' asked Jimmy.

'That a perfectly respectable Highland couple should resort to such mad violence.'

'Ah, that's where you're wrong,' said Jimmy. 'You don't know everything, Sherlock.'

'What?'

'Mary Roberts was at one time in her early life sectioned for psychopathy. Cyril Roberts used to be in the Royal Marines and spent a long time in the glasshouse and then got a dishonourable discharge for nearly beating an officer to death.'

'We never thought to dig up their backgrounds,' mourned Hamish. 'What about Penny? How's she taking it?'

'Last heard, she's selling her story to the *Sun*. She may end up on television after all.'

'That video turning up at the film show at the community centre: That bothers me. Roberts didn't mention anyone else being in on it?'

'No. He said he was frightened and puzzled because it couldn't have been Miss McAndrew. She was already dead.'

'It's a loose end, and I don't like loose ends. Go easy on the whisky, Jimmy. I shouldnae even let you drive.'

'I'll be just fine.'

Hamish studied the statement again. 'I see Cyril Roberts says nothing about fairies.'

'You mean he was gay?'

'No. Look, I'll tell you if you promise to keep it to yourself.'

'Go ahead. You know me. I never pass on anything you say because it always means, somehow, that Blair'll get to hear of it and rant and rave and I feel I've had enough of that scunner's temper to last a lifetime.'

'How's his drinking?'

'Doing great, as far as I know. Swills down doubles like water.'

'That man's liver must be cast iron by now. Do you know why more people don't sober up?'

'Why?'

'Because they don't wear their livers on the outside. If everyone wore their liver on their forehead, say, it would be on full view and people would say, "Heffens, Jock, that liver of yours is looking fair hobnailed," and they would get shamed into doing something about it.'

'I'm glad, then, mine's safely tucked away inside, hobnailed boots and all. What were you going to tell me?'

'Elspeth scared Mary Roberts into jumping into the quarry. She put on this weird voice and haunted them. Mary Roberts thought it was the fairies and lost her mind wi' terror. But if Elspeth hadn't done it, I wouldn't maybe have had a chance to get Roberts. He had that shotgun and he would have used it.'

'Pretty lassie, thon Elspeth. Got your leg over yet?'

'Wash your mouth out with soap, Jimmy.'

'Whisky'll do,' said Jimmy, and poured himself another glass. 'Roberts is trying to put all the blame on his wife. But I'll tell ye one thing that came out at the interview . . .'

'What?'

'Cyril Roberts was in love with Penny. Now, the wife, she was just obsessed with the idea of having such a beautiful child. But Roberts, it was mad obsession. He was fair crazy about her. I think *he* was the one who stabbed Miss McAndrew. And I think he'd sooner or later have got rid of his wife to have Penny to himself. I went to see her. She's a right little minx. You'd think she'd have been shattered, but she seemed to be glorying in the notoriety of it all.'

'Well, Roberts will be put away for a long time. He won't be seeing her again.'

'He doesnae know that. The crazed wee man thinks she'll visit him in prison. God help the lassie. He'll get out when she's still alive. She'd better change her name and disappear.'

'It's sad,' said Hamish. 'Amy Beattie deserved better from her daughter.'

A few weeks later Hamish returned to the police station after driving round his beat. He saw Elspeth going into the newspaper office and averted his head. He knew he had been avoiding her and felt guilty about it. He owed her a lot, but the memory of that kiss and the emotions it had stirred in him had frightened him. He didn't want another romantic involvement, particularly one right in the village of Lochdubh.

He parked the police Land Rover and got out. The rain was being driven horizontally across the loch on the screaming wind. There was a slim figure huddled in the shelter of the kitchen door.

'Can I help you?' he asked.

'I've come to confess,' said a female voice.

'Come in.' He opened the kitchen door and switched on the light and turned to look at his visitor. At first he did not recognize her, and then with a start he realized his visitor was Jessie Briggs.

Her hair was cut in a short crop and was a

natural glossy brown. She was dressed in a smart tweed suit under a cream raincoat.

'Take your coat off and sit down,' said Hamish. 'Confess what? First, do you want some tea?'

'Yes, please.'

'I'll put the kettle on. It's cold in here. I'll just light the stove.'

He took the lid off the stove and raked down the ashes. He threw in firelighter and sticks and, when they were blazing, added several slices of peat. He put the kettle on the stove and sat down at the kitchen table opposite her.

'All right. I'm ready. What's up?'

'Thon video,' said Jessie in a shaky voice. 'That was me.'

'Och, Jessie. Neffer tell me you had a part in those dreadful murders.'

'No, only that Miss McAndrew called on me right after Miss Beattie was murdered. She seemed upset. She gave me the video and said it was to be delivered to the community centre. I asked her why she didn't take it there herself and she said something about she didn't like Blakey but wanted people to help the elderly. When she'd gone, I left it lying. I was drunk pretty much the whole time. I remembered it after she was found murdered and that prompted me into doing what she'd asked. I took it round and put it through the letter box. Then when I learned what had been in the tape, I decided to say nothing about it in case the police thought I had anything to do with the murders.'

'She must have been frightened,' said Hamish. 'She must have hoped that the video would have given us some clue, or maybe she did it to warn the Robertses that she was not to be intimidated. So what prompted you to come to me now?'

'I've been going to the AA meetings and at last I told them about the tape. They said I'd better tell you and I'd feel better. Are you going to charge me?'

'No. My boss would probably curse and shout and charge you with obstructing the police in their inquiries, and it's such a delight to see you off the booze, I wouldnae want to do anything that would put you back on it. How are you doing?'

'I'm fine. I've got a part-time job.'

'Where?'

'At the gift shop in Braikie. Someone at the meeting's got three little children and she said she would look after my baby in the afternoons.'

The kettle boiled and Hamish rose and made a pot of tea. 'How's Penny?' asked Jessie, sipping at her tea and refusing Hamish's offer of shortbread.

'Last heard, she's staying with her aunt over in Lochinver.'

'She must be an emotional wreck.'

'I wouldnae say that. Did you read her story in the *Sun*?'

'No, I missed that.'

'She fairly trashed the Robertses and said she'd always been scared of them, which is a lie because, murderers they may be, but they doted on her with a passion.'

After Jessie had left, Hamish felt he should really phone Elspeth and tell her that the mystery of the video had been solved. He had behaved childishly by avoiding her. He picked up the phone. It was only five in the evening although it was as black as pitch outside. She would probably still be at the office. Her line was engaged. He felt relieved and then damned himself for being a coward and dialled again.

'Hamish,' said Elspeth in a cool voice. 'What a surprise. How can I help you?'

'I'm sorry I haven't been in touch with you lately,' said Hamish, 'but I've been awfully busy?'

'Oh, really? Your beat abounding in crimes I don't know about?'

'Nothing newsworthy, but a lot of irritating little things.'

'Like avoiding me?'

'Come on, Elspeth. Let's be friends.'

There was a long silence and then Elspeth said, 'Take me for dinner at the Italian's. I'll be there at eight.'

'See you then,' said Hamish, and rang off.

As he dressed that evening, Hamish found he was nervous and excited. He realized he had missed Elspeth's visits and company.

At ten minutes to eight, he shrugged himself into his oilskin. Lugs let out a low whine. Hamish eyed his dog. 'Oh, all right,' he said. 'You can come as well.' Taking Lugs with him, he felt, would make sure it stayed a friendly evening rather than a romantic one.

The evening got off to a bad start. Elspeth was wearing a blue silk blouse, a white jacket, and dark blue skirt. Lugs, who had got drenched during the walk to the restaurant, shook water over Elspeth and then placed his muddy paws on her skirt and gazed accusingly up into her face.

Fortunately, the cleaning-mad Willie Lamont was on hand to sponge out the stains with a new stain remover and to remove the dog to the kitchen and towel him down.

Willie reappeared to hand them menus. 'Where's my dog?' asked Hamish.

'We're just giving the wee chap some pasta. Lugs likes pasta.'

'Not too much, Willie,' admonished Hamish. 'He's overweight already.'

Hamish told Elspeth about how the video had got to the community centre – 'but don't put anything in that paper of yours.'

'I'm just glad Jessie's getting herself straightened out. Have you heard from Jenny?'

'Not a word. But I got a call from Priscilla yesterday. She said she was seeing Jenny that evening. She said she had kept clear of her for a bit because she didn't like the way Jenny took all the praise for solving the case.'

'Jenny'll be back up for the trial and she'll make the most of the publicity again. Sam says Pat is working on a paper in Dublin. He must have forged a reference.'

'Knowing that one, he probably forged several references.'

Hamish ordered a bottle of wine and told Elspeth all about Cyril Roberts's confession, and then, somehow, found himself ordering another. He felt relaxed and happy.

'Did anything come from your appeal in the paper for the old folks' club?' Hamish asked.

'Oh, that will be appearing in the next issue. Mr Blakey is getting lottery money to buy proper cinematography equipment.'

'That's grand.' Hamish studied her. 'There seems to be a bit o' worry at the back of your eyes, Elspeth. Anything bothering you?'

Yes, thought Elspeth. An offer from the *Daily*

Bugle. But I haven't made up my mind. It depends ...

The evening before, Jenny once more found herself in Priscilla's elegant flat. 'I thought you would never speak to me again,' said Jenny.

'I was angry with you for taking the credit away from Hamish.'

'But I didn't!' protested Jenny. 'I guessed it all by myself.'

'Hamish says you were listening at the police station door when he was discussing the case with Elspeth.'

Jenny blushed but said hotly, 'That's not true!'

'Have it your way. Is Hamish keen on this Elspeth?'

'Not really. They just seem to be friends. As a matter of fact,' said Jenny with a toss of her dark curls, 'Hamish rather fancied me.'

'Didn't sound like it when I spoke to him this morning.'

'Oh,' faltered Jenny, 'you spoke to him.' She rallied. 'Well, he wouldn't want to say anything about it to you in case he hurt you.'

'How on earth could it hurt me? Hamish is old history.'

'You wouldn't think so the way you go on

about him. In fact, you talk more about him than that fiancé of yours.'

'You're being silly, Jenny. Shall we eat?'

Early the following day, Priscilla sat at her computer in the City, not really seeing the figures on the screen. She was suddenly home-sick for Lochdubh. She was having doubts about getting married. Just nerves, she told herself. But she could not let go of the thought of going home. She rose and went in to see her boss and said she had just received a phone call that her mother was ill. The excuse worked and she was free to go.

I can drive up and be there before midnight, thought Priscilla.

Hamish and Elspeth finished their meal with two large brandies. When they left the restau-rant, with a pasta-filled dog rolling along behind them like a drunken sailor, they found themselves walking together in the direction of the police station. Elspeth stumbled on her high heels and Hamish put an arm about her shoulders. All Hamish had drunk sang in his brain and he hugged Elspeth closer.

He opened the kitchen door and switched on the light. They stood close together, looking at each other while Lugs yawned and slumped down on to the floor by the stove.

Then Elspeth held out her arms. One sharp little alarm bell went off in Hamish's brain, but he ignored it. He took her in his arms and kissed her rain-wet lips and then somehow they were staggering towards the bedroom, shedding clothes as they went.

At one point, Hamish dimly heard the phone ringing from the office, but he ignored it.

Priscilla tucked away her mobile phone. She had called the police station from the Tommel Castle Hotel. Why didn't Hamish answer? Then she grinned, as she remembered all the times the lazy constable had ignored its ringing. He always said if it was anything urgent, he could hear it on his answering machine. She thought of leaving a message and then suddenly, tired though she was, decided to surprise him.

She carefully washed and made up her face again. She went out and got into her car and drove down into Lochdubh. It was a filthy night. Funny, she thought, how easily she had forgotten how vile the winter could be in the northern Highlands. Horizontal rain slashed against the windscreen and the car rocked in buffets of wind.

Priscilla was just driving along the waterfront when the stout figure of Mrs Wellington, the minister's wife, leapt in front of the car, waving her arms. Priscilla braked and rolled down the window. 'Mrs Wellington!' she shouted. 'What on earth are you doing? I could have killed you.'

'I recognized the car,' gabbled Mrs Wellington, rain cascading off a golf umbrella which she held over her head, 'and I was so pleased to see you, dear. Come up to the manse and we'll have a chat.'

'It's too late,' said Priscilla. 'I'll call on you tomorrow. I'm just going to drop in on Hamish.'

'Oh, you won't find him. He was called out to Drim. A burglary over there.'

Priscilla looked down the waterfront. Through the driving rain, she could see that the police Land Rover was parked outside the police station and the kitchen light was on.

She let in the clutch. 'I can see that he's back now. See you tomorrow.'

Priscilla moved off but only got a few yards before she had to slam on the brakes again. The Currie sisters were standing in the middle of the road.

Priscilla hooted angrily.

The twin sisters came round to the driver's side of the car and rapped on the window.

'What is it?' asked Priscilla, rolling down

the window again. Rain was dripping from the plastic covering on their heads and on to their thick glasses.

'We were so delighted to hear you were back,' said Jessie. 'I said to Nessie, we must ask her in for tea, for tea.'

'I'm on my way to see Hamish.'

'Oh, I wouldnae be disturbing him this time of night.'

'The kitchen light is still on,' said Priscilla patiently, 'which means he's awake.'

'I wouldn't be going by that, by that,' said Jessie. 'He aye forgets to put it out, put it out.'

'I'll see you tomorrow, ladies,' said Priscilla firmly.

She drove to the police station and parked her car and got out. She was just about to walk up to the kitchen door when a voice hailed her. 'Miss Halburton-Smythe!'

Priscilla turned round. Archie Macleod, the fisherman, was standing there. 'I haff had a fine catch o' the fish. If you would be stepping over to my cottage, I'll let you have some.'

'What is up with everyone this evening?' asked Priscilla, bewildered. 'I'm just going to say hello to Hamish and then I'm going to bed.'

'I wouldnae be doing that.'

'Why?'

'I chust wouldnae,' muttered Archie, backing away.

Priscilla shrugged and went up to the kitchen door. It was unlocked. She pushed it open and went in. Lugs waddled towards her, his ridiculous plume of a tail waving a welcome.

She bent down to pat him and that's when she saw a shirt lying on the floor, and next to it a blouse and jacket.

Priscilla straightened up slowly and stared. A line of discarded clothing was leading to the bedroom.

She suddenly felt sad and silly. The phone in the police office was ringing and then the answering machine clicked on. 'Hamish Macbeth,' boomed Mrs Wellington's voice, 'if you're up to what I think you're up to, you'd best lock your doors. Miss Halburton-Smythe is on your doorstep.' The phone rang again. Priscilla waited, frozen. The answering machine clicked on again. 'Och, Hamish,' came Archie's voice. 'I'm probably too late but your Priscilla's at the police station.'

Priscilla turned on her heel and left the police station, closing the door quietly behind her.

Feeling stiff, almost as if she had rheumatism, she got into her car. She drove slowly back along the waterfront while the hidden eyes of the villagers sadly watched her from behind their curtains.

If you enjoyed *Death of a Poison Pen*, read on for the first chapter of the next book in the *Hamish Macbeth* series . . .

DEATH
of a BORE

Chapter One

No man, but a blockhead, ever wrote,
except for money.
            – Samuel Johnson

There used to be quite a lot going on in a high-land village during the long, dark winter months. There was a ceilidh every week where the locals danced or performed, singing the old songs or reciting poetry. Often there was a sewing circle with its attendant gossip; the Mothers' Union meetings; the Girl Guides and Boy Scouts classes; and the weekly film show in the village hall. But with the advent of tele-vision and videos, people often preferred to stay cosily indoors, being amused by often violent films with heroines with high cheek-bones, collagen-enhanced lips, and heels so high it made ankles comfortably ending in slippered feet just ache to look at them.

Therefore when Hamish Macbeth, police constable of Lochdubh, heard that a newcomer,

John Heppel, was planning to hold a series of writers' classes in the village hall, he set out to dissuade him. As he said to his fisherman friend, Archie Maclean, 'I don't want to see the poor wee man humiliated when nobody turns up.'

Hamish had seen a poster in Patel's general store: DO YOU WANT TO BE A FAMOUS WRITER? FAMOUS WRITER JOHN HEPPEL WILL HELP YOU BECOME ONE.

The first meeting was scheduled for the following week on a Wednesday evening at seven-thirty. Hamish knew that on that evening *Petticoat Cops* was showing at just that time, a cop series set in LA with three leggy blondes with large lips, high busts, and an amazing skill with firearms and kung fu. He did not know anyone in Lochdubh who would risk missing the latest episode, except perhaps himself.

So on one wet black evening with a gusty gale blowing in from the Atlantic and ragged clouds ripping across the sky, Hamish got into the police Land Rover and set out for John's cottage, which was out on the moors above the village of Cnothan. Hamish was feeling lonely. His affair with the local reporter, Elspeth Grant, had come to an abrupt halt. She had been offered a job on a Glasgow newspaper and had asked him bluntly if he meant to marry her.

And Hamish had dithered, then he had said he'd think about it, and by the time he had got around to really considering the idea, Elspeth had accepted the job and left. He wondered gloomily whether he was cut out to live with anyone, for his first feeling on hearing the news that she had gone was one of relief.

He wondered at first why John had not decided to hold his classes in Cnothan but then reflected that Cnothan was a sour town and specialized in ostracizing newcomers.

Sergeant MacGregor, who had policed Cnothan for years, had retired, and the village and surrounding area had been added on to Hamish's already extensive beat. Village police stations were being closed down all over the place, and Hamish had not felt strong enough to protest at the extra work in case he lost his beloved home in the police station in Lochdubh.

Hamish had never met John Heppel. Normally he would have made a courtesy call, but an irritating series of burglaries over in Braikie had to be solved, and somehow the man's arrival in the Highlands had gone out of his mind. Much as he loved Sutherland and could not consider living anywhere else, Hamish knew that newcomers often relocated to the far north of Scotland through misguided romanticism. Writers or painters imagined that the solitude and wild scenery would inspire them, but usually it was the very long dark winters that finally defeated them.

He drove through Cnothan, bleak and rain-swept under the orange glare of sodium lights, and up on to the moors. The heathery track leading to John's cottage had a poker-work sign pointing the way. It said, 'Writer's Folly'.

Hamish drove along the track and parked outside the low whitewashed cottage that was John's home.

Hamish chided himself for not phoning first. He rapped on the door and waited while the rising gale whipped at his oilskin coat.

A small man opened the door and stared up at the tall policeman. 'I am Police Constable Hamish Macbeth from Lochdubh,' said Hamish. 'Might I be having a wee word with you?'

'Come in.'

Hamish followed him into a living room lined with books. A computer stood on a table by the window. Peat smouldered on the open fire. Over the fireplace hung a large framed photograph of the author accepting a plaque.

'You have interrupted my muse,' said John, and gave a great hee-haw sort of laugh.

He was only a little over five feet tall, bespectacled, with thinning grey hair, the strands combed over a balding scalp. His eyes were large and brown above a squashy, open-pored nose and fleshy mouth. He wore a roll-necked brown sweater and brown cords.

'Sit down,' he said. 'You're making my neck ache.'

Hamish removed his cap and coiled his lanky length down into an armchair by the fire.

'Is that your own colour?' asked John, staring at Hamish's flaming-red hair.

'All my own. You don't seem to be surprised at getting a visit from the police.'

'I'm not married, my parents are dead, and I have no close relatives. People are only frightened when they see a policeman at the door if they're worried about a loved one or have something to hide. So why have you come?'

'It's about your writing class.'

'I'll be delighted to see you there. You can pay for the whole term or at each class.'

'I wasn't thinking of attending. I don't think anyone will. They'll all be at home watching the telly.'

John looked a trifle smug. 'I have already had ten applications from the residents of Lochdubh.'

'Who might they be?'

'Ah.' John wagged a finger. 'I suggest you come along and see.'

'I might do that. Have you had much published?'

'I received the Tammerty Biscuit Award for Scottish literature.' John pointed to the photograph. 'That's me getting the award for my book *Tenement Days*. Have you read it?'

'No.'

'Then let me give you a copy.' John left the room. Hamish looked around. A small table over against the wall opposite from the computer held the remains of a meal. Apart from the books lining the low walls and the large photograph over the fireplace, there were no ornaments or family photographs.

John came back in and handed him a copy of *Tenement Days*. 'I signed it,' he said. Hamish flipped it open and looked at the inscription. It read, 'To Hamish MacBeth. His first introduction to literature. John Heppel.'

'I haff read other books,' said Hamish crossly, the sudden sibilance of his highland accent showing he was annoyed. 'And my name is spelled without a capital B. What else have you written?'

'Oh, lots,' said John. 'I've just finished a film script for Strathbane Television.'

'What's it called?'

John looked suddenly uncomfortable. 'Well, it's a script for *Down in the Glen*.'

Hamish smiled. 'That's a soap.'

'But I have raised the tone, don't you see? To improve the public mind, even great authors such as myself must lower themselves to write for a popular series.'

'Indeed? Good luck to you. I had better be going.'

'Wait a bit. You asked about my work? I have been greatly influenced by the French authors such as Jean-Paul Sartre and François Mauriac. Even when I was at school, I became aware that I had a great gift. I was brought up in the mean streets of Glasgow, a hard environment for a sensitive boy. But I observed. I am a camera. I sometimes feel I have been sent down from another planet to observe.'

'Quite a lot of highland drunks feel the same way,' said Hamish, made malicious by boredom. 'You know, they all think they're off another planet.'

But John's eyes had taken on the self-obsessed glaze of the bore. 'You are wondering why I never married?'

'Last thing I was wondering,' muttered Hamish.

'There was one woman in my life, one great love. But she was married. We met in secret. Our passion soared like . . . like . . .'

'Buzzards?'

'The eagle,' corrected John crossly. 'She had raven hair and skin like milk.'

'Aye, well,' said Hamish, determinedly getting to his feet. 'All verra interesting, but I've got to go.'

'Oh, must you? Then I shall see you next Wednesday.'

Hamish jammed on his cap. 'Don't get up,' he said. 'I'll see myself out.'

He noticed that a wax coat hanging by the door was wet.

He was just getting into the Land Rover when John ran out after him. 'You've forgotten your book.'

'Aye, thanks.' Hamish took it from him and threw it on to the passenger seat and drove off at great speed.

He won't last the winter, he told himself, unaware at that time that John Heppel was to leave the Highlands but not in a way that Hamish Macbeth expected.

As Hamish drove along the waterfront in Lochdubh, he saw that one wire mesh waste bin had not yet been stolen by the fishermen to be used as a lobster pot. He stopped the Land Rover with a jerk, picked up John's book, opened the window, and hurled the book into the bin. The inscription had annoyed him.

He drove a little further and then noticed a small crowd outside Patel's general store. Mrs Wellington, the minister's wife, was one of the group, and she waved to him.

Hamish stopped again and rolled down the window. 'What's going on here?'

'It's dreadful,' said Mrs Wellington. 'Come and look.'

Hamish climbed down and walked over. The group parted to let him through. There on the whitewashed wall of the store by the door, someone had sprayed in red paint, 'Paki Go Home.'

'And he's not even Pakistani!' wailed Mrs Wellington. 'He's Indian.'

The door of the shop, which had been closed for the night, opened, and Mr Patel came out. 'Hamish, what's happened?' he asked.

'Some maniac's been writing on your walls,' said Hamish.

Mr Patel looked at the wall. 'Who would have done this?' he asked, looking round the little crowd.

'Do you sell spray paint?' asked Hamish.

'Yes, but never to children. I mean, I only sell it to people who're going to use it round the house.'

Hamish addressed the group. 'I want all of you to ask round the village and find out if anybody saw anyone near the shop. You closed half-day today, Mr Patel. It gets dark after two in the afternoon. So it must have happened sometime between then and now. In the meantime let's get some turpentine and wash the stuff off.'

'What about fingerprints?' asked Mrs Wellington.

'No forensic team's going to turn out for this, and the kit I've got wouldn't be able to get one off that wall. Let's get to it. And tell that new schoolteacher, Miss Garrety, that I'll be along to speak to the pupils tomorrow first thing.'

'You think it's children?' asked Angela Brodie, the doctor's wife, who had joined the group.

'I don't know,' said Hamish. 'I chust cannae think of anyone who would do this. Mr Patel is one of us and has been for ages.'

The group was getting larger, and everyone was desperate to take a hand at cleaning the wall. Hamish pushed back his cap and scratched his fiery hair. 'If it was "English Go Home", I could understand it,' he said to Angela. 'There's a lot of stupid English-bashing in Scotland these days.'

'But not in Lochdubh,' said Angela. 'It must be someone from outside. Everyone in Lochdubh knows that Mr Patel originally came from India.'

The next day Hamish put his odd-looking dog, Lugs, on the leash and walked along to the village school. The school, like his police station, was under threat. The children were taught up to the age of eleven years, and then the older ones were bussed to the secondary school in Strathbane. There had been various moves to close down the school, but each time the well-organized villagers had mounted such a strong protest that they had succeeded in keeping it.

Miss Freda Garrety, the schoolteacher, was a tiny slip of a thing in her twenties. She barely came up to Hamish's shoulder. She had straight black hair cut in a bob and a white triangular face with large black eyes. She was dressed in a black T-shirt and black trousers. Hamish thought she looked like a harlequin.

'I'm here to speak to your pupils,' said Hamish.

'About the graffiti?' She had a lowland accent. 'Make it quick. Exams are coming up.'

Hamish walked into the classroom, where the children still sat behind old-fashioned desks: the oldest at the back and the youngest at the front.

He walked to the front of the room. 'I'm here to talk to you about the racist graffiti on the wall of the general store. This is a disgrace and should not be allowed to happen in Lochdubh. Do any of you know anything about this?'

Solemn faces stared back at him, but nobody spoke. 'Now, some of you may know something but don't want to tell me in front of the others. If you do know anything at all, I want you to call at the police station with one of your parents.'

A small boy put his hand up.

'Yes?'

'My faither says there's too many foreigners in this country. Maybe you should speak to him.'

'You're Dermott Taggart, am I right?'

'Yes.'

'Is your father at home?'

'He's down on a building site in Strathbane.'

'Do you think he might have had something to do with this?'

Dermott looked suddenly frightened. 'Don't be telling him I said anything,' he said, and burst into tears. Freda rushed forward to comfort him.

'Anyone else?' asked Hamish.

Silence.

'Well, listen carefully. Racism is a serious crime. The culprit will be punished, and mark my words, I'll find out who did this.'

Hamish returned to the police station and went into his office, where he stared blankly at the computer. Who on earth would want to paint a racist slogan on Patel's shop?

There was a cry from the kitchen door. 'Hamish, the telly's here. They're outside Patel's wi' that writer cheil.'

Hamish rushed out. Archie Maclean stood there. 'Ye wouldnae think they'd bother.'

Hamish walked with him round to Patel's. John Heppel was standing outside the shop, facing a camera crew.

'. . . and that is all I have to say,' he was declaring pompously. 'I, John Heppel, will do my utmost to help the police find the perpetrator of this wicked crime. Thank you.'

Hamish's hazel eyes narrowed in suspicion. John Heppel was made up for the cameras, and yet he could not see a make-up girl anywhere around.

He pushed his way through the crowd that had gathered to where John was talking with the interviewer, a pretty girl called Jessma Gardener.

'How did you find out about this?' demanded Hamish of John.

'Ah, Constable. I just happened to be passing and saw the television crew.'

Hamish leaned forward and drew a long finger down John's cheek and then studied the brown make-up on his finger.

'Do you usually wear make-up?' he asked.

John flushed angrily. 'I am so used to television appearances,' he said, 'that I carry a kit in the car. I owe it to my readers to look my best at all times.'

Hamish turned to Jessma. 'How did *you* hear about this?'

'Someone phoned the news desk late last night.'

'Would you mind phoning up and asking the name of whoever it was phoned the story in?'

'I've got to be going,' said John, and he pushed his way past Hamish and through the crowd.

While Jessma took out her mobile and phoned, Hamish stood watching the retreat of John Heppel.

When she rang off, she said, 'It was an anonymous caller. Then John phoned and said he would be at the shop. As he's writing a script for one of our shows, we thought we may as well interview him. Me, I think it's a waste of time. You should have heard the whole speech. You'd think the wee mannie ran the Highlands. It'll probably end up in the bin.'

Hamish went back to the police station, collected his dog, and drove off in the Land Rover in the direction of Cnothan. He put the light on the roof and turned on the siren as Lugs, his dog, rolled his odd blue eyes at his master. Lugs hated that siren.

Hamish cut off several miles to Cnothan by bumping along a croft track and arrived at John Heppel's house before the writer.

He got down from the car and waited.

He searched through the rubbish bin at the side of the house and was still searching when John drove up.

'What are you doing?' demanded the writer angrily.

Hamish straightened up. 'I was looking for a can of spray paint.'

'I'll sue you for defamation of character.'

'You do that and I'll get a warrant to search your house and examine your clothes for paint. I think you sprayed that graffiti to get yourself a bit of publicity.'

'How dare you!'

'I've got enough on my plate at the moment without bothering about a silly man like you. Don't ever do anything like that again.'

'I'm telling you, I'll sue you!'

'Go ahead,' said Hamish. 'I'd enjoy seeing the sort of publicity that would get you. When I arrived at your place last night, your coat was still wet. You'd been out. Any more publicity stunts like that and I'll have you.'

'I hate that sort of person,' said Hamish to his dog as he drove off. 'Now, what do I do, Lugs? Do I tell the villagers? Och, it's chust a storm in a teacup. He won't try anything like that again. But I will have a word on the quiet with Mr Patel.'

Mr Patel's eyebrows shot up into his hair when Hamish took him outside his shop and quietly explained his suspicions about the writer.

'Are ye sure?' asked Mr Patel. 'I've signed up for one o' his classes.'

'You want to be a writer?' asked Hamish, momentarily diverted. 'What kind of book?'

'I was thinking I might write my life story. You know, how I started off selling stuff out o' a suitcase round the Hebrides until I had enough to start a shop.' His brown eyes took on a dreamy, unfocussed look. 'I'll call it *An Indian's Life in the Far North of Scotland*.'

'Maybe you should try for something snappier.'

'Like what?'

'Cannae think of anything.'

'There you are! That's why I need to go to a writing class.'

'Anyway,' said Hamish, 'I've no actual proof he did it, and in order to prove it, I'd need a warrant to search his house and I can't see me getting it. So we'll keep this between ourselves.'

'So you're not sure he did it?'

'Pretty certain. I mean, he turned up with make-up on.'

'Maybe he's . . . well, you know . . . that way inclined.'

'He's inclined to getting his stupid face on television, that's all.'

'Hey, Hamish!'

Hamish turned round. Callum McSween,

the dustman, stood there. 'I found a book inscribed to you in the bin. Here it is.'

'Oh, thanks,' mumbled Hamish. He wanted to say he had put it there deliberately but suddenly wanted to forget all about John Heppel.

He nodded goodbye to both of them. He drove to the police station, got down, and helped Lugs out because the dog's legs were too short to enable him to jump down from the Land Rover. He looked at the book in his hand.

He glanced along the waterfront. It was now the dinner hour – Lochdubh residents still took dinner in the middle of the day – and the waterfront was deserted.

He hurled the book so hard that it flew straight across the waterfront and over the sea wall.

Hamish was just frying some chops when there was a knock at the kitchen door. The locals never came to the front door. He opened it. In the days when Hamish was a police sergeant, his caller, Clarry Graham, had worked for him – or, rather, had not worked, Clarry finding that his talents lay in being a chef.

To Hamish's dismay, he was clutching That Book.

'It's quiet up at the Tommel Castle Hotel at the moment,' said Clarry plaintively. 'I was out fishing in the loch when this book fell out o' the sky and right into my boat. It's inscribed to you.'

'Thanks,' said Hamish.

'Must've been kids,' said Clarry.

'Come in.'

'You don't want to be reading something like that anyway,' said Clarry. 'Full o' nasty words. I'm telling you, there's an eff in every line.'

'That's the fellow who's going to be giving those writing classes.'

'Oh, I'd signed up for those.'

'You, Clarry? A book? I mean, what about?'

'I'm going to call it *From Police Station to Kitchen.*'

'Look, Clarry, it iss awfy hard to get a book published these days. Particularly a life story. You really have to be some kind o' celebrity. Besides, this John Heppel seems to write the sort of stuff you wouldn't want to read.'

'He's going to tell us about publishers and agents,' said Clarry stubbornly. 'I'd like to make a bit o' money. Just look at what J. K. Rowling earns.'

'Didn't it dawn on you that J. K. Rowling can *write*? Clarry, only four and a half per cent of the authors in this world can afford to support themselves. I 'member reading that.'

Clarry's round face took on a mulish look, and Hamish suppressed a sigh. Clarry obviously thought he was destined to be one of the four and a half per cent.

When Clarry had left, Hamish began to think uneasily about John's writing classes. John, he was beginning to feel, was some sort of dangerous foreign body introduced into the highland system.

He decided to attend the first class. It would upset John to see him there, and Hamish looked forward to upsetting John. He flicked open John's book and began to read. It was one of those pseudo-literary stream-of-consciousness books set in the slums of Glasgow. The 'grittiness' was supplied by four-letter words. The anti-hero was a druggie whose favourite occupation seemed to be slashing with a broken bottle anyone in a pub who looked at him the wrong way. The heroine put up with all this with loving kindness. Hamish flicked to the end of the book, where a reformed anti-hero was preaching to the youth of Glasgow. No one could accuse the book of being plot-driven. Hackneyed similes and metaphors clunked their way through the thick volume.

Maybe it was all right, he thought ruefully. Like all Highlanders, he was quick to take offence and loathed being patronized. The inscription still rankled, however.

There was another knock at the door, very faint. Hamish opened it and looked down at

Dermott Taggart, the small boy who had thought his father might be responsible for the graffiti.

'Come ben,' said Hamish. Then he cursed. Black smoke was rising from the frying pan. He'd forgotten about the chops.

'Sit down, laddie,' he said over his shoulder. 'I'll just put this mess in the bin. I havenae any soft drinks, but I could make you some tea.'

'I don't want anything,' said the boy in a whisper.

Hamish got rid of the chops. 'Sit,' he ordered. 'You didn't really think your da was responsible for the graffiti?'

Dermott hung his head.

'I think,' said Hamish gently, 'that something at home is bothering you. I think you want a policeman to call. What's going on at home?'

The child began to cry. Hamish fished a box of tissues out of a cupboard and handed it to him, then waited patiently.

At last the crying ended on a hiccupping sob. 'Dad's hitting Ma,' he choked out.

'Does he drink?'

'A lot.'

'It's hard for me to do anything unless your mother puts in a complaint.'

'You won't tell the Social?' gasped the boy in sudden alarm.

'No, I won't do that,' said Hamish, knowing

that no matter how bad the parents, abused children still lived in terror of being snatched from their homes by the Social Security. 'Leave it with me. I'll think of something.'

When the boy had gone, Hamish turned over in his mind what he knew about the boy's father. Alistair Taggart took occasional building jobs down in Strathbane. Hamish couldn't remember seeing him drinking in the village pub. Perhaps he did his drinking in Strathbane and drove home.

He was almost relieved to have an ordinary, if unpleasant, village problem to cope with instead of fretting that John Heppel would somehow bring trouble to the area.

To order your copies of other books in the Hamish Macbeth series simply contact The Book Service (TBS) by phone, email or by post. Alternatively visit our website at www.constablerobinson.com.

No. of copies	Title	RRP	Total
	Death of a Gossip	£6.99	
	Death of a Cad	£6.99	
	Death of an Outsider	£6.99	
	Death of a Perfect Wife	£6.99	
	Death of a Hussy	£6.99	
	Death of a Snob	£6.99	
	Death of a Prankster	£6.99	
	Death of a Glutton	£6.99	
	Death of a Travelling Man	£6.99	
	Death of a Charming Man	£6.99	
	Death of a Gentle Lady	£6.99	
	Death of a Nag	£6.99	
	Death of an Macho Man	£6.99	
	Death of a Dentist	£6.99	
	Death of a Scriptwriter	£6.99	
	Death of an Addict	£6.99	
	Death of a Dustman	£6.99	
	Death of a Celebrity	£6.99	
	Death of a Village	£6.99	

And the following titles available from autumn 2009 . . .

No. of copies	Title	Release Date	RRP	Total
	A Highland Christmas	Nov 2009 (hardback)	£9.99	
	Death of a Valentine	Jan 2010 (hardback)	£18.99	
	Death of a Bore	Feb 2010	£6.99	
	Death of a Witch	Feb 2010	£6.99	
	Death of a Dreamer	Apr 2010	£6.99	
	Death of a Maid	Apr 2010	£6.99	
	Grand Total			£

FREEPOST RLUL-SJGC-SGKJ, Cash Sales Direct Mail Dept., The Book Service, Colchester Road, Frating, Colchester, CO7 7DW. Tel: +44 (0) 1206 255 800.
Fax: +44 (0) 1206 255 930. Email: sales@tbs-ltd.co.uk

UK customers: please allow £1.00 p&p for the first book, plus 50p for the second, and an additional 30p for each book thereafter, up to a maximum charge of £3.00. Overseas customers (incl. Ireland): please allow £2.00 p&p for the first book, plus £1.00 for the second, plus 50p for each additional book.

NAME (block letters): _____

ADDRESS: _____

_____

_____ POSTCODE: _____

I enclose a cheque/PO (payable to 'TBS Direct') for the amount

of £_____

I wish to pay by Switch/Credit Card

Card number: _____

Expiry date: _____ Switch issue number: _____